SMART Recovery:

Science-based, self-empowered addiction recovery program

smartrecovery.org/teens

Young People in Recovery:

Non-profit that provides life skills and peer support for young people in recovery from addiction.

youngpeopleinrecovery.org

AMY REED is the award-winning author of several novels for young adults, including *The Nowhere Girls, Beautiful,* and *Clean*. She also edited *Our Stories, Our Voices: 21 YA Authors Get Real About Injustice, Empowerment, and Growing Up Female in America*. Amy is a feminist, mother, and Virgo who enjoys running, making lists, and wandering around the mountains of western North Carolina, where she lives.

TELL ME MY NAME

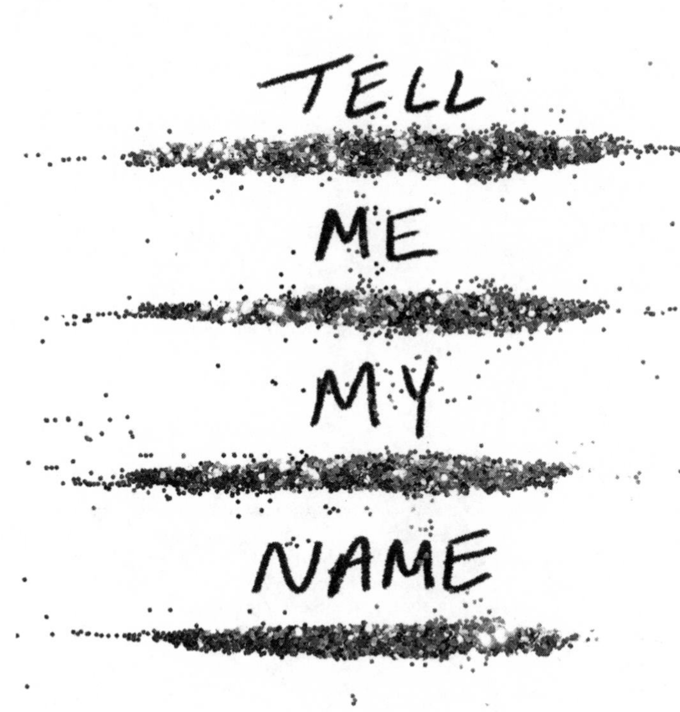

AMY REED

Dial Books
An imprint of Penguin Random House LLC, New York

First published in the United States of America by Dial Books,
an imprint of Penguin Random House LLC, 2021

Visit us online at penguinrandomhouse.com.

Library of Congress Cataloging-in-Publication Data
Names: Reed, Amy Lynn, author. | Title: Tell me my name / Amy Reed.
Description: New York : Dial Books, 2021. | Audience: Ages 14+. | Audience: Grades 10-12. Summary: Eighteen-year-old Fern's life spirals out of control after troubled former child star Ivy Avila arrives on Commodore Island, ultimately forcing Fern to take agency over her own existence. | Identifiers: LCCN 2020027808 (print) | LCCN 2020027809 (ebook) | ISBN 9780593109724 (hardcover) | ISBN 9780593109731 (ebook)
Subjects: CYAC: Identity—Fiction. | Wealth—Fiction. | Mental illness—Fiction. | Rape—Fiction. Classification: LCC PZ7.R2462 Te 2021 (print) | LCC PZ7.R2462 (ebook)

10 9 8 7 6 5 4 3 2 1

Design by Cerise Steel
Text set in Utopia Std

For Elouise

So we beat on, boats against the current, borne back ceaselessly into the past.

—*The Great Gatsby* by F. Scott Fitzgerald

I want to be held and told my name. I want to be valued, in ways that I am not; I want to be more than valuable.

—*The Handmaid's Tale* by Margaret Atwood

I'll trade your broken wings for mine.
I've seen your scars and kissed your crime.

—"All Night," Beyoncé

1

FERNS are older than dinosaurs. They've survived by growing under things, made hearty by their place in the shadows. Sucking up mud.

Fern.

Barely even a plant. Ferns don't make seeds, don't flower. They propagate with spores knocked off their fronds by passing creatures or strong winds.

They sit there, forest deep, waiting to be touched.

Papa said Daddy could have any house he wanted, so he picked an old abandoned church at the end of a gravel road in the middle of the forest on an island.

Papa says it's a money pit. Daddy says it's a work in progress.

Papa says it was Daddy's revenge for making them move for his career.

Papa says Daddy likes to make things hard for no reason. Daddy says it builds character.

Papa says I probably have brain damage from all the sawdust

and paint fumes I inhaled as a baby. Daddy sometimes calls the house his other child.

Their bickering soothes me. That they argue about such little things reminds me we have nothing big to worry about. We're the opposite of dysfunctional. We're real live unicorns.

Commodore Island is nine miles long and five miles wide. In the summer, it's overrun with tourists. Day-trippers from Seattle with their itineraries of the famous bakery and fish restaurant, the little boutiques and artisan cheese shop, all the old buildings preserved like a retro, small-town time capsule of family-owned businesses. You can barely see the tiny A-Corp logo on their signs.

Sometimes the tourists rent kayaks. Sometimes they go for hikes in the nature preserve at the center of the island. They walk around the muddy lake and take home photos and mosquito bites as souvenirs. They drive Olympic Road in its lumpy oval circuit, the mansions and luxury condos rising over them from the shore and stacking up the hill, each with its own view of the Sound, before the island's middle gives way to forest.

The tourists slow at the gates of our more famous residents, stopping traffic to take pictures of the rare wild deer crossing the road. They get their little taste of quaint, of our tiny, unscathed bubble where you can almost believe the rest of the world isn't falling apart, then they return to their gated communities in the city. There have been no deer in Seattle for a long time.

People can afford beauty here. The rich always get to keep a little of what they destroy.

Papa had a dream of becoming a fashion designer a long time ago, but he somehow ended up at A-Corp like everyone else on the island. Except he's not some big fancy executive like most of the parents here. Papa's the artistic director of the Children's Division of Consumer Protective Apparel.

Instead of high fashion and runway shows, he's in charge of making bulletproof vests for kids. It's not glamorous, but somebody's got to do it.

The tourists always end up at my work at some point on their trip: Island Home & Garden. They buy our signature T-shirts with the otters holding hands. Everyone loves otters holding hands. Even though otters haven't been spotted here in a couple decades, not since the big oil spill off the coast of Vancouver Island.

My fathers are some of the few parents on the island who believe that a work ethic must be built; it is not something that can be inherited like wealth. I am the only person I know with a part-time summer job. I'm also the only person who works on this island who actually lives on this island. Everyone who lives here either works for A-Corp headquarters in Seattle, or doesn't work. Everyone who works here lives in the giant subsidized housing complexes across the bridge to the west, on the peninsula, those miles of identical high-rise boxes strategically built on the other side of a hill so they won't cheapen the view of anyone on the island. Buses full of workers arrive around the clock for shifts at the shops and restaurants, the grocery store, and the couple of car-charging stations, to work on gardens and remodels of houses. In and out, back and forth, like the tide.

I work while everyone else my age plays. I work while they travel, or while their parents travel and they stay home to party and be tended to by housekeepers and nannies who have their own families across the country waiting for checks to arrive, in the states that have no jobs because of the floods and the fires and the poisoned earth. I work while my best friend, Lily, is in Taiwan visiting family all summer. I sell orchids and fake antique watering cans to tourists and housewives, waiting for my real life to start.

But then:

There's a rumor of a new arrival.

Moving trucks at the bottom of my hill. The gate across Olympic Road opens.

Not the usual executive rich. Not the CEOs and CFOs and COOs and CTOs of the various departments of A-Corp.

A *star*.

My sleepy town has woken up.

. . .

Rumor is she just got out of treatment. "Exhaustion," they call it, which could mean anything. Drugs, alcohol, eating disorder, sex, gambling, self-harm, mental illness. It's not so remarkable. Some kids on the island make these trips more often than summer camp.

Or she could just be tired.

"*I'm* tired," Papa says. "I wish I could go somewhere for exhaustion."

Daddy rolls his eyes in the way that means "I love you, but you can be so insensitive."

Then Papa rolls his eyes in the way that means "I love you, but you can be *too* sensitive."

We have plums, apples, pears, blackberries, wild huckleberries. A vegetable garden that gasps for the few hours of sunlight that reach our small clearing in the forest. Overgrown gardens of rhododendron and azalea. Yellow scotch broom that burns my eyes and makes me sneeze.

In the spring: cherry blossoms and dogwood. Old, forgotten bulbs of daffodils and tulips peek through the weeds, the winter-browned pine needles, the brittle cones. The first sprouts always make Daddy tender and teary-eyed. They never last long enough.

Daddy goes around with a special paintbrush every afternoon pretending to be a bee, dusting each flower, and then the next, and the next, trying to spread pollen now that there are barely any bees left to do the work. He tells me that when I was very little, there were still a few real farms left. Almost everything you can buy at the grocery store is grown in a hothouse now, those vast acres of white buildings stretching across the countryside. But there are still people like Daddy who like to do things the old-fashioned way. They can sell one artisanal apple for twenty dollars at a farmers' market.

But it is early summer now. The spring flowers are gone. We're entering drought again. It is the name of the season even here, which used to be famous for being one of the wettest places on earth.

"Should we bring our new neighbors a pie or something?" Daddy says.

"That's just in the movies," Papa says.

"And how would we even get through the gate to give them the pie?" I say.

"You sound just like your father," Daddy says.

"Meow," says our cat, Gotami.

One thing Papa and Daddy agree on is that Commodore Island is full of a bunch of people with money trying to look like they don't have money.

Seattle rich is a special kind of rich. It's jeans and hiking boots and expensive high-tech moisture-wicking shirts for people who never sweat.

I can feel something different before I see them. A shift in energy. A sucking toward.

They are not Seattle rich.

They are big sunglasses and big purses rich. Loud, bright-printed sundresses against flawless bronze skin. Sparkling jewels and heeled sandals. Nobody here wears heels until they go off the island.

They're practically matching. I don't know who is copying whom.

Mother and daughter. From a distance, they could be twins.

A hundred years ago, this used to be a sleepy rural town that had a few small farms, a few small businesses, and a few Seattle commuters. Now the A-Corp elite who live in the massive estates lining the waterfront pay a fee that goes directly to the private security force that patrols the island.

A-Corp uses the nature preserve as an example of how progressive they are and how committed to preservation. But the trees keep dying, the pine needles turn brown and brittle, and the lake is full of dead fish no matter how fast workers clean it out and fill it with new ones.

We live on one of the few country roads left. Most have been bulldozed and replaced by ultra-modern, energy-efficient, luxury housing developments. Every time something breaks in our house, Papa reminds us that we could move to one of those condos. "You could still garden!" he tells Daddy, trying to sound cheerful. "There's a community pea-patch! There's a gym with a pool!"

We are good at leaving rich people alone. They walk among us every day. Most are the kind of rich that is not famous, though occasionally you might hear their names in the news, with words like "fiscal quarter" and "acquisitions" and "international market."

They are not faces. They are not voices. They are not entire bodies and stories we've known since we were young. They are just names made out of money.

But this girl is made out of a different kind of money.

A boy asks for her autograph. Her smile is pure oxygen and sunlight. All the flowers in the store turn to her and open their petals.

For a moment, I am seeded. I have fruit.

Our house is built of old stones, covered with ivy so thick, it looks like it's holding everything together. Daddy assures us it's structurally sound. When the light hits us just right, the inside glows with dusty multicolored beams from the church's old stained-glass windows.

This is the kind of thing Papa says: "Tasteful Episcopal stained glass," with that look on his face like he's chewing something rotten. He calls it "Art Deco Christianity." At least there are no bloody Jesuses, he says.

Before they adopted me, Daddy went to school for a million years to be an interior architect. His specialty was adaptive reuse. He knows how to take old buildings and build them new insides. He likes finding broken things and nursing them back to life.

The few people in the shop steal shy glances her way. One takes a surreptitious photo with her phone.

"Can I get some help or what?" says the star's mother.

I wipe my hands on my apron.

Papa is an atheist. Daddy is a Buddhist who likes Jesus. He says maybe the Three Wise Men were monks from Tibet looking for the new Dalai Lama. I say, Okay Daddy. He has all kinds of ideas he tells me when Papa's not listening.

My job is to be handed things. I am to hold as much as I can in my arms until I have to deposit the pile on the counter by the register. I go back and forth with the mom's ceramic cats and tiny shovels and decorative blown-glass balls. I keep my eyes on the items. I nod and say okay. I try not to look at the girl, the one made of sun.

Papa likes things clean and tidy and empty. Daddy likes everything full and found and barely unbroken.

The mom goes from shelf to shelf. There is no method to her selections except for more more more.

The girl mouths "I'm sorry." I mouth "It's okay." Our whispers meet and tangle.

People love these fake antique watering cans. They're Island Home & Garden's best sellers, besides the T-shirts of the otters holding hands. Daddy says they're an abomination. He says the rust and chipped red paint are a lie. The watering cans should have to earn their rust like the rest of us.

"What's your name?" the sunlight says.

"Fern," I say.

I am made.

. . .

This is my origin story. This is my creation myth.

Some kids take ferries every morning with the A-Corp commuters to go to their Seattle private schools. Others, like me, go to the employee-only A-Corp school on the island. Some go far away to boarding schools and then come back at holidays and in summer to have parties and remind the rest of us what we're missing.

I am the one who goes nowhere.

This is the last summer.

"I'm Ivy," the girl says. But of course I already know that. I tell her I think I'm her neighbor.

The mother holds up a fake antique watering can and says, "Ooh, this is so vintage! I love the rust."

They are coming back, one by one, arriving at the airport with bags full of dirty laundry for their housekeepers to clean. They've already started their game of playing like adults with no consequences.

The local taxi service has called in reinforcements from the county across the bridge. There will soon be an island full of children getting drunk who need to get home.

. . .

I have to find boxes in the back to hold all the mother's stuff. I concentrate on wrapping each thing in paper, but my hands are shaking.

"You seem nice," says Ivy, the girl made of sun.

That's me: Nice girl. Daddies' girl. Good girl.

I am a middle-class girl from a loving, intact family. I am a fantasy. I am an endangered species. We are on the verge of extinction. I may be the last one of my kind.

"I'm supposed to recuperate this summer, and I need some company besides myself," she says. "Here, write your number on this receipt. You can be like my tour guide."

And now I have a real job. There is a use for me. I am chosen. I am touched.

2

ASH Kye. Tami Butler.

All year long, I follow their fabulous lives on social media while they forget I exist.

AshandTami. TamiandAsh. They are a unit. They are a single word.

I wonder what it would feel like to have a life that seems worthy of constant documentation.

I try not to get hung up on the fact that Tami is horrible. Ash chose her, so she must be made of at least something good. I've been trying to figure out what that is for years, ever since elementary school when we still went to the same A-Corp school, when she'd sit on top of the monkey bars and make us get in line to present her with "gifts" we found on the playground—a perfect pinecone, a special rock, a lost barrette—and no one questioned her authority. If we wanted to play with her, we had to play her game, and we always did.

It's still like that every time she comes back from boarding school—everyone waiting to see if they'll be chosen. I gave up caring a long time ago. People like Tami never choose people like me, so why should I bother wanting her to? What would I even get out of it? As far as I know, Tami doesn't have any real friends. She has people she bosses around, people she parties with. Nothing deeper. Nothing real.

Despite all of that, my heart still jumps out of my chest when I see her car pull up behind mine outside the grocery store. Since when does Tami do her own grocery shopping? I expect her to act like I don't exist, but for some reason she gets out of her car and walks up to me, her long white-blond hair trailing behind her in slow motion. She almost looks like she's smiling. "You're not fooling anyone with those sunglasses," she says, and her voice is less bitchy than usual.

"Um, okay?" I say.

"Don't act like you don't remember me," she says as she looks me up and down with what I think is approval. "It hasn't been that long since Seth Greenmeyer's party last fall."

What is she talking about? We haven't really hung out since elementary school. Is she high? She must be high. There are all sorts of designer drugs these days that make people act all kinds of weird.

"Of course I remember you," I say.

"I would love to stay and chat," she says. "But I'm running late. We have to hang out soon." She pulls out her phone. "Here, tell me your number and I'll text you."

And that's that. I give her my number and she drives off with a wave.

She didn't even go into the grocery store. She stopped just to talk to me.

The first thing I think is that maybe she's playing a trick on me. Maybe this is like one of those movies where the popular kid picks an unsuspecting loser to pretend to befriend only to humiliate later. This could be some kind of setup. But Ash wouldn't let her do that. Even if our lives don't intersect too much these days, he was still my best friend once. He's the one whose house I went to every Saturday for years while Papa and his dad would go golfing, the one I built forts with, the one I tromped around with in the forest, pretending we were explorers from long ago before everything had already been discovered. Before there was AshandTami, there was just Ash, and he was mine.

His songs were mine. He started writing them when he was thirteen, and I was the only one he played them for. Even then, there was something about his music, a bittersweet beauty. He folded his body over his guitar while he played, all elbows and knees, thick black hair draping over his face like a package waiting to be opened. He wasn't cool then. His braces were off but he still wore clothes his mother's assistant picked out for him—preppy jeans that were a little too big and button-down shirts that were a little too short. His voice squeaked sometimes when he talked.

By sophomore year, he had learned to be cool. That's when he and Tami started dating. Ash could have had his pick of anyone he wanted, but he chose her. Or he let her choose him.

His mother is Persian and his father is Korean. It doesn't seem to bother him when Tami lifts her arm next to his and compares their skin, when she makes comments about what a pretty color their babies will be. He didn't even seem to mind that time at a party when she was admiring their reflection in a hallway mirror and said, "I wish your eyes were just a little wider."

Without a beat, he said, "And I wish you were just a little less of a bitch," and then they laughed, and then they kissed, like he didn't care that his girlfriend was kind of racist, like this is just how couples talk to each other.

But I've seen glimpses—the comments in passing, parsed over time like a continuing conversation: "Isn't this exhausting?" he says to me at one party on his way to get another drink. "If only these assholes knew how I really feel about them," he whispers in my ear at another, just before a couple of guys, pills in their pockets, lead him outside. "Wouldn't it be nice to get away from all of this?" he sighs at still another, positioning his guitar on his lap, a crowd of girls seated at his feet. There have been so many glances at me across a room while Tami holds court next to him, while he's surrounded by adoring people. But he looks at me like he's alone, like he wants out, and I am the only person who sees it, I am the only one he's allowing to see *him*.

There's something intoxicating about this, about being let in on someone's secrets, like glimpsing a tiny light shining through a crack in a wall, and all you want to do is start hammering away, see what else is hiding there, be the one to find it, to claim it. All I want is to see inside. To be the one.

I wonder what Ivy Avila was like as a kid. I wonder what *she* wants. What was it that made her who she is now? If, like Ash, she started out as someone different. Or if, like me, she hasn't changed at all.

Tami called me two days after I ran into her at the grocery store and invited me over. I tried on a total of six different outfits before leaving the house, ultimately deciding on a pair of jeans and a black tank top because according to Papa, "the simplest option is always the most elegant," and he knows these things, even if all he designs these days is armor. I've known Tami since kindergarten, but this is the first time she's ever invited me over to her house, *alone*, for something other than a party that everyone else was also invited to. I try not to think too much about what this means, but I can't help but wonder if maybe Ash had something to do with it. Maybe this is all some sort of premeditated plan. Maybe he's the one who wants us to be friends. Maybe he thinks I'll rub off on her or something. Like how Ivy Avila said, "You seem nice," and asked for my number.

Ivy still hasn't called. It's been five days. I'm trying not to think about that either.

I drive to Tami's house on the east side of the island and announce myself to the security camera at the front gate. It opens mysteriously and I park Papa's little electric Honda behind Tami's Tesla. I thought Ash might be here, but hers is the only car I can see, and I suddenly want to turn around and go home. My disappointment is not a surprise, but my fear is. I have never been alone like this with Tami Butler, not socially, not on purpose.

The house is just like Tami—beautiful and perfect and cold. On the outside, it is black corrugated metal. On the inside, it is all chrome and glass and white leather. A housekeeper leads me through the living area to the back deck.

"How are you today?" I ask her.

"Fine, thank you," she says with a monotone Southern drawl, without looking back at me. She is probably one of so many workers from the southern states here on an inter-state work visa, or a refugee from the flooded coast, where things are so bad with hurricanes and poverty and diseased mosquitos. I wonder if she still has family back there, her own children maybe, while she's here taking orders from Tami. I wonder if Tami even knows where the housekeeper's from, what happened in her life that made her come here.

Housekeepers, gardeners, nannies, personal assistants. I wonder what it would be like to be able to hire people to do everything for you that you can do yourself.

Mountains frame the skyscrapers of Seattle, creating a dramatic backdrop to the covered deck where Tami is sitting with her arms stretched over the back of a huge wraparound couch.

She could be posing for a magazine. She could own the view itself.

She does not rise to greet me, but simply gives a little wave of her hand, like she summoned me and is now simply acknowledging my delivery. She is perfection in black yoga clothes, the epitome of Seattle rich—active, casual, flawless—with long platinum hair that has never known a split end, and ice-blue eyes surrounded by long black curls of fake eyelashes. She is strikingly beautiful, powerful in a sharp, slightly scary way, with a look on her face like she's sizing me up, calculating my worth with some intricate math only she knows and that I have no hope of learning.

"Luanne, bring us some snacks, will you?"

"Yes, ma'am," the housekeeper says. I will never get over eighteen-year-olds being called *ma'am* by women old enough to be their mothers.

"Well, you certainly are beautiful," Tami says to me with something like disappointment in her voice.

I have never been the kind of girl anyone called beautiful. Maybe pretty, but more often than not, nothing at all.

"You changed your hair," Tami says.

"I've been growing it out."

"I envy you."

"Me? Why?" I am nobody. I am the invisible girl who never leaves this island.

"You make it look so easy."

"Make what look easy?"

"Being special."

Special. Ash is special. Tami is special. I am not special.

I want to be special.

If Ash were here, he'd have his back to me. He'd be facing the water and the city, playing something soft on his guitar. His hair would be much longer than the last time I saw him. He would not turn around. He's the kind of person who likes to keep people waiting. He's the kind of person who likes people to come to him. And we always do.

"I love this view," Tami says as I enter the shaded U of the couch. I imagine her sliding closer to Ash now, draping her long legs over his knees, claiming him, pushing his guitar against his body so he's trapped, unable to play. "You don't need that right now, do you?" she would say. The tight muscles of his back would be defined through his thin T-shirt as he turned to set the guitar behind the couch.

You don't need that right now. Tami dismisses Ash's music, like his parents have. They're old-school, the kind that require their children to learn an instrument at a young age, not to instill a love of music but because it's supposed to make them smarter. He is not supposed to be a musician. He is supposed to continue the family A-Corp dynasty and turn out just like them. Just like Tami.

"Where's your boyfriend?" I say.

Tami looks at me with a raised eyebrow.

Now is when he'd finally look at me from behind his curtain

of hair, flicking it out of his eyes, and I would try to smile back, but my face would be crooked. He would smile with one side of his mouth like we were in on something together, like we've been carrying on some secret correspondence while he was away at school that no one, not even me, knows about.

He would say my name. He would smile that smile that feels like you're being shined on. He would get up and hug me, his body hard and sun-warmed, smelling like sweat and pine needles.

"He's stoned," Tami would say. "He's a hugger when he's stoned."

"You want to smoke, Fern?" he would offer as he sits back down, as Tami's legs stretch over him once again.

"No thanks."

"Remember, honey," Tami would say. "Fern is morally superior to you and me."

"Someone has to be." He is so adept at softening Tami's constant blows.

"I suppose you don't want a drink?" Tami says now, taking a sip of hers, something clear and icy with crushed herbs of some kind.

"No thanks," I say.

"Good for you," she says.

Tami would remove her legs from Ash's lap and he would immediately pick up his guitar from behind the couch and start playing again, his black hair guarding his eyes.

"Ash writes these little songs," Tami would say. "It's cute." And he would act like he didn't hear her.

"Your house is beautiful," I say now. I know I've been here before, but after a while, all rich people's houses start looking the same. Daddy always says if you can't figure out what to say, give someone a compliment. Everyone loves compliments.

"I heard yours is pretty cool too," she says, folding her long legs under her. "It's on the west side of the island, right? Off Olympic?"

I nod. Why would Tami care anything about my house?

"Who are you hanging out with these days?"

"No one in particular. Mostly just Lily." Lily, who moved here a year ago. My only real friend since Ash.

"Who's Lily? You should bring her sometime."

"She's always going to Taiwan."

"Ugh, I hate Taiwan. I hate anywhere you have to wear a mask. It messes up my face."

Ash would look up from his guitar for a moment and emit a laugh like a puff of air and Tami wouldn't even notice.

The beauty of the view is interrupted by a decrepit boat puttering by, in such bad shape, it looks like it shouldn't even be floating. Laundry hangs off a line on the back next to a few bicycles chained together, surrounded by stacks of various crates and boxes secured by bungees. I see a skinny man and a smudgy little girl. Then a little boy, even younger. I wonder how long they've been sailing from place to place, hauling anchor as soon as they become unwelcome. Boats like these in Puget

Sound—they're not so different from the people living in cars or tents on land, except these people can fish for their food, and they can sink.

An island security boat motors up behind it, lights flashing, a voice announcing over a loudspeaker: "You're too close to shore. Move away from the shore or you will be issued a citation." A few nearby birds squawk at the interruption and fly away.

"Island security really needs to step up their game," Tami says. "Did you hear they found a whole family living in the nature preserve? They'd been there for weeks and nobody noticed. We pay good money to not have to deal with that kind of thing."

The two sunburned children look out the grimy windows of the boat's cabin as it turns away.

"This island is so boring. How can you stand it?" Tami says.

"I kind of like it here. It's beautiful. The air's still breathable." I almost add, "People are nice," but that's not true. People here are not nice.

"I guess," she says. "But no offense, Commodore Island isn't exactly the cultural capital of the world."

Tami's one of those people who says "no offense" before she says something offensive.

"God, I am so bored," she moans. "I just got back, and I am already so bored." She smiles, and something opens, a crack in her façade. "But now Ivy Avila's here."

My chest seizes. Has she met her already too? Has Ivy called her and not me?

"We're going to have a good time this summer," Tami says, looking at me, and her face is different—not so sharp and intimidating. "You and me."

"Okay," I say. *You and me.* There has never been a Tami and me.

"I don't have a lot of friends," she says. "I know a million people, but none of them are real friends, you know?"

"Yeah," I say, because in some strange way, I do.

"I think we could be friends," she says.

"Me too," I say, but I feel something heavy in my stomach.

She laughs. "You want to hear this thing my mom always says? She's been saying it ever since I was a kid. She always tells me, 'It's lonely at the top.' I mean, it sounds so conceited, right? But it's true. You know what I mean."

Tami is lonely at the top. That's what this is about. She wants to see what it's like to have a friend who's beneath her.

"When you get down to it," she says, "most people aren't really friends. Mostly we're all just using each other."

She forces a smile and sits up tall. She tilts her head and just like that, all her cold perfection clicks back into place. "Are you hungry?" She types something into her phone. "Where is that goddamned maid?"

I am not hungry. I want to leave here. I want to see Ash.

Maybe the reason Ash can stand to be with her is because of his talent for closing himself off, his strange knack for acting like he's alone even when surrounded by people.

"We should have a party," Tami says.

We both have this talent, Ash and me. We have our own worlds nobody even knows about.

"That's all there is to do on this island," she says. "Party. Get wasted and have sex."

Maybe now is when I would look at Ash and he'd be staring right at me, and our eyes would meet, and Tami would fade away. And maybe she would go inside to check on the housekeeper, because no one ever does anything fast enough for her or the right way. And as soon as she disappeared into the house, I'd feel myself unchained, and Ash would tuck his hair behind his ear and say, "You just took a deep breath."

"What?"

"As soon as Tami was gone, you took a deep breath," he says. "Like all of a sudden you could breathe again." He smiles. "I feel like that too sometimes."

"Then why—"

"How've you been, Fern?" he says, with those eyes that make this feel like an incredibly important question. Like *I* am an incredibly important question.

I have been fine. There has never been much else besides fine. My existence is defined by fine.

"How are your dads?"

"Good. Papa's working a lot, as usual. Dad's thinking about writing a cookbook."

"Isn't he supposed to be an architect?"

"The only house he ever managed to actually build was ours."

Ash laughs, and for a brief moment, I don't feel so hopeless.

"How's your dad?" I say. I've heard the rumors about him being back in rehab again.

"Oh, I don't know," he says, looking out at Seattle. "He likes the place he's at. They have equestrian therapy there. He says he's thinking about retiring early and buying a horse farm. We've talked on the phone a little. I don't think he wants to leave."

"Why not?"

"He's safe there."

What I want to ask is: Do you talk to Tami about stuff like this?

What I want to ask is: What makes a person safe?

"She's not in there getting food," he says.

"No?"

"She's calling her boyfriend in Seattle."

I stare at him, look for some shred of feeling, but it's trapped somewhere deep inside, and all I see is a beautiful boy who deserves so much better.

But I already know Tami has another boyfriend. I'm not proud of it, but I've done some research. It's not difficult to find things out about people.

"You've changed," he says.

"It's the hair." I've grown it long. It's lightened in the sun.

"It's more than that."

"Maybe," I say. Then, "Yes." Then, "You've changed too."

He doesn't say anything for a long time. I like being quiet with Ash. I like watching the sky darken to strips of orange.

"I bet the sunset looks different on your side of the island."

"Yes."

"Do you still climb that tree by your house? Can you see the sunset from it?"

"Yes."

"Let's do that sometime, okay? Let's climb that tree and watch the sunset."

"Okay."

"Let's keep in better touch when we go to college."

I say nothing because I can't keep saying yes, yes, okay. I must have something to say besides what I have always said. Besides just doing what I'm told, besides just agreeing, besides just validating everyone else's existence.

Ash sighs. His eyes are glassy and tired. He drains his drink, crunches on an ice cube.

"You'll chip your teeth," I say.

"What?"

"Papa always says that when I chew ice."

"But that's what dentists are for. There's always someone to fix everything."

We look at the sky a little longer. Sunsets take forever in the summer.

"None of this is real," Ash says out of nowhere, and I look at the orange and pink reflected in the windows of the Seattle skyscrapers.

"You're real," I say, even though I know he's not, that this entire conversation has taken place in my imagination.

I feel my skin tighten, an oppressive weight in my chest. I

know before I even turn around that Tami has returned and Ash is gone.

"Put the food on the table," she tells the housekeeper, who is following her, carrying a tray of tiny sandwiches and intricately sliced raw vegetables.

"Thank you," I say.

"What are you going to do now, tip her?" Tami says, laughing.

"Anything else, Miss Tami?" the woman says.

"No." It's like she makes a special effort to not say "No, thank you."

Before the housekeeper is outside hearing range, Tami says, "That accent makes them sound so stupid."

"I think I'm going to go," I say, standing up. The heavy feeling in my stomach is worse now. "I don't want to be late for dinner," I say, even though I already told Daddy I'd be home late.

"Oh," Tami says, and for a moment I see her edges softened, her shoulders not so yoga perfect. She is disappointed, maybe even embarrassed. She is maybe a small piece of human. Maybe all people, even the Tami Butlers of the world, get lonely sometimes.

"Okay," she says, making an effort to sound chipper. "I'll feed your food to the fishes, then." She rises and walks to the bar to make herself another drink. That's two just since I've been here. "Seattle is so far away," she says to no one in particular. "I wish I had my own helicopter."

I almost say "Tell Ash I say hi," but stop myself.

“Let’s do something wild,” she says. “I’ll think of something.”

“Okay,” I say, even though I am the girl who never does anything wild. She should know that. But maybe she knows something I don’t.

And I walk away, leaving Tami to drink alone. And just like that, I am gone, like I’d never even been there.

I drive home but I don’t go inside just yet. It’s almost dark. Daddy and Papa are probably drinking herbal tea and watching some kind of smart show, probably a documentary or critically acclaimed dramatic series. Gotami is getting her fur all over the throw blanket in the nest she’s made between them on the couch. Daddy has some dried garbanzo beans soaking in water to make homemade hummus in the morning. My sweet little family doing their sweet little family things.

I climb the giant old oak tree on the edge of the property, between the fruit trees and where the real forest starts, with thick, strong branches in all the right places. A curved one near the top is a perfect perch, with another branch behind it that serves as a backrest. I could probably fall asleep here and be safe from falling.

I listen to the bugs and night sounds, leaning back to look up at the sliver of moon peeking through the branches of the taller trees overhead. I think how this would be a perfect place for a teenager who wanted a place to get away, a place to have secrets.

I think it is time for me to start making some secrets. I'm eighteen years old and I've done nothing yet.

It's almost lunchtime in Taiwan. I can't remember if it's today there, or tomorrow, or yesterday. Lily and I promised to call or at least text each other every day, but I have no idea what I'd even say to her right now. She'd want to know what happened at Tami's, and I don't want to talk about that, don't want to tell her how disappointed I was that Ash wasn't there, don't want to tell her Tami says she has plans for us. I don't want to tell her how this both terrifies and excites me.

From here, I can just see over the trees down the hill toward the shore. I can see the lights on at Ivy Avila's house, the walls of which are almost completely glass. A dark figure is in an upstairs window, looking out at Seattle, and everything about it, objectively, is beautiful. But something about the scene makes me think of Alcatraz, another island, how the prisoners there must have felt so many years ago, behind bars with the most beautiful view in the world.

3

EVERYONE on the island is talking about Ivy Avila, and I am good at listening.

I put on my sunglasses and turn invisible. I become silent and still and the light passes right through me.

Coffee shop. Monday. 10:47 a.m.:

"Isn't her mom like some kind of crazy stage mom?" Woman 1 says. "Like she totally lives off her daughter?"

"Getting rich off your own kid is as bad as getting rich off of welfare," says Woman 2.

"I'm pretty sure no one ever got rich off of welfare," says Woman 3. "And when's the last time you had a job?"

"I hate you after Pilates," says Woman 2. "You turn into a liberal snowflake."

"If I'm a liberal snowflake, then you're new-money trash," says Woman 3.

"We're all new-money trash," says Woman 1. "How long have either of your families had money? Three generations? Old money is not tech money. It's from way before that."

Woman 2 and Woman 3 both roll their eyes.

"And what about the American dream and all that?" says Woman 1.

And then they all laugh.

Island Home & Garden. Tuesday. 2:11 p.m.:

"Here, I have it," says a boarding school girl I vaguely recognize as she reads from her phone. "This is such bullshit. Her mom totally wrote this. It's all about her. She was a poor single mom, boo-hoo-hoo, cleaning Seattle high-rises for a living. Then she saw a spark in her daughter and sacrificed everything to bring her to Hollywood at age nine and devote herself to supporting her daughter's dream."

"Sacrifice what?" says her friend as she inspects a fake antique watering can. "That woman didn't have anything to sacrifice. She's just mooching off her kid."

"'After several commercials and small parts,'" the other girl continues, "'Ivy landed her first big role at age eleven as a recurring character on *The Fabulous Fandangos*. Then her big break came at age thirteen when she got a starring role in *The Cousins,* a popular teen drama on A-Corp's video streaming service. Ivy then launched her music career at age sixteen with her debut album, *This Is Me,* which went platinum.' Boring. Where's the juicy stuff?" The girl types and swipes and reads some more.

"Ooh," she says. "Apparently there are rumors that she's had affairs with all these old, like *much older*, people in Hollywood, men and women. Some problems with drugs and eating disorders, the usual. God, what is it with these Hollywood losers that they can't handle their drugs?"

Grocery store checkout line. Wednesday. 5:23 p.m.:

"I'd do her," says a middle-aged guy to another middle-aged guy. "Hell yeah, I'd do her in a second."

Home. Thursday. 7:09 p.m.:

"Celebrity culture certainly is fascinating," says Papa, swiping through a feature about Ivy on his phone. "It's like they live on a different planet. But now she's trying to live on ours."

"That poor girl," says Daddy.

"Meow," says Gotami.

She is a girl made of rumors and gossip and other people's desires. They swirl around her until they lose all meaning, until there is just an outline left.

But she is more than that. Ivy Avila is more than just her outline.

Somehow I know this.

4

"I see you," a voice says, and suddenly I'm falling, like I'm in some kind of funnel and life is swirling dark around me, attaching its shadows to my transparent skin. I'm being conjured into being at the same time I'm being destroyed, going down, down, down while I'm being formed, and it's infinite how far I can fall. I will be falling forever. I will never hit the ground.

"Hello?" the voice says, and at first I think it's Lily. I open my eyes and all I see is the shadow of a face with a burst of sunlight behind it, and I remember I am in a hammock under Daddy's fruit trees, it is my day off work, I was reading, and then my eyes closed, and then I was flying somewhere not here, and now there's gravity again and my eyes are open and I'm squinting, trying to find detail in this new, unfamiliar light.

"Sorry," the voice says. "Did I scare you?"

The light changes as the figure moves and I can see her face now: *Ivy*.

Finally.

I suddenly feel my body.

"No, hi," I mumble, trying to sit up, but the hammock won't let me, binding me in an awkward position where I can't use my arms. "I guess I was napping. Sorry."

"Please don't apologize for napping. No one should ever apologize for napping." Her dark eyes sear into mine. I wonder if she can see herself reflected.

I manage to set myself somewhat upright. "Did you walk here?" I say. She is wearing cutoff jean shorts and a wide-shouldered, thin white shirt that shows the outline of her black bra, and the kind of expensive athletic shoes that aren't meant for actually exercising.

"Yeah, it's a nice walk. I like walking. I think. I don't know. I'm trying to figure out what I like. It's an assignment I have. Isn't that weird? To not even know what I like? I mean, besides the obvious things that I'm not supposed to do anymore. That I don't want to do anymore." She pauses, looks at me, tilts her head. "Sorry, am I oversharing? I just don't get a lot of opportunities to talk about anything real, so I'm like starving for it. And you seem like someone who does."

"Does what?"

"Talks about things that are real."

"Yes. I mean, I do. You can say whatever you want."

She smiles and I feel my skin tighten, like I have been zipped up and put back together. Those eyes again, unblinking, staring into me. I want to look away but I can't.

"Walking is good exercise and it helps clear your mind," she says. "Like you can meditate while you do it. I'm supposed to meditate."

"My dad meditates," I say.

"Really?" She seems excited. "Do you?"

"No. He tried to teach me one time, but all that breathing just made me anxious."

I should have lied. I should have told her I meditate. I will sit in the quiet with her for thirty minutes if she wants me to.

"I'm supposed to go to these meetings where you meditate and talk about your suffering."

"That kind of sounds like the meetings my dad goes to."

"Is he an addict?"

"No. Just a human."

"Same thing really. Everybody's addicted to something. It's the human condition." She smiles. For a moment, I'm pretty sure this is one of those dreams where I think I wake up but really it's just the start of a new dream.

"I lost your number," she says.

"It's okay."

"But I remembered you said you were my neighbor. So I wandered around and here you were."

Here I am. She found me.

"Tell me your number," she says. "I'll text you mine." I do. She does.

"I may have a party this weekend," she says. "I don't know. I'll text you if I do. I may not even go."

"You may not go to your own party?"

"It's my mom's idea. She's always the one who wants to throw the parties. If she wants a party so bad, why doesn't she throw one for people her own age? Why does it always have to be my party? She says it's a good way for me to make friends, but I know she doesn't give a shit if I make friends. She just wants to show off."

"And you don't?" I say. Where did that come from?

But Ivy smiles, and the music of her laugh makes everything shine. "Maybe I do," she says. "Want to show off a little. But not like that. Not like her." She looks at me with approval, and everything around us brightens. "I like you, Fern. You're real. You're not full of shit like everyone else."

"Thank you." What I want to say is, "You make me real." What I want to say is, "I don't even know who I was before this moment."

"Can you make me a promise? Don't lose that, okay? Don't treat me like I'm special. Always tell me exactly what you think. Don't let me get away with anything."

"I don't think I have that power."

She puts her hands on my cheeks, cups my face, makes me a tulip.

"Oh, Fern. You have more power than you know."

I want her to hold my face like this forever. I want the warmth of her hands around my jaw, her fingertips on my cheekbones, her thumbs so close to my lips I could put them in my mouth.

“I have to go,” she says, just as I realize my eyes are closed, just as I decide to open them.

“I’ll text you,” she says.

“Promise,” I call after her.

“I promise,” she says, looking at me over her shoulder, and the trees whisper their commentary, but I don’t know what they’re saying.

5

WHEN I told Lily I was going to the city tonight with Tami Butler, she almost hung up on me.

This is what Tami said when she invited me: "Let's get off this pathetic hunk of rock."

"Is your boyfriend coming?" I said.

"Why do you keep asking about my boyfriend?"

"Why are you going?" Lily said. "You don't even like her. Does this relationship nurture you in any way?"

Who talks like that?

She makes it sound so easy. As if it's just a matter of liking or not liking someone. What matters is I've been waiting my whole life for girls like Tami Butler to acknowledge my existence. Even though I tried to convince myself I wasn't. Even though I told myself I didn't care. But I do care. Everyone cares. Anyone who says they don't is a liar.

And maybe I do like Tami, just a little. Maybe I got to glimpse a part of her people don't usually see. Maybe I want to see more of it, more of what else she's hiding. As cruel as she is, there's something about Tami that I admire. How does it feel to not care about being nice or liked, to be so sure of your place in the world, you feel no threat of losing it?

Lily looked at me through the screen of my phone, from the other side of the earth. She said, "You know they're all narcissists, right? Tami, Ash. I could diagnose them right now. You're not still hung up on *him*, are you?"

"No," I lie.

"As you can probably guess, I'm not a big fan of this decision."

I didn't say, "But you are not here."

I didn't say, "What choice do I have?"

I didn't say, "I'm bored and I'm lonely and I want to feel worth something."

I want to feel something.

I check my phone.

I look in the mirror and I don't know when I started looking like this. Like someone who might be friends with Tami Butler.

. . .

I check my phone again.

No one remembers nice girls.

Tami sends a prepaid car for me. I get a text that says, *Your car is here. Driver's name: Norman.* Norman probably has at least two other jobs. Norman probably moved here from someplace that's underwater now or that's been poisoned by busted oil pipelines.

Papa says, "Be safe."

Daddy sniffles, "Where did my little girl go?"

Gotami says, "Meow."

No one says anything about a curfew. I have never needed one.

"Quite a place you got here," says Norman.

Ivy Avila hasn't texted. I'm beginning to think I dreamed our whole conversation.

Daddy talks about "the middle path." But the middle path is boring. Buddhism is boring.

. . .

We do not take the tourist ferry. We take the private A-Corp boat. We climb the steps to the VIP lounge. The woman at the door scans Tami's ID and adds me as her guest. She looks at me like I do not belong here, like she knows just by looking at me that my own ID only gets me access downstairs.

I have always been the middle path.

I do not say to Tami, "Why me? Why'd you pick me?"

There are so many other girls on the island, private school girls, girls home from other boarding schools, girls so much more like Tami than I will ever be. But Tami is tired of those girls.

The casual rich of the island have transformed into their cocktail dresses and diamonds, their heels and pearls. The city glimmers across the water, promising something.

We are moths rushing toward the light.

I was supposed to be Ivy's tour guide.

. . .

"You know why she wants to hang out with you?" Lily said. "Because you're not a threat. Because you're not competition."

Tami pours a flask of something into my lemonade. "You know why I like you? I think we have a lot in common. We're *special.* Not like all the basic bitches on the island."

I am the girl homeless people ask for money. I wear a giant flashing sign that announces to the world: "I will listen to you. I will not be mean. My patience is endless." I am a magnet for people's secrets, but I don't have any of my own. Not yet.

Tami called me special.

Maybe tonight I will make some secrets.

The city approaches quickly.

. . .

Tami says, "All the other girls on the island are jealous. I can't trust them. You know what I mean."

My patience is endless.

6

"WHERE are we going?" I ask Tami. She does not answer. She's texting someone and smiling.

The Seattle boardwalk sparkles with shops and restaurants and the big ancient Ferris wheel. It is a place made for tourists. Security guards are everywhere, hired by the businesses to keep the vacationers safe.

A car is waiting for us. The driver already knows Tami's destination, but I do not.

Our car exits the boardwalk, and a few small storefront shops and restaurants line the quiet streets, all mostly closed for the evening. Skyscrapers soar above us, majestic and expansive. This part of the city is spotless, everything high-tech and shiny, everything tidy and calm and orderly. Everything safe.

There are billboards everywhere, advertisements of things to buy: the latest high-tech gadgets, expensive jewelry, self-improvement seminars, do-it-yourself Botox home injection kits. There are notices from the government reminding us of our patriotic and legal duty to turn in undocumented immigrants. During the day, the sidewalks are packed with people, but at night, this part of downtown is empty. The walled section of the city is strict in its laws against sitting or lying on the sidewalk, against panhandling and scrounging through garbage cans. The street is devoid of human life, but there is still movement—the cars on their way to other places, the advertisements flashing, the little scrubbing Beauty Bots constantly cleaning the sidewalk, and the security drones buzzing just overhead, always watching. I get the feeling the city would still go on after all the people disappeared, like it doesn't even need us anymore.

Before I left tonight, Daddy told me to be careful. There have been a lot of protests in the city lately. "There have always been protests," I told him. Seattle is one of the few cities that still allows them.

"But they're turning violent," he said. "People are tense. A bomb was found in the parking garage of the Smith Tower."

"I'm not going to the Smith Tower," I told him. He did not find that funny.

I look at the sleeping city around me and see no sign of the unrest everyone's always talking about. Everything looks peaceful.

"Where are we going?" I ask Tami again. She just hands me the flask and I drink without thinking whether I want to or not.

It tastes like fire. My voice is gone. Something lost burns inside me, something both remembered and brand-new. I feel a momentary shock of terror, like that feeling you get in a dream when you're falling, when you have no idea where the bottom is but you're pretty sure whenever you hit, it's going to be the end of you. But then I jolt awake and remember where I am—in a car, in Seattle, with Tami Butler, on my way to who knows where.

"You're not going to go crazy on me, are you?" she says. "Now that you're drinking?"

"Why would I do that?"

She just arches her eyebrows like she thinks she knows me better than I know myself.

We continue up the hill, away from the water, through the dark gleam of the financial district, asleep for the weekend. Every time we pass an intersection, I see glimpses of the lights a few blocks to the north, the part of the city where people go to play. I do not ask why we are driving this way and not that way, why we are not turning, why we are staying on the street that will take us out of downtown and into the residential areas.

I look at Tami, and she's texting again, with that same smile on her face that has nothing to do with me.

The office buildings and expensive condos give way to the massive apartment complexes on the other side of the hill, and we breeze through a security checkpoint that only checks people coming the other way. As soon as we leave the gated part of downtown, everything becomes suddenly dingier, older. Massive apartment buildings loom over the narrow streets, blocking the night sky. Paint peels off the dull streetlights.

Garbage on the sidewalks. Homeless camped wherever they can find an empty spot. Between downtown and the walled communities of mansions by Lake Washington are these vast blocks of people packed tight, pedestrians and bicycles rushing everywhere, street after street of identical apartment buildings with businesses jammed side by side on the ground floor. Billboards display ads for no-interest A-Corp credit cards, synthetic beer, employment recruitment for a new mega-prison being built in New Mexico. It's like a different world here. We're allowed to come to this part of town whenever we want, but they have to scan their IDs and pay a toll to drive into downtown.

My dads remember when things were different, when there was still the possibility of having a life that existed somewhere between poverty and wealth, when there were more options than being born rich or being one of the people who serve them. But that world was already dying when my fathers were born. They are the last of their kind.

Only the exceptional ever break out of the life they were born into.

So what does that mean for me? I don't know the answer, but I do know that compared to the quiet slowness of the island, the busyness of this neighborhood feels almost refreshing. Maybe in a place like this, a person would never have to feel alone.

"Have you ever seen anything so depressing?" Tami says.

Maybe that's the trade-off. Tami can afford to buy anything she'd ever want. She can buy all the space and security she needs to not have to bump into anyone. But maybe there's a downside to that. Maybe we need to bump into people sometimes.

We drive through several blocks of apartment buildings and through a small commercial area. An armored Immigration and Customs Enforcement bus packed full of prisoners drives by, their faces pressed against the wired windows, bodies packed together tight. People on the streets throw garbage and yell insults, though many of them came to Seattle as refugees from other places within the U.S., forced to move for the same reasons. The only difference between the people on the sidewalk and the people in the bus is what side of a line they were born on.

Our car stops at a stoplight, and for a few very long seconds, I feel suddenly vulnerable. We are not on the protected island anymore. We are not in the walled part of the city. We are stopped in the middle of the street, and a group of people a little older than us are standing on the sidewalk, glaring. One woman gives us the finger. Another guy spits in our direction. I know they cannot see inside the tinted windows, but they can guess from the car that we do not belong here, that we are not like them.

Or am I? I am somewhere in the middle. Am I closer to them or closer to Tami?

Something hits the window by Tami's head and we both jump. What looks like coffee drips down the glass. The people on the sidewalk laugh, but then they're illuminated by flashing red lights coming from a police drone hovering above them. As they start running, sirens sound in the distance.

The light changes, and just like that, we drive away, leaving them behind.

"God, don't those people have anything better to do?" Tami says. "It's not like throwing shit at cars is going to make them less poor."

All we did was drive through their neighborhood, but somehow I still feel responsible.

We turn onto a street of old houses. Not old like the stately mansions by the lake. Old as in crumbling. Old as in leaking roofs and unmown lawns. Barking dogs. Bars on the windows.

The car turns a corner and starts to slow.

I don't say, "What are we doing here?"

Tami looks at me now. She is strangely calm. Her eyes shine with the reflection of a corner store advertising a sale on bottled cocktails.

"Have you heard of Freedom?" she says. For a moment, she reminds me of one of those people handing out flyers for their weird cult churches who always seem to find me.

"It's a new pill," she says. "It's *amazing*."

"Is that why we're here? Why don't you just buy it from someone on the island?"

Tami smiles. "I can't get this on the island."

The car slows to a stop in front of a drooping two-story house with a couch on the front porch and half a dozen bicycles chained up inside the wrought-iron fence.

I know for a fact she can get any drug she wants on the

island. If no one has it, she could pay to have a drone fly it out to her any time she wants. There must be something else we're here for.

A dog barks and a police siren wails somewhere in the distance as we open the gate and walk the weedy path to the front door. "Don't worry," Tami says. "I told Vaughn you're coming."

"Who's Vaughn?" I say. "Why does he need to know I'm coming?"

Is it too late to turn around? Is it too late to get in that car and tell the driver to take me back to the terminal?

"Am I not supposed to be here?"

I want more of whatever was in that flask.

7

ARE other people's lives like this? All of a sudden you look up and realize you're doing something you don't remember ever choosing?

What I can't understand is how just this morning I was at work unpacking a new shipment of fake antique watering cans, and now I'm sitting in some house in a questionable Seattle neighborhood buying drugs with Tami Butler.

But the living room is cozy, with soft, if worn, furniture, colorful rugs, art on the walls, and books on the shelves—the old, actual paper kind. It isn't anything like what I pictured a drug dealer's house to look like. The guy sitting on the couch across from us is about three times the size of the girl sitting next to him. He tells me he's an MMA fighter.

"Pre-professional," he corrects his girlfriend, who says "amateur."

He's all muscles and tan and trendy tattoos of various fitness brands and sports team logos. Her light brown skin is free of makeup, black hair in tight braids. A cup of tea and a reading tablet sit in front of her. The guy says, "Raine's in community college—got dreams of being a social worker."

"Who *dreams* of being a social worker?" Tami says.

Raine just looks at Tami and blinks. It's like she doesn't speak sarcasm.

"If they had *this*, no one would need any kind of therapy anymore," he says, zipping up a plastic baggie with a dozen golden pills that glimmer in the soft lamplight.

I look at Raine, trying to process what she's doing versus what he's doing. She returns to her tablet, like this is some kind of study group and not an illegal drug deal. She highlights something with her fingertip and glances up. "Vaughn," she says. "I forgot to tell you—Lita's about to get evicted. I offered to let her sleep on the couch, just till she finds a place."

He leans close to her. "We don't have room," he says in a low voice, as if we won't hear. "We barely fit the people who live here already, and they pay rent. You can't just take in everybody."

"It's not everybody," she says. "It's Lita."

Why would someone get into this in front of company? Because she knows he won't pick a fight or make a scene with us here? Or does she genuinely not care what we think?

"We can talk about it later," Vaughn says. He smiles at us a little too big, and changes the subject. "Raine, tell them about how Freedom was invented by scientists for medicinal use."

She looks up from her tablet again, her eyes focusing like she'd already forgotten we were here. "Oh, yeah. It got all the way to clinical trials," she says. "So much poison gets approved by the FDA, you know? With all kinds of terrible side effects. My theory is they gave up on it because the self-help and coaching industries are big business and rely on people staying sick. But Freedom could help a lot of people."

"How noble," Tami says, and no one but me knows she's kidding.

"How does it help people?" I say.

"Don't get them started," Tami says.

"It helped my cousin," Vaughn says, and Raine is looking at him in a way that reminds me of how Daddy looks at Papa sometimes. "When he came back from the war in Brazil, he was broken. And of course the VA wouldn't do shit to help him. He was on a waiting list to see a therapist for like three months. But a therapist couldn't help him with what he was going through. No one could."

"But then I did a bunch of research and found out about Freedom," Raine says. "We had to eat nothing but rice and beans for two weeks to save up enough for one dose." She smiles. "It changed everything."

"My cousin's like a totally different person now," Vaughn says. "But he needs a dose every day. And the only way to afford it is to sell it." He holds the baggie out to Tami.

"Well, it certainly helps me," she says, grabbing it and putting it in her purse.

"We're not talking about people like you," Raine says flatly, and looks back down at her tablet.

"What is that supposed to mean?" Tami says. "'People like me'?"

I look around the living room, but I find nothing that will

save me from this. Just mismatched chairs and sheets for curtains.

"No offense, but I don't think you need it," Raine says.

"No offense," Tami says. "But you don't know anything about me."

"How about we bring it down a notch?" Vaughn says.

I want to change the subject. I want to ask where all the roommates are. I want to know how so many people live in one house with only one bathroom.

"Raine, how did you and Vaughn meet?" I say, because it's the first thing that pops into my head, but now it's Vaughn who looks uncomfortable. He steals a quick look at Tami and I catch a moment of eye contact between them and suddenly I get it. There's something else going on here. Now I know what Tami can't get on the island or delivered by a drone.

"We went to the same high school," Raine says. "Garfield, just down the street."

"Bulldogs!" Vaughn barks. "Class of sixty-three."

"It was sophomore year. I'd noticed him, but we weren't really friends or anything. We hung out with different crowds."

"She rolled with the brains," Vaughn says. "I did not."

"And then one day I saw a kid getting picked on by some asshole, and Vaughn stepped in and defended him." She smiles. "And I was a goner." Tami is pretending to ignore the story. She's tapping on her phone with a scowl on her face.

"That's a lovely story," Tami says. "But we have to get going." I don't think I've ever seen her so uncomfortable.

"I'm hungry," Vaughn says. "Are you hungry?" he asks Raine.

"A little, I guess."

"Do you want to get us something from the kitchen while I finish up in here?"

"Sure," she says, looking a little confused. "Okay."

"It was nice meeting you," I say as she stands up.

"You too," she says, but she's looking at Tami, and not kindly. Tami matches her stare, draping her arm over the back of the couch like she owns this place and everyone in it.

Raine is the first to look away.

As soon as Raine is gone, Tami leans in and starts giving orders: "Come to my place downtown. Invite some people. Bring someone for my friend."

Vaughn reaches over and touches Tami's face, and she slaps his hand away. "Not here."

He says, "Sorry."

Tami has this effect on people. She makes them say "sorry" for no good reason.

She stands up. I stand up. She walks out the door. I walk out the door.

We leave without saying goodbye, or thank you, or anything.

"He's hot, right?" she says as we return to the car. I have no idea what I'm supposed to say to that.

A haggard man of indeterminate age, possibly drunk, limps by us. He points at me and says, "I know you from somewhere."

I am the girl who always looks like somebody else.

The car is still parked at the curb, waiting for us. Tami tells the driver the address of her family's condo downtown. She takes one of the golden glittery pills out of the baggie and washes it down with one of the car's complimentary bottles of water.

"Two hundred dollars a pop," she says. "And totally worth it."

She holds the baggie out to me. "Try one?"

"No, thank you," I say.

She laughs. "It's sweet how good you're trying to be. Don't worry, it's not like other drugs. It doesn't get you high. I don't know how to describe it. It just makes you feel . . . unburdened."

I hear Lily's voice in my head: "You are not seriously thinking about it, are you? *Are you?*"

"No," I say. "Thanks. I'm okay."

"You're okay." Tami laughs. "Of course you're okay. Everybody's A-OK."

She passes me the flask and I at least take a drink of that. It's starting to feel familiar. Warm instead of burning. Like a hug from the inside.

"That girl cracks me up," Tami says. "Studying all the time and talking like she's some working-class intellectual with a moral high horse stuck up her ass. But the truth is, her husband sells drugs and beats people up for a living. She's such a hypocrite."

"They're married? How old are they?"

"I may be a bitch, but at least I'm not a hypocrite," Tami says, taking a swig from the flask. "I know what people think of me.

But that's how you get what you want. That's how my mom got where she is. Girls like Raine don't get anywhere." She looks at me and smiles. "You're so *nice,* aren't you?"

I have no idea what to say to that.

"You never thought I'd be someone into slumming it, did you?" She says this almost proudly, like she took me here, in some twisted way, to impress me. "Did you see his arms?" She laughs. "I'm totally just using him for his body. It's an incredible body."

But then something shifts. She looks out the window, and I get the impression that she's trying to hide her face. "He's good to me," she says. "He treats me like a queen." She's silent for a few blocks, then turns back to me and says, "Ash is such hard work. Everything in my life is such hard work." She says this as she's drinking expensive bourbon out of a silver flask in the back of a hired car, after swallowing a two-hundred-dollar pill that's supposed to make her forget all her worries. "Sometimes I feel like I'm not good enough for him. Can you believe that? *Me?* Not good enough?"

I don't say, "What if that means you're not supposed to be together? What if that means you don't fit?" Admitting that would be a failure somehow. And Tami is someone who refuses to fail.

"I can relax when I'm with Vaughn," she says. "Do you have any idea what it feels like to never be able to relax? To always have to be in control?"

"But no one's making you," I say.

"I don't have a choice."

"Yes you do," I say. "You can choose anything you want." What about Raine and Vaughn? What about their choices?

But Tami just laughs. "I don't have time for that shit. You slow down for one minute in this world, you stop for just a second to have a feeling or wonder what it all means, that's how you end up a failure. That's what makes you weak. I'm not ever going to end up like that. My mom has never cracked. Not once."

Yes, but where is she?

And what is the alternative to cracking? What if there are things that build and build until there's so much pressure they need to be let out?

What if there are things that need to be let in?

"You want to know a secret about desperate people?" Tami says. "They fuck like their life depends on it."

Tami laughs and laughs, and I don't know if the pill already kicked in, if it's the booze, if it's some kind of nervous response to everything she just told me, or if it's the high of doing and saying whatever she wants and knowing she can get away with it.

For a moment, I hate her. I think, *This will be the last time I hang out with Tami Butler. I will go home early and call Lily and confess my temporary lapse in judgment and everything will go back to normal.*

But then we enter a new section of the walled part of the city, and the glittering lights of the exclusive clubs lining the street pulse against Tami's flawless skin. Her face throbs in and out of shadow, split-second snapshots of a glamorous girl in profile, and then I see something shift in the frame-by-frame of her, something drain out, like the shadows are lapping up the light.

I don't think the pill has kicked in yet. As she stares out the window I am struck with the knowing that I have never met anyone so utterly alone in my life.

Maybe Tami and I do have something in common after all.

8

I'VE never been to Tami's family's condo in the city, but it looks exactly as I'd imagine it—same sparse, modern furnishings as her house, near the top of a high-rise, with a wall of windows looking west.

"There's my house," she says, pointing toward the northern tip of Commodore Island. "Do you see it?"

"Yes," I say, though all I see are a line of indistinguishable, identical lights on the shore reflecting back at themselves.

Vaughn comes up and puts his arms around her waist and kisses her on the neck.

"Why don't we ever go out?" he says. "I want to go out."

"You know I can't be seen in public with you."

"I should go," I say, and turn around. It is the right thing to say, but I don't know if I mean it.

"Nonsense," Tami says. "Vaughn's friends will be here soon. He has a friend I want you to meet."

I have only been tipsy a handful of times in my life and never really understood the appeal, but the few sips I've had from Tami's flask have seemed to turn on a switch inside that I don't remember ever feeling. A yearning for more. A spark of something new and wild and reckless.

I think maybe I will get drunk tonight.

They arrive in a pack, Vaughn's friends. He introduces them to me one by one while Tami stands looking out the window, her back to us all.

They are too excited to meet me. I almost feel sorry for them, for their misunderstanding. They think I am another girl like Tami.

Kayla and Amir are both low-level coders at A-Corp. Esteban is a bartender at a nice restaurant downtown, and his girlfriend, Tracy, is in community college and is a server at the same restaurant. Jordan is training to become a junior real estate agent, the only one without a partner, no doubt the one intended for me. They are all friends from high school, which they graduated from two years ago.

"Do you want a drink?" Jordan asks me. There's something vague about his face. He looks like the image that would come up if you searched "average white young man."

"Sure," I say. He has a face that is meant to be forgotten. I understand why Tami thought we'd be a good match.

Tami and Vaughn disappear into one of the bedrooms down the hall, and I am left with strangers to sit around a glass coffee table that looks sharp enough to cut someone. I try to follow the conversation but it's all gossip about people I don't know. I look out the window and count the few stars strong enough to shine through the light of the city. I let Jordan make me another drink.

There is a brief moment, after the second drink, when I think I finally understand the appeal of alcohol. I am in a miserable situation but somehow not miserable. I am not on this hard couch listening to a conversation into which I have no entry; I am floating out of this building altogether, over Seattle and the Puget Sound, over the hills in the middle of the island, back to my home and maybe snuggled on the couch in between my dads, or in my bed, where I will call Lily and be comforted by her tough love as I tell her all the strange things I've been up to. But first, I have to pee.

As I walk back to the living room from the bathroom, I hear someone say, "Ivy Avila," and stop in my tracks. I lean against the wall and listen.

"I read that she was down to like ninety pounds and her hair was falling out," says Kayla.

"No," says Tracy. "It was drugs. She had a thousand-dollar-a-day coke habit."

"It was drugs combined with bipolar disorder," says Amir. "She went off her meds."

"She's not as pretty as she used to be," says Kayla.

"I think she's hot," says Jordan.

That's when I come in and sit down, and everyone smiles, and no one says anything more about Ivy Avila.

I want to tell them about how she has my number, about

our plans, about how she chose *me*, but then Tami and Vaughn emerge from the hallway, Tami looking as perfect as usual, not a hair on her head displaced. She doesn't seem to feel any need to directly acknowledge or speak to any of the people sitting in her living room, like she just wants us here as filler.

Jordan puts his hand on my knee and I don't push it off.

If Lily were here, she'd say something about this being Tami's castle, about how she is the queen and we are all her servants, her hired fools. Just like the games she used to make everybody play in elementary school.

She pulls out her baggie of Freedom and pops one in Vaughn's mouth.

"You ready?" she says to me, holding up a glittering pill. "Or can't you afford it?"

"She can't afford Freedom," says Kayla, giggling a drunk girl giggle.

"Join the club," Jordan says.

I think I will let him kiss me tonight.

"I know you're trying to be good," Tami says, walking over to the hallway table and picking up my purse. "But in case you change your mind. See, I'm putting one in this pocket here. It'll be there in case you want to do something naughty. You can thank me later."

"It still trips me out that Raine lets you deal this stuff," Amir says.

"This shit saves people's lives," Vaughn says. "And I don't need Raine's permission to do anything."

"Don't let her hear you say that," Tami says, and everyone laughs. Is this something people do? Laugh about someone's wife with the girl he's cheating on her with?

"She's just so . . . principled," Kayla says, and everyone laughs some more.

"You mean uptight," Tracy says.

Tami just watches, a satisfied smile on her face, as she leans against the kitchen island, stirring her drink. She's being strangely quiet, like it's beneath her to join us, but it's okay to have us here to watch.

"Raine is still so determined to be good," Vaughn says. "Like that gets you anywhere."

"Being good is entirely overrated," Kayla says.

"Like last month," Vaughn says. "She gave our last fifty bucks to her cousin who was about to get his electricity turned off. So then *our* electricity got turned off."

"Damn," Esteban says. "That's cold."

"All these things I used to love about her just make me tired now," Vaughn says.

"Everybody's tired, man," Amir says. "You know how many hours I worked last week? Sixty-one. I don't even know if I can pay my rent this month."

Tami's not tired like this. These are things she's never had to think about and never will. My family's not anywhere near rich by her standards, but somehow we've been spared too.

"She's pretty and everything," Esteban says. "But seriously dude, why'd you even marry her?"

I realize everyone is drunk. I'm getting there too, but they've all been drinking much faster than me. These are the kinds of conversations people have when they are drunk.

"She's smart," Vaughn says. "Much smarter than me. For a while, being around her made me feel smart too. But now it just makes me feel stupid."

"And being with me doesn't make you feel stupid?" Tami says, and all heads turn in her direction.

Vaughn seems to panic. "Well, you don't make me feel bad about it at least," he says. "You don't want me to be someone I'm not. Raine is just always trying to make me . . . better."

"What's wrong with trying to be better?" I say for some reason, and everyone looks at me like they're trying to figure out what exactly I'm doing here.

Tami laughs and the rest of the group decides it's okay to laugh too. "*She*'s trying to be better," she says. "It's admirable, really. But some of us are lucky and don't need to work that hard."

Before I can figure out how to feel, Jordan hands me another drink. I am long past the point when I should stop. But I'm also nowhere near the point of feeling like I belong in this place or with these people, and those two things seem to even each other out in some weird way that I think I am starting now to understand.

Vaughn walks over to the wall of windows. "Just wait," he says to his reflection in the glass. "I'm going to start winning all my fights, and I'll shoot up in the ranks, and then I'll get sponsored and buy a house on Commodore Island too. And it'll just sit there empty while I fly around the world in my private jet."

"Where you going to go?" says Esteban.

"You're not going anywhere," says Amir.

"Fuck you, man. I'm going more places than you."

"At least I got a marketable skill."

"What skill? Being an asshole?"

"Make me a drink, Esteban."

"Make your own damn drink, Amir."

"Lazy immigrant."

"Look who's talking. My parents paid good money to buy their place here. My mom was a fucking neurosurgeon back in Colombia. Your people just hopped on the bus in Arizona."

"Dude, there was no water left. It was a hundred and forty degrees in the summer."

"At least people weren't chopping off each other's heads with machetes."

"Are you really having a pissing contest about whose parents had it worse?" Kayla says.

Tami's face is pure amusement. To her, we're all just a bunch of puppies, brought here to tumble over each other and make a mess and chew on each other's ears.

I try to get up but I can't. It's the drinks, or it's Jordan's hand now farther up my leg, or it's the laser beams of Tami's eyes, holding me in my place.

“But what about Ash?” Vaughn says, walking in our direction from the windows. He is shrinking. He is shriveling up. All his muscles are deflating balloons.

“What *about* Ash?” Tami says, her eyes darkening.

“You have goose bumps,” Jordan whispers.

“I’m cold,” I say.

“Why are you with that loser?” says Vaughn.

“Any second now,” Amir says, “Vaughn’s going to start talking about how he can bench-press him.”

“I looked him up once,” Kayla says. “He’s *beautiful*.”

“You looked up my boyfriend?” Tami says.

“No,” the girl says. “I mean, yes. I’m sorry.”

“I have to piss,” Esteban says, standing up, then wobbling.

“You don’t get to talk about Ash,” Tami says to Vaughn in a calm voice.

“I think I’m going to go,” I think I say, but no one can hear me.

“But I don’t understand!” he says. “What do you even see in that guy? He’s just . . . limp. It can’t just be that his family has money. Your family has money. You don’t even like him. You think he’s pathetic. You—”

But then Tami punches him in the face, with a closed fist, and the sound of impact reverberates. We all just stare, in total silence, as the tableau unfolds in front of our eyes—Vaughn’s hand reaching for his cheek, the tears welling in his eyes, the blood seeping out of his nose and dripping onto the wood floor.

"Darling," Tami says calmly. "Go get some paper towels. I don't want the blood staining the bamboo."

She looks at me and smiles, and I get the strange impression that she's done all of this for me.

Esteban sits down again. Tracy stumbles into the kitchen for paper towels. Amir just keeps saying "Damn" over and over again. Kayla reaches into her purse and starts poking around on her phone, like she suddenly realized she had some important correspondence to conduct.

"No phones," Tami says. "You know that. No pictures of me and no pictures of her." She glances in my direction. "You know what'll happen if any photos of us get online. Our lawyers will destroy you."

Lawyers? I don't know what she told them, or if anyone's buying it, or why she's doing it. But I do know Tami gets bored easily. This could be some new game for her that she'll lose interest in any minute now—selling me to strangers like I'm someone and seeing if she can get away with it.

Maybe the glimpse of her I thought I saw in the car was just a trick of light and shadow.

But then she walks over to where Vaughn is kneeling on the floor, trying to hold a wad of reddening paper towels to his nose while helping Tracy smear the blood drops on the floor. Tami puts her hand on his shoulder, gently, and looks down at him with the closest thing I have ever seen to tenderness on her face. He tilts his head toward the touch, already forgiving her.

Vaughn looks up for a moment and our eyes connect, and

I see his humiliation flare, I see this giant man made suddenly small, and I realize no matter how big he gets, even if he becomes a star fighter and makes a bunch of money, he will still be this guy on his knees wiping up his own blood.

He will never end up with Tami, not for real. Maybe he and Ivy are alike in that way. They were both born on the outside of this world, and no matter how hard they try, they will never really belong in it as anything besides entertainment.

And what does that mean about me?

I stand up and the apartment swirls. We are so high up, higher than humans were ever meant to be. Our bodies are not made for sky.

Tami doesn't even bother watching as they clean up the mess. She's making herself another drink. She doesn't ask anyone else if they want one. I have lost track of how much she's had to drink tonight. How is she still upright? How is she still so in control?

I grab my purse from the table by the front door. The gold pill sparkles inside it.

I walk over to the window to tell her I'm leaving, but before I have a chance to speak, Tami says to me, "You know these would be your people if you weren't so *special*."

She says "special" like a curse. I have no idea what she's talking about. How am I special? Because by dumb luck I was adopted out of poverty?

"How does it feel to be so *loved*?" she spits, then she walks away, down the hall, and closes a bedroom door behind her.

If I could fly out that window, I would.

But instead, I have feet. I have gravity that does not know how I got here.

All I want is the ground. I want what is beneath the street and sidewalks. I want the soil to fill in the holes burrowed inside me.

This is the part of drinking that happens after the split second of warmth and invincibility: *want, want, and more want.*

9

THERE is a hallway. An elevator. A street. A car. Nodding off in my sunglasses in the middle of the night, in a blurry daze at the public ferry terminal with all the other people on their way to a hangover, going home with their dresses slightly rumpled, walking barefoot with their heels in their hands.

I type "freedom pill" into my phone.

I wait for the boat. I am made out of waiting.

Maybe I am not in the elevator alone. Maybe Jordan the junior real estate agent gets there just in time, just before the doors close, and we go down to the ground together.

The only life Tami knows is one of wanting something and getting it.

. . .

Freedom: It says something about clinical trials. Something about researchers wanting to find a way to help people live without shame. Rape and abuse victims. PTSD. Cult deprogramming. Drug addicts and alcoholics. Victims. Survivors. People who need real help.

The night is cool. Maybe it sobers me up a little. Maybe I'm thinking a little more clearly.

I have never asked myself what I want.

Freedom: Trials stopped when people showed signs of not wanting to distinguish between right and wrong. Not that they lost the ability, but that they didn't care.

What do I want?

Tami said, "How does it feel to be so loved?"

Maybe he says, "I live a couple blocks from here." Maybe I tell him to stop talking.

. . .

Freedom: A small percentage showed signs of personality disorders. Grandiose delusions. Psychosis. Violence. Extreme behavior.

I don't want to be the middle path.

Maybe as he touches me I fly away. Into my memories, the past all swirling and lost. I write my own history. I piece together the boyfriend I had because it seemed appropriate, the friends I let drift away until I only had Lily, how everyone else eventually faded to acquaintances, to blurry, anonymous classmates I'd see at school, who'd occasionally invite me to the parties everyone got invited to.

High school was the time when everyone became filler.

Freedom: There is a fine line between guilt and shame, and the drug could not tell the difference.

Those friends are the images that come up when you search "generic high school students." They are nothing but filler.

...

Everyone is filler. The guy taking off my clothes is filler.

How does it feel to be loved?

I am the one who is always in control.

I imagine I am Tami. I imagine I am Ivy Avila. My body moves and suddenly I become more than filler.

How does it feel?

Freedom: Conclusion: There is no cure for shame.

My body knows exactly what to do. I am made out of instinct. I am not tamed.

Maybe there is no elevator, no car, no ferry. Maybe I fly all the way home. Maybe my body is made for sky.

. . .

Maybe I want to be wild. Maybe I want to feel something, anything.

Wrinkled dresses. Wrinkled sheets. Sleeping men. Women, barefoot, carrying shoes.

Me, alone, all the way home.

10

I wake up to a pounding head and oceans churning inside my stomach. Before the memories come of what I did last night, first there's a wave of nausea to deal with. I hop out of bed, Gotami meowing in protest as I knock her to the floor and run to the bathroom, where I make it to the toilet just in time for last night's drinks and whatever food I shoved in my face when I got home to come right back out again.

When I am done, I stay there for a while, the tile floor bruising my knees, my head lying on my arms crossed over the toilet seat. Thank god Daddy likes to keep the house so clean.

It's not shame I feel, not exactly. More like disappointment. Isn't rebellion supposed to be fun? Isn't that supposed to be the reason people do things like stay out all night and get drunk and sleep with strangers?

I brush my teeth, drink some water, and go back to bed. I wake up again around noon to the sound of Papa and Daddy arguing in the kitchen. Their version of arguing, anyway. One that involves speaking calmly and using "I" statements.

I lie in bed listening to Papa say he heard me come in

around three a.m., that he heard me throwing up at ten a.m., that this isn't the daughter he knows. Daddy reminds him I've never broken a rule, not ever, that a little rebellion is healthy, that trusting me to make my own choices will help me grow into a responsible young woman.

They both do their jobs so well. The protecting and the nurturing. But as understanding as they are, I doubt even they would have a hard time saying what I did last night was healthy.

I hear Daddy laugh. "Honestly, I was starting to worry we'd raised her to be too sensible."

I don't come out until I know Daddy's left for his Sunday meditation group. I find Papa sitting on the couch reading, Gotami asleep in his lap. He looks up at me and smiles, and I am nearly knocked down by the impulse to throw myself into his arms and fall apart. Daddy is the one I usually go to for comfort, but here is Papa, smiling at me with a kindness I don't know I deserve.

"Good afternoon, sweetie," he says, getting up, displacing Gotami. I have to hold my breath to keep from crying, which just makes my headache worse. Papa pulls a tray out of the oven. "I had this in there staying warm for when you woke up." He dumps the pile of glistening, greasy, cheese-smothered tater tots onto a plate and sets it on the table. "Have a seat."

He brings over a bottle of ketchup, a couple ibuprofen, and a glass of Daddy's homemade kombucha, a fermented tea that's supposed to have all kinds of nutrition in it but tastes like carbonated vinegar mixed with snot.

"Best hangover cure ever," Papa says. "Perfected it in college."

"Thank you."

"I was ready to ground you for a month, but your dad talked some sense into me."

"Are you mad at me?"

"I just want you to be safe and making healthy decisions." He waits to continue speaking until I look up and into his eyes. "Were you safe last night?"

"Yes," I say quickly.

"Do you need any sort of . . . protection?"

"You mean like a gun?"

That makes us both crack up, but then I almost cry again. He should be making me feel worse, not better.

"I'm fine," I say. "Really." They bought me a pack of condoms when I was sixteen that is still unopened and dusty somewhere in the back of my closet. I don't remember everything from last night, but at least I remember he had a condom. It scares me that I might have been drunk enough to not care.

But then I suddenly remember the ride home from the ferry, the car I could not afford, the grumpy old driver who mumbled the whole time about kids these days thinking they're so special, kids these days getting away with murder, as we twisted around the dark corners of the island, as I opened the window in hopes that the cool breeze would keep me from barfing, the way the sky turned a shocking orange as we approached my road and I feared for a brief moment that the forest was on fire. But then I noticed the cars parked along Olympic Road far into the distance, I heard the bass of the music and the sound of drunken laughter, and I realized the light was coming from behind the wall of trees that were not on fire at all.

There was a party at Ivy Avila's house last night, and I was not invited.

"I trust you, Fern," Papa says now, and I cringe at the sound of my own name.

I heard you had fun after you left, Tami texts.

Worst hangover ever, I write back. She's probably fine this morning. She's always been able to drink everyone under the table and wake up perfect the next day. I wonder what exactly she knows. I wonder if she told Ash.

I wonder what happened at the condo after I left, if she woke up in Vaughn's arms this morning, if his face is bruised from her punch, how he's going to explain that to his wife.

When Daddy gets home, I help him weed in the garden. He doesn't mention my coming home late or throwing up this morning. We work silently together in the late afternoon shade, the birds chattering around us, a soft breeze rustling the trees. My head is still cloudy and my stomach is not in prime condition, but I feel something like peace settle over me. After the madness of last night, this is the most opposite of places—all this order, all this wholesome life. I inhale a deep breath of pine needles and warm soil and a whiff of salt water, and I am starting to feel like myself again.

"*Psst*," Daddy says, and I look up to see two identical does staring right at us. As many times as I've seen deer in our garden, I still catch my breath. There's something about their big dark eyes that makes me feel seen in some brand-new way. They tilt their heads in tandem, considering us, then walk off as if having decided we're not worth their time.

After dinner, I video-call Lily in Taiwan, where it's midmorning. I give her all the details about last night and then tune her out as she goes off on her tirade about "those people," just like I expected. She's like a voice in the back of my head, constantly giving her opinions about whatever I do. I know she does this because she cares. In some weird way, it comforts me.

"Don't you get it?" she finally says. "You're better than them. You're better than all of them. You're one of the few honest people I know."

But that's only because I've never had anything I've needed to lie about.

Tomorrow morning I'll be back at work, fully recovered from my hangover. The sun will be shining, and it will still be the sweet spot of summer when it's not too hot. I can find comfort in knowing last night was an anomaly. A onetime experience.

My one wild summer night that I never have to do again. I'll spend the rest of these weeks until college starts going to work, maybe drop by a couple parties where I'll have one or two drinks, weekend outings with the family, a few trips into the city. My life back. My boring, safe, island life. This is what I know I should do.

I imagine going to work tomorrow and overhearing what the gossip has morphed into over twenty-four hours. A woman of indeterminate age with unfortunate plastic surgery will put a fake antique watering can on the counter. She will say with an interrogating tone, "I read online that Ivy Avila had a party."

"That's the rumor," I will say, scanning the watering can's barcode.

"I heard people came in by helicopter," she will say. "Celebrities. Seattle socialites. People came by boat."

"Is that so?" I'll say, scanning the potted orchid that she will throw away as soon as it stops flowering.

"Were you invited?" she will say, eyes squinting, her Botoxed forehead unmoving.

When I tell her no, she will look me up and down, from my unremarkable face to my messy ponytail to my dirt-stained smock, and say, "Yes, well, I guess you wouldn't be," and then hand me her credit card.

11

"WHY didn't you come to my party last weekend?" a voice says.

I have been here before. In this exact place. This same voice in my ears. The same darkness opening up to a halo around Ivy's face as I blink my eyes open, as I feel my waking body sway in this hammock. Why does she appear like this, in this space between sleep and awake?

"You didn't invite me," I say.

"I didn't invite any of those people." She laughs. "There were even a few that didn't leave until Tuesday. My mom found one in the hallway closet. So will you come? To the next one? I don't want to be there unless you are."

"Okay." I have a vague feeling like I'm supposed to be hurt, or mad at her, but it is just a small nagging compared to the warmth spreading through my body.

She wants me.

"We should go walking sometime," Ivy says.

"There are trails all around the forest," I say. "The nature preserve starts right behind my house."

"Don't you get scared in there?"

"In the forest? No."

I don't tell her I feel safer there than I feel anywhere. Because no one can see me.

"I guess I'm a city girl," she says.

No, I think. *You are someone who likes being seen.*

"I went hiking in rehab. They had this whole thing about getting in touch with nature. They made us camp overnight once."

"Did you like it?"

"I wanted to."

"Did you get in touch with nature?"

"I got in touch with some mosquitos and poison oak."

She smiles. I smile. I am her mirror.

"Is that a vegetable garden over there?" she says. "Can I see it?"

"Okay." I manage to get out of the hammock without falling on my face. I try to match her footsteps as we walk over to Daddy's garden together.

We stand at the edge of the garden, looking over the deer fence at the tidy rows, the perfectly spaced plantings, all the nurtured things growing.

"We had a garden at my treatment center," Ivy says. "We all had chores taking care of it. We called it weeding therapy. I learned as much about plants there as I learned about recovery."

"Sounds pretty cool," I say.

"The guy in charge of the garden and all the grounds was this guy named Boots who was like this ex-junkie from Oakland who became a monk in Burma for a while before he came to work there. Rumor was he was dating this counselor named Bob, but they'd never deny or confirm because of professional boundaries or whatever, but we all knew." She laughs. "Sorry, I talk a lot. I don't have a lot of people to talk to, except my therapist."

"It's okay."

"Boots would like this garden."

I wonder if Ivy had to water their garden, if she had to distribute compost, if she had to weed and thin and tidy and pollinate by hand and worry over every little thing the way Daddy does. Sometimes I wonder if all his effort is really necessary, if it would grow just fine without anyone tending to it.

"Tell me about yourself," Ivy says.

"There's nothing to tell," I say.

"So make something up."

"Like what?"

"I don't know. Anything. My therapist says the way we lie says a lot about us."

"How do you lie?"

But she just smiles. "I have to go back," she says. "I'm supposed to have a call."

"What kind of call?"

"With my therapist." She looks up from the garden into the wall of forest behind it. "I'd like to go hiking with you sometime."

"Okay."

"I'm supposed to be taking a break. From work. I'm supposed to be doing healthy things."

"We could go hiking now."

Am I a healthy thing?

"I should get back for my call."

"Okay."

"Will I see you this weekend?"

"Yes."

"Bring your friends."

Okay, okay, yes. I'll do anything you ask.

And then she walks down the road, and I am left, once again, in this space between the garden and the forest.

Papa and Daddy are in the kitchen getting dinner ready, listening to the soothing voices of public radio talking about horrible things:

Members of a religious compound in North Dakota committed mass suicide, with fifty-seven deaths reported. This is the eighth major mass suicide of the year in a legally exempt independent community in one of the libertarian states.

The National Guard has been called in to the North Carolina city of Asheville to enforce a quarantine in the midst of an outbreak of a super-strain of measles that has so far claimed the lives of thirty-two children and three adults. Asheville has one of the highest unvaccinated populations in the country.

North African refugees are dying of heat stroke in immigrant detainment centers in Spain.

The separatist siege of Portland, Oregon, is entering its eighty-seventh day. Seattle officials are concerned about the possibility of similar violent uprisings in the city as protests continue to increase in number and intensity, though they are still mostly peaceful at this point.

Algae blooms in the Gulf of Mexico, the water a toxic sludge as thick as stew.

The usual hurricanes in Florida, Texas, Louisiana. The usual poor left behind to weather the storms while everyone who could already moved north and west.

Daddy chops carrots. Papa does a crossword puzzle. The bad news is so relentless they can't even hear it anymore.

Stocks reached record highs today.

"I'm going to a party tomorrow night," I say. "At Ivy Avila's house."

In tandem, they look up from what they're doing and stare at me like I'm speaking a language they don't understand.

"First of all," Papa says. "You don't *tell* us you're going to a party. You ask us."

"Can I go to a party tomorrow night?"

"I'm not sure after what happened last weekend," Daddy says.

"But I'm not grounded, am I? I'll be just down the road."

"But those Hollywood types and their lifestyles," Papa says.

"Their *lifestyles*? Do you have any idea how you sound?"

"Will there be drinking there?"

"I don't know."

"Will there be drugs?"

"She's sober, remember? She's really nice. You'd like her."

"We should meet her if you're going to be spending time together. Maybe I should talk to her mother."

"No one else's parents worry this much."

Papa and Daddy share a look that means "Well, maybe they should." They're not exactly quiet when it comes to their thoughts about the parenting styles of the families on the island.

"So what do we think is an appropriate curfew?" Daddy says. Papa likes to worry. Daddy likes to find solutions.

"How about one?" I say.

"Not going to happen," Papa says.

Daddy and I both give him the "You're being way too serious" look.

Daddy puts his hand on Papa's shoulder. "She's eighteen, love. She's not in high school anymore."

"But nothing good happens after midnight," Papa says, his voice tight. "Nothing."

"How about let's work with twelve thirty?" Daddy says. Always the peacemaker.

Papa clenches his jaw and nods.

12

EVER since I was little, as soon as it'd get warm in the spring, I'd start walking everywhere barefoot outside, even on the gravel of the driveway. I took special pride in how the bottoms of my feet would harden so much that by the end of the summer, I'd have a layer of thick leather skin impermeable to sharp rocks and even the barnacles of the beach. It's the only way I have ever been tough.

I walk down the road barefoot now, the only pair of low heels I own sticking out of my purse. Each step makes me cringe. My feet aren't nearly as tough as they used to be.

I'm wearing a vintage dress Daddy found at a thrift store and altered to fit me perfectly. It's been hanging in my closet for months because I've never had any occasion to wear it. Papa's supposed to be the fashion designer in the family, but I don't think he's touched a sewing machine in years. "Doesn't it show a little too much leg?" he quietly complained when I modeled it for them tonight, along with the makeup that I had to watch online videos to learn how to put on.

"You look beautiful," Daddy said, and kissed me on the cheek. Papa gave me a way-too-long hug. Gotami meowed.

I could hear Lily's voice in my head: "You look like a girl who is overcompensating for a lack of confidence in her intelligence."

I say, "Shut up, Lily."

I think I may actually look like someone who belongs at a party at Ivy Avila's house. Lily may not think that's anything to be proud of, but maybe I'm done caring what Lily thinks.

I can hear the music before I even get to the road. When I reach the pavement of Olympic Road at the bottom of the hill, the horizontal beams of the setting sun blind me, and I pull my sunglasses out of my purse. I dust off my feet and stuff them in my shoes, pausing for a moment to look out at the water. It is calm and the sky glows with bright golden light. In a rare moment of stillness, there are no boats on the water, neither yachts and speedboats nor floating shacks. A convertible full of beautiful strangers drives by slowly, squinting their eyes to see if I'm someone worth noticing, but I am invisible in my sunglasses, and they park way down the road at the end of an already long line of cars.

The gate to Ivy's waterfront property is open, with a stern-looking man in a suit standing next to it. I say, "Hello," and he nods without looking at me.

As I walk up the short, flower-lined driveway, the sound of the party gets louder, and I feel something pulling at me, and I am simultaneously chasing it, some indescribable thing I want, and I get the feeling that I am crossing over into a new reality, a new world, one that will change me forever. Even though I've never been here before, it feels somehow familiar. Like I was meant to be a part of it.

It's just a party, I tell myself. I've been to plenty of parties before. But then the house opens up before me, a huge glass structure, full of people and light and music and flowers, everything inside illuminated, everything alive and burning with an intensity I have never felt in my safe, wholesome life.

Everything feels *special.*

Tami called me special.

I want to be special.

I could watch the whole thing from out here if I wanted to. That would be the safe thing to do.

Or I could walk forward. I could take one step after another down the path that leads around the side of the house to the huge outdoor space, more like a resort than an actual home, with various levels of patios and decks and covered seating areas, a pool and a hot tub, two full bars with bartenders, tables with hors d'oeuvres, people dressed in black walking around with trays of drinks and food. A private dock has a few speedboats tied up to it, and a group is currently stepping off a water taxi, with another boat idling nearby, waiting for its turn.

It is still early, but the place is already packed with young, beautiful people, many of whom I recognize as varying levels of famous, and the others are people who look like they should be famous; all mixed in with a few boarding school kids and locals from the island, some of whom are huddled in the corner by a fountain, looking terrified and young and terribly out of place.

Most of the people here are much older than me. Much older than Ivy. They do not belong on this island. But this place, this property, has somehow turned itself into something with its own rules, its own agenda.

I don't see Ivy anywhere.

Maybe I stay on the edges, hiding behind my sunglasses, watching. Maybe I make myself invisible, become a voyeur, and live through everyone else.

Or maybe Tami finds me. She grabs my arm a little too hard. She says, "There you are," claiming me. She says, "Where have you been hiding?" I'm the one who told her about the party. I wanted to show her I'm friends with Ivy Avila and she's not.

I told her because I wanted her to bring Ash. But he's not here. Again. I'm starting to think he's avoiding me.

If Ash were here, he'd be holding court with Tami on some centrally located couch where everyone would be sure to see them. Everyone is dressed in their socialite best, but he'd be in some obscure band T-shirt and jeans, just to show how good he looks without even trying. He'd be leaning back in that entitled, cocky way boys do, legs spread because they never question how much space they have a right to take up. But there's almost an elegance when Ash does it, like a lion or tiger or some other purring beast, beautiful, on the verge of dangerous.

His eyes crinkle in a private smile only I can see, like this is all a joke and we're the only two people in on it, and the lights flicker, and the room darkens, and there are spotlights on just the two of us. With this smirk, he has invited me to an elite, secret club, and we are its only two members. We will sit on a cloud somewhere together, watching everyone below us, and we will know exactly what's going on, and we will be the only people who do.

"So Jordan, huh?" Tami says, breaking my trance. "How was it? Are you going to see him again?"

"No," I say, and I'm surprised by the disgust in my voice.

"You surprise me, girl. There may be some life left in you yet. Let's get a drink."

"What happened with Vaughn?" I say. "Is he okay?"

Tami laughs. "Oh, Vaughn is fine. Just a little lovers' quarrel. We kissed and made up."

Did she tell him she was sorry? Has Tami Butler ever told anyone she's sorry?

I imagine Ash holding the thin straw from his drink between his teeth, biting down, his white teeth gleaming. His tongue is hiding somewhere behind that smile, and I feel the teasing pressure of his teeth like a phantom stalking down deep into my body, the promise of his tongue warm and soft.

And then Ash would turn his attention back to the group huddled around him, back to telling some story about that band he hung out with backstage in Vegas, about some epic five-day party he went to in Rio, about his adventures with shamans in Peru. I'd be released, and he'd go back into disguise, and so would I, leaving a little piece of me with him.

I wonder what Vaughn and Raine are doing now. I try to imagine them at this party, but I can't.

Maybe I sneak away when Tami's not looking. Maybe I

hide behind my sunglasses and eavesdrop on a pack of Seattle socialites sitting with their feet in the pool, as they talk about Ivy's previous party, dropping names of the people they saw there. I half listen as I look around the crowd for Ivy. The only person I recognize in the vicinity is the girl who came in second on the last season of that singing competition show.

"Have you seen Ivy?" someone says.

"No," another one says. "Didn't see her at the last one either."

"Someone said she has cameras installed all over the place," says another. "And she just sits in her room watching everyone. She's crazy, you know? That's why she was in rehab. She went crazy on set and tried to kill a boom operator."

"No," says the other one. "She just tried to kill herself."

"All I know is she tried to kill someone."

"Who cares? Where'd that cocktail waitress go?"

"I did see her mom lurking around, though," says a young man. "She looked hungry. She's on the prowl." The girls laugh.

"You're technically legal."

"Gross," he says. "But I'm sure she could snag an island boy easy."

It goes on like that for a long time. Everyone at the party is having different versions of the same conversation.

It wouldn't matter if I stayed outside, looking in. If I perched somewhere in the corner and eavesdropped on other people's lives. It would not be much different than if I followed Tami around the party as the night gets darker, nursing my soda while everyone gets drunker.

Another young celebrity arrives and everyone pretends to not be impressed. One of the island's local drug dealers is propped up in a throne-type chair with a line of people waiting for their turn to conduct business. The reality show runner-up plays piano and sings, but no one is listening. I can feel the party collectively getting drunker. The heat rises. Articles of clothing are strewn about the house.

A woman who is older than all of us stands at the top of the grand staircase looking down with a drink in her hand, hair extensions piled on her head and cleavage piled on her chest, surveying the party with a hungry, prideful look in her eyes. Something seizes inside me as I see this vision of Ivy in thirty years. Something like fear. Something like disgust.

The music has gotten louder. People yell to be heard, but they say nothing. A girl falls down the stairs and no one comes to help her up. Someone runs by, fast, nearly ramming into me. Someone else lunges forward and I have to jump out of their way. Arms grab a boy and pull him into a shadowed corner. The lights seem to flicker and spin and I wonder if my drink has been spiked.

The magic has shifted. What felt so special at first has tipped over into some other realm. A frenetic energy has inserted itself into the party, like the stakes have suddenly been raised, like everything has become more desperate. And I just watch from wherever I am, either by Tami's side or alone, in shadows, hiding behind sunglasses, the light shining through me, the night turning more surreal even though I think I am completely sober.

It does not matter if I found Tami or if I watched from the shadows. She would not notice when I got up to leave. No one would see me walk down the hall. They're all looking for someone else.

I find a drunk girl slouched in the bathroom who doesn't know where she is. "I was in a boat," she says. "I think. Now I'm in here. But the floor's still moving like a boat. Is this a houseboat? Are we on Lake Union again?"

I just stare at her, wondering what I should do, when I feel the presence of someone new behind me. The hairs on the back of my neck stand up. My skin feels warmed. Without looking, I know it is Ivy.

"Do you know her?" Ivy's voice asks. I can feel her breath on my bare shoulders.

"No," I say, turning around. "Do you?"

"I don't know any of these people." Her face is calm, friendly. "We can put her in one of the bedrooms. She'll be safe there until she sobers up."

What if I'm the only one who's seen Ivy all night? The whole world thinks they know her, but here, in this bathroom, I am the only one.

"I know you," the drunk girl says, and I can't tell if she's talking to Ivy or me.

Ivy texts something into her phone and almost immediately two large men arrive. "Take her to the south bedroom," she says. "And someone check on her regularly to make sure she's okay.

Don't let any assholes into her room. Got it? If anyone hurts her, you're both dead." The men nod and carry the girl away.

"You sound like a feminist mafia boss," I say.

She smiles. I have pleased her.

"I'm not in the mood for a party, are you?" she says, then takes my hand. "Let's go upstairs." And I don't even think. I would follow her anywhere.

Nearly the whole bottom floor is made of glass and steel beams, almost completely open except for a couple of bathrooms, while the second floor is more private, with actual walls. No one seems to notice us as Ivy leads me upstairs to a secluded bay window with a built-in bench, like a reproduction of a quaint little reading nook in an older, traditional-style home. We sit there together in silence for a while, the windows open so we can hear and see the madness below and the stars shining above.

"Do you want to know a secret?" Ivy says.

"What?"

"I wasn't even at the party last weekend. My own party. I had nothing to do with it. It was all my mom."

"What'd you do instead?" I say.

"We should hang out soon," Ivy says, looking out the window like she's looking for something, or someone, specific. I wonder if she knows how mysterious she's being, if she's like this on purpose.

"We're hanging out now."

"I mean go fishing or something."

"Fishing?"

"I'm kidding," she says, turning to look at me. "But let's go for that walk we were talking about. Or a hike. I'll even go in the forest. I don't know. Something nice. Something not this."

Nice. I am her source of something "nice."

"You're not drunk, are you?" she says.

"Not at all."

"It's refreshing, right? Being sober? Seeing clearly?" She raises her glass, and I have a feeling she's trying to convince herself more than me. "Club soda and lime. Doctor's orders. I think we're the only sober people here. By a long shot."

"I feel like I'm on an alien planet," I say.

"I feel that way all the time."

"I wish I could put on some kind of disguise and go through the world being the opposite of me."

"Me too."

"But that only works in the movies."

She looks at me and just like that there is no party, there are no people, there are just the two of us suspended here in space, molecules and atoms connected by molecules and atoms, and I forget time, I forget history, I am only what her eyes make me, I am only the sound exhaled through her mouth, perfectly articulated.

And suddenly the party is transformed again. This is a new kind of magic. This is the other world I was meant to enter when

I walked down the driveway, as I stood in the shadows in my sunglasses, watching, waiting for entry. I am on a side with Ivy that no one else is on.

"There's something I want to talk to you about," Ivy says. "Like a favor." She seems for a moment unsure, almost nervous, just as I am fortified with a sudden, shocking confidence.

"Okay."

She will make me useful. I feel myself leaning in, ready to catch her need.

But then the electricity of the moment is stolen as her mother arrives, a little wobbly on her feet, with a drink in her hand, the low cut of her tight dress showing bronzed skin pulled over very fake breasts. "Honey, darling," she says. "Can I talk to you for a minute?"

"I'm busy, Mom," Ivy says, her face clouding over. I feel my own heart pulled toward her, like it wants to piece together all the parts of her that are breaking.

"What are you doing up here? The party's downstairs. Nobody important is upstairs."

I look at Ivy and she's looking out the window again. She hasn't yet found whatever, or whoever, she's looking for.

"Is he here?" her mom says.

"I don't think so," says Ivy, hardened.

"Who?" I want to say. I feel something twist inside me. Is that jealousy?

"Come on," her mom says. "Talk to me. It'll be just a minute."

"Fine."

So I drift away. Just like that, I am erased. Ivy has been claimed by her mother and it's nearing midnight.

The light of the party has dimmed. Everything is darker, more shadowed. People are closer to the ground, huddled, almost horizontal.

A couple is fighting.

Two boys are kissing while their girlfriends egg them on.

A girl is puking in the bushes.

Lights turn on in rooms upstairs, then dim back down.

The corners are full of people who couldn't make it to chairs.

I remember what Daddy said: "Nothing good happens after midnight."

Spilled drinks everywhere.

Broken glasses and dishes.

A chair, half charred by some mysterious, now extinguished fire.

No one is having fun anymore, but no one is leaving. Maybe they think they'll camp out here, wake up in the morning, and start it all over again. They'll keep doing the same thing over and over, hoping they'll get lucky and something will change.

The reality show star is crying, alone. People back away slowly, like they don't want to catch what she has.

A sound of raised voices, a fight brewing, a glass breaking.

Limbs grasping in the shadows.

Boats rocking on the dock.

Small, consistent, forever waves, lapping against the rocky

shore, the clicks and rolls of the rocks as they collide, a tiny fraction of the time it will take for them to break each other down into fragments, into sand.

As I walk away from the house, I turn one last time and see, through the glass, Ivy standing at the top of the grand staircase, with the lurching and comatose debauchery winding down around her, a transparent home full of so many strangers.

How can she live in this house made of glass? What is the architecture that keeps it standing?

Her face displays a private softness, an opening, but no one is looking, no one but me. But then it's like she remembers she is not alone, not safe, and in a split second she transforms, conjures a second self and dons her like a shroud. She is once again the star everyone wants, an actress, someone who is always someone else.

I walk away, through the graveyard of stranded cars on Olympic Road. I stand in the middle of the road and look up into the clear sky, searching for the moon, but it is not there.

A raccoon runs across the street. Daddy would say that means something. He'd look it up: the spiritual significance of a raccoon on a new moon.

He will be sleeping on the couch when I get home, will startle awake at the sound of the door and say something like "I must have dozed off while reading." He will hug me and try to hide the fact that he is sniffing my breath for alcohol. I will find comfort in this as I pretend to be annoyed.

...

I start my climb away from the shore. Old pine and fir trees creak as I pass, despite the lack of breeze. They send messages below the surface, over mycelium highways, alerting the trees farther up of my approach. There is the sense that everything freezes right before I get there, like I keep walking in on a secret party I am not invited to and no one wants me to know is happening.

The forest crowds around me as I make the ascent up the hill, returning, changed.

Bare feet hardened by gravel, shoes in my hands.

Maybe I am made of forest.

Maybe I want to be wild.

Me, alone, all the way home.

13

I still haven't seen Ash. I'm trying not to think about this. He's probably busy, and seeing me is not at the top of his priorities list. He has a girlfriend. He has a life. I'm just the bored and boring girl from his hometown who has nothing better to do than think about him.

Except now I have Ivy. Now I have her text from last night inviting me on a day trip today. She called it an adventure. I called in sick to work. There are more important things than that fraction of a paycheck.

When Lily asked me how the party was, I told her it was just a few people from Ivy's sober meditation group and we ordered pizza and played board games. I could tell she was thinking about not believing me, but luckily she still thinks I'm the most honest person she's ever known.

I don't know if I'm going to tell her about today's outing. Maybe I want a secret.

Papa's at work and Daddy's volunteering somewhere, and I've been sitting on my front porch ready to go for nearly an hour. Ivy said she'd pick me up this morning. I don't know what her idea of morning is, so I made sure I was ready early.

Daddy says the fruit trees are stressed. They talk to him. They tell him they need more water because it hasn't rained in a long time. It's only June and everything is already starting to feel dusty. He says when he was a kid this didn't happen.

I hear her before I see her. The crunch of gravel beneath tires. The trees sway as they whisper her approach like a game of telephone up the road, and I am the last to know.

She's in one of those new cars I've only seen in ads, in a mirror-like silver that reflects the forest around it. As far as I know, she's the first person on the island to get one, which is saying a lot. People love their high-tech toys here, and they love people knowing they spent way too much money for them, though they'd never admit it.

The car stops and the driver's-side door opens upward, like the hatch of a spaceship. Ivy's head pops up over the top, her long brown hair in a messy bun and her face free of makeup, but still breathtaking, still the most beautiful girl I've ever seen.

"Hey!" She smiles and waves. "You ready?"

Of course I'm ready.

"It's ridiculous, isn't it?" she says as I climb into the car. It's all shiny chrome and flawless white leather inside, like the car version of Tami's house, with buttons and displays and lights and mysterious gadgets I've never seen in a car before. "I don't know what half these things do," she says.

As soon as I close my door, a seat belt shoots out of somewhere and clicks silently into place. "The first time that happened, I screamed," Ivy says. "My mom bought me this car. With my money. I don't even like it."

I don't ask where we're going. I don't say, "Why'd you pick me?"

"Car, on," Ivy says, and it starts purring.

"Would you like to engage automated driver assistance?" a robotic but mildly sexy voice says.

"Yes, please," says Ivy.

Ivy Avila is the kind of person who says "please" to a robot.

"I'm supposed to be learning how to become comfortable with silence," she says. "So I'm not going to turn on any music. Okay?"

"Okay," I say, and then we don't talk for a long time. But Ivy fidgets a lot, like she has to move her body extra now to make up for the lack of noise. She adjusts her seat, rubs her eyes, fusses with her hair, touches buttons and dials without actually pressing or turning them.

We drive north on Olympic Road, past all the gated waterfront mansions on the left and the forest on the right. The car makes no sound. Gravity doesn't seem to exist as we turn corners. I feel like I'm strapped into a soft, unmoving bed. We could be going two hundred miles per hour and I wouldn't even notice.

I hold my breath as we drive over the bridge to the peninsula, just like I've done since I was a little kid. It's supposed to be good luck. You're supposed to make a wish. My lungs are bigger than they were back then. I can hold my breath for a long time now.

I thought we were going to Seattle. I half expected we'd drive straight into the Sound and the car would turn into a submarine.

"I'm supposed to be relaxing," Ivy says when we reach the other side of the bridge, and I realize I forgot to make a wish and now it's too late.

We speed by the checkpoint that only cares if you're driving onto the island, not off it, and I let out a big sigh.

I think I'm supposed to be doing the opposite of relaxing.

Papa said there used to be an Indian reservation here. Now it's just miles and miles of subsidized housing for thousands of people who work in Seattle and on Commodore Island but can't afford to live there. The street is lined with bus and shuttle stops, marked by signs listing different destinations, the sidewalk crowded with people on their way to work, private security guards stationed at the end of every block in little kiosks. Immigration cops patrol on foot, automatic rifles strapped to their backs.

"I used to live in places like this," Ivy says. "The one in White Center when I was little. Then one in LA before I got *The Fabulous Fandangos*. Mom moved us out of there as soon as she got my first check."

"What was it like?" I have only ever lived in the middle of the forest, with no neighbors. I wonder how it compares—being surrounded by strangers, versus being surrounded by trees.

She's quiet for a while. "Crowded," she says. "And loud. Even at night, you could still hear people moving around getting ready for night shifts. You could smell everybody's food cooking. Mom was always yelling at some neighbor, like their lives were constantly in her way. Like she was better than them, even then, when we were nobody. Always talking about the day I'd make it and we'd get to move to Commodore Island like she always dreamed and we'd finally be happy." She laughs. "And she's still just as miserable. Except now instead of yelling at the neighbors, she yells at the cleaning ladies and gardeners. She even yells at the birds when she thinks they're being too loud."

"My dad says we're lucky to still have birds around here," I say.

As soon as we get to the other side of the sign that says "Leaving A-Corp Property," the road is lined with people holding signs saying they're available for work or asking for help, some of them sitting on folding chairs with coolers next to them, typing away on tablets like they're at the office. We pass a large playground full of children with no adults in sight. People stare at us as we go by with a look on their faces I cannot read. It's not scary, exactly. But it's clear that no one is in charge here, like anything could happen at any moment and there's no one around to stop it.

I think about Raine and Vaughn. Jordan and the others in Tami's condo that night. I wonder how close they are to a bill they can't pay or losing a job that could end them up here, like this. I know Tami and Ash never could. But what about me? What about Ivy? Even she probably doesn't have the kind of money that never runs out. Does she know that?

"It wasn't lonely," Ivy says, and it takes me a second to remember what we were talking about. Living in the developments. Surrounded by the noise and smells and lives of strangers.

Outside the windows, trees and people fly by, but inside, it feels like we're staying still. Lights illuminate the dashboard but I have no idea what they mean. We pass through the preserved, quaint main street of a historic small town—an attempt to lure the business of tourists—but I can see the sprawl of strip malls extending behind it.

Then, out of nowhere, Ivy says, "What do you think of me, Fern?"

"What?" I say.

"I know what people say. I know about all the rumors." She looks at me for too long, like in the movies when you can tell it's fake because if they were really driving they'd have crashed by now. "I don't care what they all think," she says. "But I care what you think. I want you to know the real me."

Why aren't we swerving into a ditch? Why is she looking at me like this? Why does she care what I think?

"I think you're more than anyone knows," I say. My breath is not mine. I have given it to her. I am a vacuum.

She smiles and finally looks back at the road. "Exhaustion is real," she says. "People act like it's this fake thing, but I had just finished shooting the fourth season of *The Cousins*, was on the European leg of my tour with the band, and my agent was sending me all these scripts to read and my mom was there the whole time, breathing down my neck. I slept less than five hours a night every night for three years. Some nights I'd just skip sleep altogether because I had so much to do, and all these appearances. Who wouldn't get exhausted by that? People aren't meant to work that much for that long. That's what my therapist says. We're physically not capable. But I just thought I had to work harder. That's what they tell you. You miss one opportunity, and your career stalls. Your career fails. People forget who you are, and then you're over. And there were all these pills to help me do it all, you know? It was survival. But then I couldn't do anything without them. And that just made me more exhausted."

"And now you're not exhausted?"

"Now I don't know what I am."

"Do you miss it?"

"I'm not supposed to, but yeah. I do sometimes. I miss knowing what I'm supposed to do with myself. I miss feeling like I was good at something."

We drive a little longer, past a line of old, boarded-up buildings and rusting cars without tires, shacks built around them from discarded parts, homes made out of hollowed-out buses with a few people sitting around like piles of rags and ashes, more broken than even the buildings. Most don't raise their heads to watch us go by. They are not like the people sitting by the road just outside the housing development, probably with full-time jobs they still need to supplement in their off-hours.

"Don't worry," Ivy says. "This car is pretty, but it's also built like a tank."

We drive so fast, the people are nothing but a blur.

"The thing about being a performer," Ivy says, "is that you're always performing, even when you're by yourself. After a bunch of years of that, you forget who you are. Fame becomes its own addiction, maybe even more than the pills and booze. I don't know if I'm okay unless other people think I'm okay. Ever since I was little, I've defined myself by the jobs I get, the interviews, the fans, how much people want me. If they don't want me, I don't know who I am."

She has asked me nothing about myself. Daddy would say that's bad manners. Papa would say it's the sign of a narcissist. But I'm almost relieved. This way she doesn't have to find out how little I have to say.

"I thought I knew who I was once," she says. "For a little while, a couple of weeks, I thought I knew exactly who I was. But I'll tell you about that later." She smiles now, lost in some veiled memory. A billboard for a new housing development flashes by—a suburb of a suburb of a suburb.

"Maybe you just need some rest," I say. "Then you can figure all this stuff out."

"Yeah. That's what my therapist says. All I want to do is sleep, but I can't. I have this anxiety and insomnia, and I'm getting acupuncture and doing all these herbal tinctures that taste like shit, because my doctor won't let me have anything resembling a sleeping pill. And I'm supposed to be taking a break from work for a while, or A-Corp is never going to hire me again. They can even sue me. So I'm always *awake*, without anything to do but think, because I'm not working. I'm not doing anything. I don't know how you all do that."

"Do what?"

"Not you. You're different. You have a job. But the rest of them. They just . . . do nothing while their parents are off who knows where working their asses off. How amazing that must be. To be so sure of your own worth that you don't think you have to earn it. It's like they're incapable of feeling shame."

"Have you heard of this drug called Freedom?" I say. "My friend Tami does it. It's supposed to take away shame."

"I don't want to talk about drugs," she snaps. "Or Tami."

"Have you met Tami?" I say. "She came to your last party."

Ivy says nothing. There's a new tension in the car, like the electricity went sideways. Neither of us says anything for a while. All I see are trees and more trees.

"There's a fine line between shame and having a conscience," Ivy finally says.

"She's kind of awful," I say. "Tami."

"I know."

The car is quiet for a long time.

"Oh, I've heard about this place," I say as we approach a huge gated compound with a sign that says "Ray of Light Ministries."

"What's this one about?" Ivy says.

"I think it's the one about no procreation. The men and women live on separate sides of the compound and have no contact."

"Sounds nice." Ivy laughs. "I totally get it. All these people giving up everything they have to go live somewhere where they don't have to think for themselves anymore. Where all their choices are made for them. They're just giving up one kind of freedom for another. I dated this girl for a while—Lorelei Simmons? She was in that movie *Cold Heat*?"

It takes me a moment to realize Ivy's asking me a question. I've gotten used to her talking without needing much participation from me. "It sort of rings a bell," I say.

"One day she just disappeared. I called her agent and he told me she decided to join that big cult outside of Santa Cruz, the one with that guru with the gold teeth and neck tattoos who used to be a drug addict and claims to be a reincarnation of the original Buddha. Lorelei just emptied her bank account and handed it over. No one's heard from her since."

"Is that the one where they all have sex with him?"

"Probably. All cults end up like that. As soon as someone calls themselves a guru, it's over. It's so weird when you think about it. All the rich people with their protected, sparkling sci-fi lives trying to leave the cities and live off the grid and go back in time. And all the poor people trying to do exactly the opposite, all those people in places without electricity or internet or clean water or food. That's what going back in time is really like. It's not camping. But the rich people think it's some vacation, and they can just go back home when they've had enough." She grips the steering wheel. "Because they can."

For someone who's supposed to be cultivating silence, Ivy sure does talk a lot.

"I think part of me wanted to die," Ivy says. I don't know how she got to this statement, how the map of her mind led her here, but it's a ride I think I'm starting to get the feel of.

A sign on the side of the road says 45, and I see the number 73 on the dashboard. But whoever designed this car made it drive so smooth, you can't even feel danger.

"The *exhaustion*," Ivy says, and she takes both hands off the wheel to do air quotes around "exhaustion" and we swerve, but the car corrects itself on its own. The car says, "Autopilot engaged."

"I'd do a bunch of one thing to keep me awake and a bunch of another thing to calm me down," she says. "And then it'd be time for a party and I'd do a bunch of whatever was there. I'd just keep doing it until I couldn't anymore, until some manager would intervene or I'd pass out, or whoever I was dating at the time thought they could save me and tried a few times but gave up after they realized they couldn't and figured out I was way more trouble than I was worth."

After a pause, she says, "But I have a strong constitution. Just like my mom. That's what she says. I'm a survivor. Whether I want to be or not."

That's when I see the police lights pulsing in the side mirror.

"Damn," Ivy says, and for a moment she just looks ahead and doesn't slow down, like she's thinking about just driving until she finds a cliff to fly off of, and she would do it without thinking about me, without even asking if I want to go down with her.

But then she sighs and slows the car down, pulls over to the side of the road. "Shit," she says. "Shit, shit, shit." I pick her purse up off the floor and hand it to her. Then we sit in silence and wait.

After a couple minutes of him doing whatever he's doing in his car, the trooper gets out and walks slowly toward us. Ivy rolls down her window when he arrives and hands him her ID before he even asks. He inspects it for a moment, then crouches down for a better look at her face, and his eyes light up.

"You're Ivy Avila!" he says.

"Yes, sir."

"Quite a car you have here. Haven't seen one in person yet."

"Thank you."

"Did you know you were speeding, darling?"

I cringe at "darling," but Ivy is all smiles.

"I'm so sorry," she says. "I guess I forgot to turn on the speed limit sensor. I always turn it on. I don't know what happened." She is playing dumb and cute.

"Well," he says, putting his hand on her arm, which I am positive is against protocol. "Promise me you'll be more careful next time, okay?"

"Yes, officer."

"And one more thing." He hands Ivy his little notebook and pen. "An autograph. For my daughter."

"Of course."

Before he walks away, the officer takes one last lingering glance, peering into the car and resting for a moment on Ivy's lap, at the place where her thighs meet the fabric of her short skirt. We are out here in the middle of nowhere, two girls alone on the road, and he has all the power. You hear stories about things like this. Stories about his word against hers.

"Be good" is the last thing he says, his voice low, hungry.

He is walking away. He is feet crunching on gravel, the ghost of a lingering stare, his eyes going places no one invited him to.

As we drive away, Ivy says, "Middle-aged men love me," with a hardness that makes me lose my breath, and for a split second I see her turn into stone, into something impermeable and solid and forged by fire, flying through the sky at 73 mph, capable of doing serious damage and not caring who it touches.

I realize I am breathing fast and shallow, that fear has lodged itself in my chest. Not fear of getting arrested for speeding, not fear of crashing, but something else that I cannot name. I look at Ivy and she is holding some other kind of feeling. Maybe I'm afraid because she is not.

I look out the window, at the trees lining the road, one after another after another, creating a kind of rhythm as we pass by. It's a hypnotic pulse of green and brown, but then occasionally a flash of some other color deep inside the layers, the weathered blue or red or orange of a tent or tarp of the people living out here in the forest because they have nowhere else to go.

"Ah!" Ivy says after a few more minutes of driving. A carved wooden sign on the side of the road reads "Shoji Japanese Spa." The car turns into a heavily guarded driveway and Ivy scans her wrist under a sensor that opens the locked gate. Two armed security guards nod as we pass through. "Here we are." Her voice is light now, as if forcing cheerfulness will make it real.

We drive along a river for a while, then turn uphill on a windy road surrounded by rhododendron bushes and towering evergreens until we get to a small wooden building that resembles a Japanese pagoda, with bamboo and ornamental maples and flowers all around. A pretty blond woman with thick-lined eyes wearing a black kimono-like dress comes out to greet us. "Nice to see you again, Miss Avila," she says, and leads us inside.

"What is that smell?" I whisper to Ivy.

"Sulfur," she says. "From the hot springs. You'll get used to it."

The waiting room is all tatami mats and cushions and watercolor paintings of cherry blossoms. Soft flute music plays behind the gentle trickle of an indoor fountain. A wall of shelves displays merchandise for sale. At first I think the place is old, maybe a preserved relic from the turn of the last century when pockets of Japanese settlers dotted the areas around Seattle. But on closer inspection, I realize everything is brand-new, freshly painted and then distressed with meticulous detail to look authentic. If Lily were here, she'd say something like, "How is this a Japanese spa if there are no Japanese people running it?" then she'd give me a speech about cultural appropriation and I'd tune it out even though I know she's right. Lily's always right about everything.

Ivy picks up a tiny porcelain teacup from a shelf. "All these tea sets are imported. My mom bought like five and they're sitting in boxes she'll never open."

After we change into slippers and robes, the woman leads us down a wooden boardwalk along the side of the mountain hundreds of feet above the river rushing below, which periodically splits off to other trails that lead to small bamboo huts. Cloudy, steaming streams flow under the boardwalk, the rocks and soil beneath them multicolored from various minerals. Our guide tells us a rehearsed speech in hushed tones about how there are seven natural hot springs of varying temperatures and sizes, and how we have the largest one on top of the hill. I don't know how much Ivy's paying for this, but I'm guessing it's not cheap.

"Apparently all these pools used to be just out here wild in the middle of the forest, free for anyone to use," Ivy says. "Can you imagine? It must have been a mess."

I'm used to seeing security guards everywhere, but they seem particularly out of place here, in the middle of this oasis that's supposed to be so peaceful. They are scattered around the property, patrolling with guns strapped to their backs.

"Why does a spa need security guards with guns?" I whisper.

"There's so many people living in the forest. There was a problem with people jumping the fence at night and using the pools."

"So they need to be shot?" I say.

"People do all kinds of crazy shit when they don't want to share."

The woman leads us to our own little hut, and another woman brings a tray with tea. The door closes behind them, and I am left alone with Ivy, surrounded by three thin bamboo walls and an open view off the side of the mountain. Birds chirp and the river rushes below. To the side is our hot spring—a pool the size of a couple extra-large hot tubs stuck together, in the earth, surrounded by large rocks. Steam rises off the opaque chalky water, and the smell of rotten eggs is overpowering. It's beautiful, but something feels off. Like we are not supposed to be here. Like we're intruding.

"So we just, like, get in?" I say.

Ivy smiles, amused. "I thought you were a nature girl," she says. "This is nature."

"But how deep is it?" I say. "Is the bottom just mud? There must be all kinds of bacteria in there."

"The water's medicinal or something. The pools are self-cleaning because the springs pump fresh water in all day. They put smooth rocks on the bottom, and there are all those boulders you can sit on. Any more questions?"

I don't say, "And we're supposed to be *naked*?"

I don't say, "Why did you take me here?"

Ivy unties her robe and I look away before she takes it off. I pour us tea and the smell of jasmine sweetens the stench of the water.

I feel her watching me as I get in backward, as I try to cover my breasts with my arms in a way that looks like I'm not trying to cover them up.

Ivy laughs. "No need to be modest around me. Relax, Fern. This is supposed to be relaxing."

I step into the water and quickly sit so I'm covered with the gray-white water up to my shoulders. It feels like a hot, smelly, silty bath.

"Are you relaxed yet?" Ivy teases.

"Don't rush me," I say.

She smiles, closes her eyes, and leans back against her boulder, so I decide to do the same. I have to admit, it does feel good, and I can feel the tension in my body let go a little. Maybe my body will convince my brain to relax too.

When I open my eyes, Ivy's staring at me. I don't know how

long she's been looking, or how long my eyes were closed. She smiles, and I think she's going to ask me if I'm relaxed yet again, but instead she says, "So I have something to tell you. Remember how I told you I have a kind of favor to ask?"

I am the person people tell things to. I am the person people ask for favors.

I sit up on my rock a little taller, but my nipples poke out over the water, so I slouch back down again.

"We have a mutual friend, you and I." Ivy sits up straighter now, her breasts fully exposed, and I try not to stare. I don't understand how she can be so comfortable in her own body.

"Who?" I say. Everywhere I look there is bamboo and rocks and moss and water the color of dirty milk.

She pauses for a moment, like she's thinking about changing her mind, like uttering the name will start something she can't undo.

"Ash Kye," she finally says.

My chest constricts. The smell of sulfur seems to get stronger.

"He's a friend of yours, isn't he?"

"Yes," I say. "We've known each other for years. Our fathers used to golf together. I didn't know he knew you. He never said anything." But when was the last time I even talked to him? When was the last time he told me anything?

"No," she says. "He wouldn't have. I guess I'm kind of a secret." This seems to make her sad, and I wonder what that would feel like—being someone's secret.

"We met on vacation a year and a half ago," she says. "On this A-Corp island in Brazil that's a big vacation spot for the rich and annoying. He was there with his family. I was there with my mom. It was supposed to be my relaxing vacation before shooting the last season of *The Cousins*, but going anywhere with my mom is not relaxing. She was off chasing pool boys or something when I met him on the beach. He was trying to avoid his family. His dad was drinking too much and embarrassing him. His sister was on the phone the whole time and his mom was on her laptop working. We were both lonely and needed someone to talk to, I guess. So that's what we did." She smiles a private, inward smile not meant for me. "It was like we knew we were soul mates within ten minutes of meeting each other. I told him things that first day on the beach that I never told anyone."

I cringe at "soul mates." But maybe that's what happens when people fall in love—they have no choice but to turn into clichés.

I wonder for a moment if I should say something, if I should interject, ask a question. What kind of a conversation is this? Is it one where I just let Ivy talk for as long as it takes to tell her story, until she's emptied out? Is this a monologue? Am I her audience?

Ivy is somewhere inside her head, sifting through her memories. She has no use for me in there. So I decide to say nothing. I decide to just let her talk. It's like I'm not even here.

I am strangely not jealous. Somehow sharing Ash with Ivy does not feel wrong the way Tami having him does.

Sharing Ash. How ridiculous. He's not even mine to share.

"We were together there for two weeks," she continues. "They were the best days of my life. We spent every possible moment we could together, every single night. He told me how much he hated boarding school and doing what everyone expected of him, how he felt so much pressure to fit inside a box. We told each other about our childhoods, about who we were before the world started eating us up. And it's like we got to be those people together. Like we got to be innocent again. This one night, I remember it was a full moon, we talked until the sun came up. About running away, all these elaborate scenarios of the life we'd have away from everyone who wanted something from us. When the sun rose it felt like the beginning of a new world, like we had just *created* a new world. We were going to be free. Together."

I am starting to feel too hot, but I don't know what to do with my body. Ivy seems like she's in a trance, like she's channeling something, like she has no idea where she really is.

"I thought it was a plan," she says. "A real plan." There is a sad, almost desperate, tinge to her voice now. "He said tomorrow, we're doing it tomorrow. We talked about starting over as brand-new people, getting an apartment somewhere, reinventing ourselves, building lives besides the ones everyone else has already figured out for us. He wouldn't have to follow his mom and dad into some executive A-Corp career, and I could take the money I made and invest it smart and we could live off it for a long time, maybe forever. And he could write songs, and I could sing them. We would have *real* lives. So the next night I packed my suitcase and brought it to our meeting place on the beach. Just rolled it out there on the sand. Can you imagine? I was ready to leave. I was ready to run off with him." It's then that Ivy looks me in the eyes. "And he laughed. He said he was kidding. He looked at me like I was crazy."

I want to go to her. I want to reach across the water. She is so small on the other side of the pool. But I don't know what kind of friend I'm supposed to be. One who just listens to her monologues, or one who touches her?

"Is that what you want?" I say. "To leave your career and everything behind?"

"No," Ivy says. "I don't think so. My career is all I have." She pauses, and for a moment I catch a glimpse of her as a child, lonely and shattered and needing something no one can give her. "I just want him."

We both want the same boy who's already taken.

She tries to make herself bigger, tries to paint confidence on her face. "I don't blame him. I was a mess when I met him. I was exhausted and I wanted out. I wanted to run away from everything. From my mom. My contract with A-Corp. Everything. I was crazy for thinking he would do that with me. We had just met. And he has nothing to run away from."

"So you don't want to run away anymore?"

She sits up a little straighter. "I know what's real. I know how the world works, how people work. I'm not going to ask anyone to change for me. I just want to know him again."

My skin is starting to get pruney, and I'm feeling a little nauseated from the heat and smell. I wonder how long we're supposed to stay in here to get the supposed medicinal effects, how long it takes to get to prime relaxation, if there's some magical equation for us to get Ivy's money's worth. I wonder what it was like here before it got turned into this place with bamboo walls and imported tea sets and white women in geisha dresses and security guards with guns, if it was just mud and rocks the way nature intended. Maybe if it was still like that, I wouldn't feel such a strong impulse to leave.

I count back in my head a year and a half, to the winter Ash got back from his trip to Brazil. I remember he seemed shaken, quieter than usual, drinking and smoking more. He confided in me at one party that he was thinking about breaking up with Tami. He said she didn't understand him. But then he arrived at the next party with a split lip and he wouldn't tell anyone where it came from. Tami was overly affectionate with him that night, by his side the whole time, offering to get him things, holding his hand like she was someone who liked holding hands instead of who she really was—someone who makes fun of those kinds of couples. Her eyes burned with something that did not quite look like love. He looked at her like someone possessed. The look on his face did not look like love either.

Later that night, I saw them in the shadows, Tami in his lap, straddling him, moving slowly, whispering something into his ear, and I remember it struck me that I was witnessing something like magic being performed, an incantation, a powerful spell being cast, and I wondered how people learn to do these things. Where do they get that kind of power? How does Tami just know what it takes to control him? His eyes were shut tight and her whispers were conjuring him into being. She was making him. He was hers.

She reclaimed him from Ivy, and he has belonged to her ever since.

"So that's why you moved to Commodore Island?" I say. "For Ash?"

I don't say, "But what if he doesn't want you? What if you're wasting your time? Why are you planning your life around a boy you knew for two weeks? What if there's nothing for you here? What if Tami is more powerful than all of us?"

"It sounds ridiculous, doesn't it? My mom has been obsessed with moving to Commodore ever since she was a little kid. She'd hang out inside the ferry terminal in Seattle, waiting for her mom to get off work, watching all the people getting on and off the boat, and she thought they had everything she didn't, and she's been fixated on it ever since. She knew that spot where I met Ash was where a lot of Commodore's most important families own vacation homes. Her idea of making it was to find someone to take care of her and own a big house on the water on Commodore Island and never have to work again."

"And she got her wish," I say. Ivy is that someone. Ivy is the one who has to take care of her.

"Yeah, I guess so. Sometimes I don't know where her dreams stop and mine start."

"Is she happy?"

Ivy laughs. "Of course not. She's fucking miserable."

"Maybe she was wishing for the wrong thing."

"She wants me to be with Ash too. For her own reasons. No matter how much money I make, it's never enough. She won't be happy until we have old A-Corp money. She wants to be part of a dynasty." I do not know how to read the look on Ivy's face. I do not know the secret language of hating a parent.

I decide I can't stand it anymore. I'm too hot. I lift myself out of the water, and Ivy does too, like a mirror image of me on the side of the pool, and now here we are, naked, dripping wet, sitting on rocks, staring at each other, and I do not look away.

"I need your help," she says, throwing me a towel. "I need you to organize a meeting at your place. With me and Ash."

"Why can't you do it?"

"I can't just invite him over. Can you imagine what Tami would think of that? And you know how this island gossips. You two are already friends. It makes more sense if people think we meet through you. Plus, I want you to be there."

"Why?"

"I trust you. I trust myself when I'm with you."

I don't say, "But you don't even know me."

"I don't have his new number," I say. "Tami will think it's weird if I ask her for it."

Ivy looks at me, a war of yearning and disappointment on her face.

"Yes," I say. "Okay, yes. I'll figure something out. I promise. I will."

AshandIvy. IvyandAsh.

She drops her towel and I try to burn into memory the perfect back of her body before she puts on her robe.

Maybe what Ash needs is a love like Ivy's.

Maybe what I need is to be the glue that binds them.

14

TOURISTS and bored housewives. Family time. Skyping with Lily.

That's what my summer should look like.

Ivy materializes as soon as I get home from work, like she was waiting for me in the bushes, like she fell from the sky.

Tami says come over. I say yes, hoping.

But Ash is not there. Again.

Ivy says, "Did you call him yet?"

Daddy drives Papa around the island to the ferry terminal every morning and picks him up every night. That is what they are like.

. . .

I let Tami make me a drink even though it's only afternoon.

"Do you think it's possible for a person to love two people at the same time?" she says, like it's a rhetorical question.

Yes. Yes, I do.

"Do you love Vaughn?" I say.

She turns her back to me. "Isn't this a great view?" she says.

Daddy takes me out for lunch and clothes shopping in the city. He pretends he's not crying as I pick out a new coat for college.

"You know I'll call you every Sunday," I say, but that makes him cry more.

"Come over," Ivy says.

"I can't. I have to have dinner with my family. Do you want to join us?"

She has no idea what I'm talking about.

Tami makes me another drink. It's her way of being generous.

"Come over after dinner," Ivy says. "I've been doing this thing where I jump into the Sound and then get in the hot tub. It's supposed to be good for your heart or something. The shock from cold to hot."

Tami says, "Let's go for a drive. Let's take your car." Why in the world would she want to take my car?

Daddy sniffles. "You look beautiful. Let me take a picture to send your father."

"It's just a coat, Daddy."

"But it's a great coat. It will keep you warm."

Slumming it.

That's what I am to Tami. I am the friend version of Vaughn.

"No," I tell Tami. "Let's take your car."

But maybe she loves him.

The tram speeds Daddy and me over the parts of the city where people like us don't go, fast through its noise and bustling anonymity, back to the ferry terminal to go home. A tall chain-link fence topped with barbed wire protects us from the masses, lined with protest posters and graffiti that will be removed soon, and replaced, and removed again.

"Do you like your job?" Ivy says.

Tami sideswipes a car in the coffee shop parking lot.

Someone throws a rock that makes it through the fence, and I jump at the impact as it hits the window of the tram, right by my head.

The island is starting to feel small, claustrophobic. The trees tilt inward. Vines consume the house.

"I could give you a job," Ivy says. "You could be my assistant or something. I could basically pay you to do nothing."

Tami keeps driving after she hits the car. "Aren't you going to leave a note?" I say.

. . .

The rock only made a small ding in the tram's window. Nothing was shattered.

My home, once a haven, feels like a tiny boat drifting out at sea, with no motor or sails or oars, at the mercy of whatever tides push it around or whatever stillness it gets stuck in.

I tell Ivy yes.

Goodbye, fake antique watering cans. Goodbye, T-shirts of otters holding hands.

"Why would I leave a note?" says Tami.

"To exchange insurance information or something. So that person can get their car repaired."

"That's their business, not mine."

"But you hit their car."

"But no one saw me."

"You should be more careful," I tell her. I try to make my voice strong, but it sounds like pebbles bumping into each other under a wave.

"Other people are careful so I don't have to be."

We have no motor or sails or oars.

. . .

"Hey Tami, can I see your phone? I'm thinking of getting that kind."

"Knock yourself out."

Contacts:

Search:

Ash.

Share contact.

Papa said dinner will be ready in fifteen minutes. I am in my tree, looking west, waiting for Ivy's silhouette in the house made of windows.

I am a boat drifting out to sea.

Ash's reply is immediate: *I was wondering when I'd hear from you.*

15

IT is not difficult to betray Tami. I know she's in the city tonight, with Vaughn. She is making this too easy.

But I didn't want Ivy and Ash's meeting to happen at my house. I love my home, but it's so small and open, and the thought of Daddy undoubtedly being there hovering and wanting to talk to Ash and ask him about his dad, and being all starstruck and overly friendly to Ivy—it's too embarrassing to think about. So I came up with an even more ridiculous idea.

Why not orchestrate a surprise reunion of lovers at an old army fort? What could be more romantic?

I think of them on some Brazilian island that will soon be erased under rising sea levels, but for now is still a perfect place with umbrella drinks, a cool ocean breeze, pristine soft sand, and a horizon full of blue sky and smooth water. And now they'll meet *here*, at these moss-covered ruins slowly being reclaimed by the earth, at dusk, after the sun has already slipped behind the mountains, when all the shadows across pockmarked concrete walls are even more sharp, the angles more weird, with all the tufts of grass and tiny ferns growing out of crumbling holes, the canopy of trees blocking the sky, the stairs covered with pine needles, the bats starting to stretch their wings and get ready for the night, the old gun turrets full of rusty, mysterious metal that was too heavy to remove, the cigarette butts and graffiti all over the place, the occasional used condom or hypodermic needle buried in a corner.

What is wrong with me?

During the day, people come here for picnics. When we were kids, Ash and I would climb all over it, like a big concrete maze full of dark rooms with tiny, too-high windows, while Papa rattled off some facts about U.S. Army Coastal Artillery Corps at the turn of the twentieth century and top secret World War II operations. I tried to imagine soldiers in here but I couldn't. The only thing I could imagine this place was good for was hide-and-seek with my best friend.

But now this. Waiting. With an actual picnic basket packed by Daddy, full of crackers and salami and fancy cheeses and fruit, and a handwritten note from Papa to give to Ash's parents. "We'd love to see you both soon. Hope all is well!" it said. I crumpled up the note and threw it in the recycling.

I'm sitting on some kind of big metal stand. Maybe there used to be a cannon here. But now there's just me.

"Fern?" says a voice in the shadows, and I jump. Ivy emerges from behind a corner, overdressed in a black sleeveless minidress. Her legs are long and flawless, and she makes even an old army fort seem glamourous. "What is this place?" She climbs crumbling stairs to meet me. "It looks like the set of a horror movie."

I get the impression that under her perfect butterscotch skin, all her muscles and tendons are tying themselves in knots. "Do you have anything in there to take the edge off?" she says, eyeing the picnic basket.

"My parents don't usually drink," I say. "There's nothing in the house."

She looks confused. She does not live in a world where parents don't keep alcohol in the house.

I don't say, "Aren't you supposed to be sober?"

"I was just kidding," she says, her eyes darting around the structure, as if she might find a bottle hidden here.

Ivy sits down next to me, smooths her dress, pulls her phone out of her purse, and looks at it. "So he's supposed to be here in, what? Fifteen minutes? Is he usually on time?" He's supposed to be her soul mate, but she's asking me if he's the kind of person who's usually on time.

"Yeah, I think so. Are you ready?"

She gets up and starts pacing. She doesn't know what to do with her hands. I want to jump up and wrap my arms around her and hold her still. "Are you sure he's coming? He confirmed it? It wasn't like one of those 'maybe I'll stop by' kind of things?"

"Yes, he's coming."

She moves around our strange little stage, touches the moss on the waist-high half-walls that surround us on three sides, inspects the metal bars that jut out in various places for no apparent reason, walks down a small flight of steps and peers into a dank and windowless pitch-black room, then comes back up and looks over the top of the wall, where you can barely make out a view of the water through trees that have grown tall and thick since this place was meant to be a lookout.

"Are you hungry?" I ask.

"I couldn't possibly eat," she says. But she walks over to me and opens the picnic basket anyway. Inside are Daddy's little glass containers in their tidy arrangement, the linen napkins and bamboo napkin rings, the compostable cutlery and plates.

"This looks like something a sane person put together."

"Um, thanks?"

"Do you think your family would adopt me?"

She looks at me and the raw hope on her face betrays the joke she was trying to make, and something about it strikes me as incredibly sad.

She takes a few steps back and I feel her inhale, feel my skin pull toward her, feel every molecule in my body want to be consumed by her, absorbed into her bloodstream.

Then footsteps on dried leaves. Ash's low voice from behind a corner: "Hello?"

Wings flutter inside my chest. I close my eyes and when I open them, Ivy's gone.

It's just me, sitting here, on this broken old turret, facing Ash as he emerges from the shadows, shirtless and dripping with sweat.

I feel the weight of years of wanting. I feel all the miles between us. I feel Tami's presence like some parasite inside him. And what am I? A memory? Someone he used to know that he will forget, someone fading away even as I sit here right in front of his eyes?

I stand up. I don't know what to do with my hands. Everything inside my skin is gnarled and kinked.

"Ash," I say. "It's been a long time."

"It's good to see you," he says, his voice so low, I can feel the vibrations of it in my chest, those same piercing dark eyes behind thick black lashes. He is the boy I imagined. He is the boy I've been following online while he's been gone, living a life that doesn't include me, growing into himself, growing into the world's expectations.

He takes a tentative step forward. His lip twitches like he wants to smile but doesn't remember how, or like he hasn't decided if he wants to yet. He looks me in the eye, then looks away, then looks me in the eye again. I can't tell if he's genuinely nervous, or if this is all an act—the adorably bashful boy—calculated, showing me what he thinks I want to see.

We are out of practice. We have forgotten how to be friends.

We are just friends. We have only ever been just friends.

"What happened to you?" I say, and I'm not quite sure what I'm asking.

"I ran here."

"Why?"

"I felt like it."

Really? Do human beings really do these kinds of things? Just go through the world half-naked, expecting to stay safe?

Ash has been known to run through the trails across the island and then emerge sweat-drenched and blinking at various spots along the shore, where he'll order a car on his phone to pick him up whenever he feels done. How strange to live like that, with no return plan, to trust your place in the world so completely that you know someone will be there to help you whenever you get too tired to make it home on your own.

Wandering the forest around my own house, I have always secretly hoped to see him break through the trees like the deer, invisible and hidden until they are suddenly right in front of you, sleek and beautiful, staring straight into your eyes.

"You don't have a shirt on," I say. I am trying not to look. Not at his smooth, hard chest. Not at the chiseled bone and muscle under the glowing sun-browned skin of his shoulders. I am trying not to imagine licking the sweat out of the well of his collarbone.

"That never bothered you before."

I don't know what this is. I don't know if he's trying to make a joke. I can't tell if the movement in his lips is an attempt at a smile, or if it's irritation. I don't know what I'm doing here, why I agreed to do this. And where the hell is Ivy?

"Wait," I say. "I have to go get something from my car."

"Your car?"

“Something for the picnic. Here,” I say, pushing the picnic basket toward him with my foot.

“Wait,” he says. “I don’t understand.” I feel his eyes on my back as I run away.

I find my way through an old doorway, into a black room that smells of soil and secrets. I stand there trying to catch my breath, in the shadowed corner, where no one can find me. This is what caves feel like. This is where bats live. This is where dark things are born. It is where things go to die.

When I emerge, it feels like a new world. I don’t know how long I was in there, but now the trees are rustling with their evening conversations, the sky has darkened, and I can hear the waves rolling the rocks around on the other side of the trees. The breeze off the water smells of seaweed.

Somehow I know to peek around the corner before making my presence known. Somehow I know I’m not welcome. I am a watcher now. A witness. I have done my job. Ivy has found her way out of the shadows.

She stands before him, cocktail party ready, while he’s in nothing but running shorts. The breeze changes direction and I catch a whiff of his sweat and musk, and for a moment I think I know how animals feel.

The moon is half-full. Ivy is half-lit.

They are electricity, frozen. They are energy, bottled up, ready to explode.

“You invited my girlfriend to your party,” he says. I can’t

decipher the meaning of his voice. Anger and passion have the same tone.

"I thought you would come."

"This isn't how to do this."

"How am I supposed to do this? I tried emailing, I tried calling, but you changed your address and number. God, I sound like I'm crazy."

This is what makes him step toward her. This is what softens him. "You're not crazy." He lifts her chin gently with his hand so her eyes meet his. I can almost feel the warmth of his touch on my own face. I can almost see his eyes staring into mine, seeing all the things no one else ever does. We are the only two people in the world, and this is our cloud, high above it all, and I am safe, and nothing can touch us here.

I don't know why, but I start crying. Something about this tenderness releases me.

"I feel crazy," Ivy says. "You're the only one who's ever made me feel sane." For some reason, I think of Daddy, of being hunched over in the garden with him, weeding. Those are the moments he was always most likely to go off about his Buddhist stuff, and I would never really listen to his words, but the sound of his voice would soothe me. I remember his words now, something about how it's not people and experiences that create pleasure and suffering, it's our responses to them. No one can make us feel anything.

I hear bats. I hear the sounds the night makes. I hear

Daddy's voice telling us "All beings are responsible for their own actions."

But what about feelings? What are we supposed to do about feelings? Who's responsible for those?

"I see you," Ash says.

"Yes," Ivy says, breathless.

"No one else does," Ash says.

"You're the only one."

Ivy steps forward, putting her face only inches from Ash's, and I am struck by how brave she is. Her want is brave because it makes her vulnerable. It gives him the power to hurt her, but she does it anyway.

She has put herself in front of an audience for most of her life, has faced ridicule and gossip since she was a little kid, and she keeps doing it, keeps putting herself out there, over and over again, and the world keeps beating her up. Her want, her need, bare and naked, for all the world to see.

"How are we supposed to do this?" she says softly. The trees rustle with her breath. "We're doing this, right? I'm here now. Ash, tell me we're doing this."

And then I can't watch any more. My skin feels wrong and the electricity is catching. I am behind a stone wall but I am also somewhere between them, sandwiched between his sweaty chest and the thin layer of expensive fabric covering hers. I am somewhere between their lips, no longer talking, breathing each other in. They are not kissing, not yet, but it is only a matter of time. And then they will not need me. Then I will be irrelevant.

I close my eyes and find my way back into the cave. It is a place for underground creatures that don't need light. The silence is heavy with fear and disappointment. I wait. I know Ivy is coming.

Her shadow blocks the pale light coming in from the doorway and for a moment there is total darkness, and I do not feel the floor, and I do not feel my skin, and I am floating in space between here and not here, and now the only thing that's real is Ivy's body against mine, pushing me into the wall. And I'm suspended in the split second during which I return to my body, and a memory's created in this place where time sits still: a scene like in a show, soft music playing, a game played in middle school, minutes spent in a dark closet on a dare, with a boy who was one hundred percent gay. We were supposed to be kissing, or whatever almost-teenagers are supposed to do together in dark closets, but instead we talked about our pets. He had a dog named Peanut and I had a cat named Gotami, and it was safe and warm and the definition of innocence, and I want to go back there, I want to live there forever, but that place does not exist, and I can never, ever go there again.

Cold, wet stone with mysterious slimes and textures. Ivy's hands grabbing my shoulders. Her pelvis pressed against mine, her hot breath against my lips. I can't even hear what she's saying. Something about Ash. Something about this being a disaster. I am consumed by the darkness erasing the distance between our bodies. She is shaking me. She wants to make me feel what she feels. My mouth is full of the almost taste of her.

"Shhhhh," I say. It is white noise. It is the sound babies hear in the womb.

I have power in this darkness. In here, Ivy needs me.

"You're both nervous," I tell her. I use a voice I didn't even know I had. I think one day I will be a mother.

"You think he's nervous?"

"Of course he's nervous."

"He doesn't have a shirt on," she says. That makes her laugh. She giggles uncontrollably for a few moments, shallow puffs of adrenaline on my neck. Her hands all over me, desperate for contact, grabbing my back like she wants to hold me but also wants to claw at something, to break skin, to make my skin hers.

"Okay," she finally says, and just as quickly as she came on, her hands fall against her sides and she takes a half step back. I feel myself sucked away with her. I lose some of my skin. Dim light seeps through the doorway and I am left in the half shadow, half panting.

She is gone, on her way to Ash. She is not mine.

I don't tell them I'm leaving.

I don't know if they hear my car crunching over pinecones and rocks. I watch them as I back away, sitting across from each other, face-to-face, foreheads touching, whispering incantations. I do not exist in the space between them. This place from my childhood is no longer mine. Every memory becomes paper thin. Their one meeting here has more gravity than my whole life. They now own it.

It is not a long drive home along the waterfront. My mind is strangely clear, empty, like part of it is missing, left back there in the ruins.

Before I go inside, I take a minute to walk through Daddy's vegetable garden, his perfect rows of beans and carrots and greens and squash, and I am suddenly irritated by what I have always admired about him—his determination to do things the hard way, his faith that working for something gives it more value than if it comes easy. What a waste of energy it is to create things with his hands that he could so easily buy. All his little projects, all these extensions of him. He makes things difficult so he can create the illusion that they have meaning. That doing them gives his life meaning.

I pull a couple of small weeds. He calls this his weeding meditation. He calls doing dishes his dishes meditation. And laundry his laundry meditation. He says everything is a meditation if you're mindful. It is strangely relaxing, the repetitive action, knees down in the soil, helping to make things grow by killing the things that might crowd them out.

But is any of this really necessary? The forest grows just fine without him. Maybe it's an illusion that the plants need him at all. Maybe he just wants something to control.

Maybe relaxing is the same as boring.

Am I one of his little projects? Am I something to control?

Am I Ivy's?

I don't go inside the house. I take off my shoes and walk down the gravel road. The soles of my feet are getting stronger.

Scotch broom. Flowering blackberries. Chamomile growing

among the rocks on the side of the road. All half lit by moonlight.

If Ash were here, he'd say something like, "I can't believe you used to have to walk up and down this road every day for school."

Ivy would say, "It's like authentic country living. People pay good money for this." They would laugh and I wouldn't know what's so funny.

Now here they are, exactly where I knew they'd be. Ivy's space-age car in the driveway. Ash, his chest now covered with something borrowed from Ivy, a cool vintage T-shirt with the neck cut out, a showcase for his collarbones. I can see them through the glass walls, on display, like a giant television. But they can't see me out here in the darkness.

The house looks different without the dozens of guests and blazing party lights, without all the extra staff. It is empty and sterile, like what's left after some kind of viral apocalypse, a mass extinction that happened so fast, no one even had time for looting and destruction. Everyone's just gone, their world left shining and intact and useless.

Ivy is making him a drink at the bar in the expansive living room. Even though I am outside, I can hear the ice tinkle in the glass. "Is this still your drink?" she says, pouring something brown. He nods. They are awkward again. Whatever connection they made at the fort has to be remade here.

"It's just you and your mom here?" Ash says, taking his drink. Ivy does not make one for herself. She is still trying to be good.

“Yep,” Ivy says. “We both finally realized LA wasn’t the best place for us. I’m ready for some stability, you know? So I can really think about what I want for my future. Make some smart decisions.”

“Smart decisions are good,” Ash says.

“But not too smart.” She looks at Ash with so much desperation in her eyes, I feel nauseated, woozy, like I’m on a boat and the sea just dropped.

Before he has the chance to say anything, Ivy says, “I want to show you something.”

The front door is unlocked. I follow them into the grand entryway with the giant front doors that probably rarely get opened. It is not hard to be invisible. I am here in the place between places, in the place between before and after, the place where ghosts are born. Daddy says there are some Buddhists who believe in a place between death and the next life, a place where a soul can get stuck if it’s not careful. But he also says Buddhists don’t really believe in a soul, not the way most people do, so who knows what to do with that.

I swear I see figures out of the corner of my eyes, remnants from Ivy’s party who never left. They are hiding behind couches, under chairs, peeking out from closets and around corners. They follow us wherever we go. They feel familiar. They are the parts of us that get left behind. Now that I know how to be a ghost, I can see the others, the people without skin, the ones like me who are stuck in the in-between place.

Lining the walls are framed movie posters, photos of Ivy with some of the most famous people in Hollywood, photos of her onstage singing, photos of her accepting awards. The whole place is a shrine to her. I hide around the corner as she leads Ash to the centerpiece—her framed platinum record, sparkling under its own spotlight.

He is speechless, his face twisted with emotion. Ivy slides next to him, their shoulders touching as they stare at the platinum record. "Remember when we talked about making music together?" Her voice is thin. It sounds as breakable as glass. "None of the songs on that album come close to what you write."

"Can I touch it?" he says.

"I didn't think I'd ever see you again," Ivy says.

I feel something wet on my cheek, and Ivy wipes hers, and a tear streams down in a perfect straight line to Ash's chin, and she is staring at him, and he is staring at the record with a look of pure want on his face, and I am watching both of them, and all of our want has nowhere to go. It is too big for even this great empty room. It is stuck here like the not-souls between after and before.

Ash could have everything on that wall if he wanted to. I've heard his music. I've heard his voice. Maybe his being a musician wouldn't be his parents' first choice, but all they'd have to do is make a phone call and he could have the attention of anyone in A-Corp Entertainment. All it would take would be for Ash to say this is what he wanted, that he would risk everything he has to have it. But that would require him to make a decision. It would require him to fight for it.

Ivy reaches over and gently wipes the tear from Ash's cheek, but he does not turn, does not lean into her hand, does not look away from the record on the wall. Ivy thinks his tears are for her, and maybe they are, but maybe they aren't.

"I need another drink," he finally says, forcing a smile, but it's too late. Something has cracked. An opening. A fissure.

Me too, I think. But I am not here.

How easy it is to erase a moment. How easy it is to walk away.

I follow them to the outdoor bar. They live in a world where houses have bars, one for outside and one for inside. They live in a world where kids know how to make drinks besides shots of cheap vodka and beer in cans.

"You have a good view," Ash says, sitting down on the outdoor couch, even though it's night and we can't see much of anything beyond Ivy's property except the lights of distant houses facing us from the other shore. "It's nice to not see Seattle all the time. You can pretend you're not near a city at all. Are those palm trees?"

Ivy laughs as she hands him his drink. "That's why I picked this place. It's like my own tropical island. Like our island."

He is a construction of her memories. She is trying to shape him into the details of the boy she knew a year and a half ago. He is only two weeks old. He exists only on a tiny strip of beach, under a different view of the stars.

"I could climb those trees to pick you coconuts," Ash says. "How many do you want?"

Ivy smiles. He is finally playing her game. "How many do you have?"

"I can't believe you're here," he says. Something has softened. Maybe Ivy has awakened the part of him that remembers. Maybe he is already forgetting how to be cool. Maybe his want is making him brave.

"Me neither." Then she swallows. Then she clenches her fists. Then she tries to smile her famous smile, but it comes out all lopsided.

Ivy turns to the bar and picks up a bottle of wine. She pretends to read the label but I know what she's really doing is marking this moment as the space between after and before, a point in history that cannot be erased.

You would think relapse would have fireworks, that it would be some grand explosion of desperation and destruction. But maybe sometimes it is a series of small adjustments and unconscious decisions that have already been happening beneath the surface, laying the foundation, so that by the time the ultimate decision comes, it's anticlimactic. Sometimes relapse is not one big break but a series of small fractures that all add up to a soundless shattering.

"This is one of the last vintages that came out of Napa before the Great Fire," Ivy says, pouring a glass. She swishes it around for a while and smells it. She closes her eyes and takes a sip, and I can taste the warm comfort wash down my throat and spread through my whole body, the feeling of rightness, of relief, of escaping the place between places, feeling my feet firmly on the ground. Oak and cherry, and a little bit smoky. The taste of knowing who I am.

"To reunions," Ivy says.

"Reunions," Ash says.

Their glasses clink, and then Ivy looks straight at me where I'm hiding in the shadows. The look in her eyes says "I've known you were here the whole time. You are my secret." And the warmth hits my stomach, and I want more.

"To us," I whisper, and I know only she can hear me.

And that's when I hear footsteps and hide behind a bush just as Ivy's mom saunters out of the darkness in a see-through robe over a swimsuit. "Well, if it isn't Ash Kye," she says without any surprise. She must be as good at spying as I am. "How are you, young man? I've been meaning to get ahold of your mother, but I've been so busy since we arrived, and now with this remodel." She waves her arm at nothing in particular.

"I'm sure she'd love to hear from you," Ash says, such a gentleman. "She's in Buenos Aires now, but will be back for a few days next week before she leaves again for Tokyo."

"Lovely, I'll be sure to make some time for lunch. Please tell her I say hello."

Ivy takes a long sip of wine, and I am thirstier than ever.

"I see you're drinking again," her mother says.

"It's just wine."

"Last time I checked, wine had alcohol in it."

Ivy looks her in the eyes defiantly as she refills her glass.

"Well, don't hog the good stuff," Ivy's mother says, and grabs the bottle out of her hand. "You know, Ash, this is one of the last vintages to come out of Napa before the Great Fire."

"You don't say?" says Ash, and Ivy giggles.

"Well, I'll leave you kids. Don't have too much fun." She gives Ivy a look that says "Don't fuck this up again."

She takes the bottle with her to the pool, illuminated in the darkness by underwater lights. Ivy immediately opens a new one.

I don't know how long I wait there in the shadows. Long enough for their conversation to die down, long enough for Ivy's mom to pass by again on her way back from swimming, long enough for the new bottle of wine to half empty. Ivy is in that perfect place between too drunk and not drunk enough, that moment of equilibrium before the scales tip.

They are alone now. They are whispering things I cannot hear. The words are not important. What matters is their leaning into each other. What matters is Ash taking Ivy's hand and kissing the tip of each of her fingers. What matters is Ivy's lips, stained red with wine from now extinct grapes, finally touching his.

16

"COME with me," Ivy says.

I do what I'm told. I work for her now.

Lily says she doesn't think it's a good idea. "That's my professional opinion," she says from across the ocean.

Professional what? Professional pain in my ass.

"I was invited to this thing," Ivy says. "A charity event. I wasn't going to go. My therapist doesn't think I'm ready. But I think I want to. I want you to come with me."

She says she just wants to make an appearance. She says we won't be long.

Is it my job to believe her?

This is the makeover part of the story. This is the part when I get turned into someone else. When it becomes clear I wasn't enough before.

Ivy plucks my eyebrows. She does my hair and makeup. I am her doll. I bend to her.

"Here, wear this," she says, handing me a shimmery forest-green version of her own sky-blue cocktail dress. I lift my arms over my head and shiver as the fabric falls against my skin. I have never felt anything so soft in my life.

We look at ourselves in the full-length mirror. We could be twins.

"My perfect little doppelganger," Ivy says.

I am the paler, more transparent version of her.

"Can you believe we're exactly the same size?" she says. "Even our feet match."

"Like Cinderella," I say.

Ivy smiles. "So when do you turn into a pumpkin?"

"Are you nervous?" I say as we climb into the water taxi.

The boat's engine rumbles and we start moving toward the lights.

"The problem with these water taxis is what they do to your hair," she says as she ties a scarf over her head.

"Are you going to be okay?" I say.

"Ash is with Tami tonight," she says, looking out over the water at Seattle.

"Oh," I say.

"He doesn't love her."

"Okay," I say.

"We've been getting reacquainted." And she smiles and smiles and smiles.

The stars glitter overhead somewhere but we can't see them. There is a barrier between us. There is a faint smell of smoke.

I don't know where we're going. I never know where we're going.

"Don't worry, I'm not going to drink anything tonight," Ivy says. "Can you imagine what people would say? But I can take it or leave it. That's how you know you're not an alcoholic."

There is a red carpet on a sidewalk. There is a cordoned-off area leading to doors. Security guards. Photographers. Long legs extending out of cars and limos.

"Ivy! Ivy!" the paparazzi yell. I recognize some of them as the ones who park outside her gate on Olympic Road. It is their job to stalk her. They get paid to do this.

What is my job? What exactly does it mean to assist someone?

Time speeds up. Our hearts beat faster. The flashes and whispers are their own kind of drug.

. . .

Lights and lights and other shimmery dresses. People I've seen on so many screens, people I've seen in movie theaters with their faces two stories tall. So many cheek kisses. So much posing for photographers. So many limp one-armed hugs. Hands on the smalls of backs. Identical smiles for this picture, that picture. Everyone made two-dimensional. Everyone flattened for consumption.

The captions will say, "Ivy Avila's first appearance in public since rehab."

The captions will say she was drinking club soda all night.

The captions will say she was radiant.

They will say nothing of her pale assistant.

The crowd parts for her. Whispers swarm around us like moths.

I don't speak. No one needs to know who I am.

"Look at you," she says. "You are my arm candy."

I start laughing. People look. They raise their eyebrows. So I grab a prawn from a passing waiter and shove it in my mouth to shut up.

I wonder if anyone here actually knows what charity this is for.

...

Light descends in particles, in waves. Ivy is denser than us all. She absorbs their glow, and the little sequins on her dress turn into their own tiny illuminations, a million mirrors, blinding everyone who looks. And everyone looks.

We move around. Ivy has the same conversation with different people in different places. There are various stations. By this ice sculpture. By this table of silent auction items.

By this couch, but not sitting. By this hors d'oeuvres station, but not eating. By these stairs, but not going anywhere.

I hear Ivy say the same thing a million times: "Oh it's so good to see you! It's been forever! I'm doing great, I really am. Self-care is so important, you know? I've been meditating. It's changed my life."

She is such a good actress. She should win an Academy Award for this party.

Every light turns and points and there are no shadows to hide us.

There's an older man, potbellied and vein-faced, following us with his rheumy eyes like lasers. I keep my eye on him. I am Ivy's bodyguard.

Ivy always seems to know where he is, dancing around the party so she's always as far away from him as possible. But then she makes a mistake. She finally takes a breath, and in that split second we manage to get stuck near the wall, we are cornered, and I feel her heart beating fast in my chest.

Suddenly the lights are too bright. We are too exposed. They are no longer spotlights but searchlights, and we've been caught, we've been blinded like a deer frozen in the road, just waiting to get hit.

I don't know who he is, but he is coming, and Ivy is scared. I can feel her panic in my own chest, can see the faint, disjointed shadows of memories, can feel my whole body sick with wrongness. It is my job to protect her, so I grab her hand and pull her to the coat check, I get our things, and we are off, in the car on our way to the water taxi, and my arm is around her, and I say "Who was that man?" and she says "What man?" and I say "The man who scared you?" and she just smiles and says "What are you talking about? I'm not scared of any man."

She stands up on the boat as we leave the dock, holding on to the edge of the canopy. She closes her eyes as the wind fans out her hair behind her. I stand next to her and feel the wind pass right through me.

She hooks her arm through mine and pulls me close to her side. "That was great," she says. "Wasn't it great? We left at just the right time. I made my appearance and I was the first to leave. That's what you want to do. You have to be mysterious. You have to always leave them wanting more. That's the thing about making people want you. You can't let them see you needy."

"Okay," I say.

"I didn't even want to drink. I can't wait to tell Dr. Chen. I think she's going to be proud of me. I'm fine. I'm totally fine."

"That's good," I say.

"I couldn't have done it without you, Fern." She looks me in the eyes and I see the night sky reflected. For a moment I think the city lights are stars. "You make me better."

"Stay with me," she says, pouring her third shot.

We are sitting on her bed. She says she is having a nightcap to help her fall asleep. She says everybody does this, no problem.

She lies down and closes her eyes. In a few moments, her lips part and I can hear the faint sound of her breath. I lean in close and breathe with her, smell the sweet and sour coming from inside. I should have reminded her to brush her teeth. It is my job to help her remember these kinds of things.

I take off her shoes and unzip her dress so she'll be more comfortable. I put the blanket over her and lie next to her on top of the blanket, careful not to touch her. We breathe in and out.

. . .

Inhale. Exhale.

Ivy, you made me. My job is to love you.

17

ONCE upon a time, Ivy Avila was a little girl who just wanted to be loved.

Isn't that how all stories start?

And then her mom found a way to make her lovable. As if her simple existence wasn't enough.

And then she quit school and worked and worked and forgot how to be a child. She gave everything she had and everything she didn't know she had.

Or was it taken?

Did she throw herself to the wolves, or was she thrown?

Is a child even strong enough to do that kind of throwing? Is it a child's job to make themselves lovable?

And we did love her. We do. Or whatever it is you call the feelings we have for the faces made two-dimensional by our screens, the lives made two-dimensional. We love her talent. We love her voice. We love her body and her beauty. We devour what we have been thrown.

And what about Ivy? What is left for her? Is she still hungry?

. . .

Lily was not proud of my going out last night. She's not impressed by Ivy's celebrity. She's not impressed by my new job. She's never understood what I see in Ash. She's not impressed by anything I do or anything I love.

But Ivy thinks I'm special. Tami even called me special. Maybe it's my turn to be special.

Lily doesn't have to know about Ivy's party tonight.

I don't understand this strategy. Is this how Ivy plans to win Ash back—by befriending his girlfriend? Her logic is upside down.

But Tami is acting like she already knows her, like they go way back. This is probably one of Tami's games, one of her ways of acting like she's the one in control. Even though this is Ivy's house, Tami's walking around like this is her turf too.

Ivy is giving them the tour, even though they've both already been here. The house, the grounds, the magical people. I follow, silently, like a chaperone, a referee, the neutral party.

But am I? Neutral?

Tami has her arm through Ash's. She is not letting go. She wants everyone to know Ash belongs to her. He could be any of these actors, these socialites, these rock stars. They are beautiful together.

This party is different from the last. It is hot even after the sun sets, and smoke from forest fires in the north is making the air hazy, burning eyes, closing throats. But people act like they're still invincible, despite their new dry coughs.

Ivy's mom is on a trip. She is not here, behind the scenes, running things. This party is all Ivy.

The night is darker. The magic of the last party has rotted away, and these are the dregs, like a civilization on the decline. People are drunker, grasping at shadows. There are men far too old to be at a teenager's party. They lurk in the shadows. Everything is shadows. But still, it is impressive.

And Ivy leads Tami and Ash around like everything is radiant. She shows them the pool, the gardens, the private dock. She introduces them to the most famous guests—an entire K-Pop band is here—and then looks back to check their reactions, to gauge how much she's impressed them.

As we walk, Ivy expands. Every time a head turns to look at her, she collects some new shiny thing, and it attaches to her, it gives her weight. She is a magnet. She is made out of her collections.

She is made out of her secret with Ash, swaggering with the audacity of parading him around as someone else's love when she is confident his heart is hers. He is the prized centerpiece of her collection, being polished and shined, waiting for the perfect moment to be revealed.

She is the shine of chrome and glass and mirrors. She is the diamonds and gold of so much jewelry. She is the electric blue of someone's eyes, the gloss of a girl's lipstick, the shine of a leather jacket. She is Ash's eyes, watching her, wanting her.

"These people are all your friends?" Tami says. I can tell she's trying to sound nonchalant, but she is not as good an actress as Ivy.

"Not really. I don't know. They're just people I know."

"Oh, there's Celia La*motte*," Tami says, trying to sound unimpressed and doing a bad job of it, as she waves at a B-list actress across the patio. The girl doesn't even bother to smile when she sees Tami looking at her expectantly, but as soon as she sees who we're with, her face lights up.

I never thought it'd be possible for me to feel sorry for Tami Butler.

Ash puts his arm around her and pulls her close, but he's looking at Ivy when he does it.

Something shifts in Tami. "So this is what you do?" she says, her voice low and hard. "Throw parties?"

Ivy opens her mouth. A few of the shiny things she's collected fall out.

As we walk, everything shrivels and turns gray in Tami's wake. That is the power she has.

Ivy walks us through the small museum of herself, and Ash acts like it's new to him, while Tami acts like she couldn't care less, like her insides aren't being torn open with jealousy. Maybe Tami is part of an A-Corp dynasty, but Ivy made this all by herself.

"Ash, did I tell you I bought another rental property in Bellevue?" Tami says. "I've already tripled the money my grandfather left me when he died."

"Uh-huh," he says. Is this really what rich teenagers talk about? They could be forty years old.

There's the picture of Ivy with that actor who won the Oscar last year. There's the picture of her with that famous director, that famous musician, that famous chef, and on and on. I think of Tami with Vaughn, with her empire of people she can demean without consequence, the supposed friends she treats more like they're her employees, and I wonder about the difference between power and fame. The difference between old money that's inherited and new money that's earned. I wonder which has more weight.

Here is Ivy, raw and vulnerable, at the mercy of whoever deems her worth noticing, defined by the eyes that see her. And here is Tami, born knowing how to take whatever she wants. And there is Ash in between them.

And where am I?

There is something desperate in the air. Glasses get filled and emptied, filled and emptied. People hide in corners, doing harder drugs. Eyes bulge out of faces, searching for something.

Ash betrays his usual cool when he spots members of a band waiting in line for a bathroom. They are in sunglasses even though it's nighttime. "You're friends with them?" he asks Ivy. "They're good. They're really good." What he doesn't say is, "I love them. I don't want any of you to know how much I love them."

Ash's dark eyes sparkle for a split second, then Tami looks at him, and the light goes out. "Really, Ash? What are you going to do, go ask them for their autographs? While they're waiting in line for the bathroom?"

"Why don't you go ask Celia Lamotte for her autograph?" he snaps back.

Ivy smiles and smiles and smiles. A fight breaks out somewhere. A girl appears to be OD-ing, but is quickly whisked away by her friends without much fanfare. The party goes on.

Ash is a statue by Tami's side, made of stone. He is a trophy, heatless. Objects can't feel.

But I see a faint outline of a shadow beneath him, thrown by the artificial light above, and it is twisting itself inside out, trying to break free.

Ivy grabs another glass of wine from a passing server. Tami says, "Aren't you supposed to be drying out?"

Ash opens his mouth but only pebbles fall out. The impotent *tink, tink, tink* as they hit the ground is percussion, making a song with the melody of a girl, unseen, crying softly in the distance.

"Oh, there's Madison," Tami says, and she disappears around a corner, eager to escape us, to be on her own so she doesn't have to compete with Ivy's light.

As soon as she is gone, Ivy grabs Ash's wrist and whisks him in the opposite direction, and I am left in the vacuum of their absence, on hold.

I don't know how long I stand there. Time seems to stop and I am just a series of observations without thoughts attached—the sound of that girl crying, the faint smell of smoke and spilled drinks, the sour taste of wine in my mouth, even though I've been drinking nothing tonight but water.

And then Ivy and Ash return, their noses sniffling, with pupils the size of pinpricks, a halo of electricity surrounding them as if they are walking in a different reality, they are vibrating with it, and Ash can't keep his eyes off her, and I think she must have found the right spell, the right potion, to finally make him hers.

But then Tami comes back, and she pulls him away just in time, before Ivy can claim him, and his shadow clings to hers for a few extra moments before it has to break away.

"We have to go," Tami says. Ash says nothing, just stands there vibrating next to her, his shadow flickering in and out.

"Oh, okay," Ivy says. "Let's hang out again sometime."

"I'll text you," Tami says as she pulls Ash away. He turns his head back, his eyes searching for Ivy, but she is already gone.

The only thing I can think to do is to follow Tami and Ash, but I am so quiet, they don't know I'm there. I imagine Ivy somewhere in the bushes. She must know all the best hiding places.

The gravel makes no sound under my bare feet as I follow them to the end of the driveway. I watch Ash pull Tami into him as they wait for their car to arrive. His kisses are wild and all teeth. He is hunger and more hunger. Whatever potion Ivy gave him is working, but it is all wrong.

Tami pushes him away, a pleased smile on her face. His want gives her power.

"Not now, Ash," she says.

His breaths are quick and shallow. He is all wound up with nowhere to go. "God, that girl is a train wreck," Tami says, and Ash just vibrates next to her. "Acting and music are bullshit professions."

"She's made a lot of money," Ash says. "More money than you."

Tami laughs and the flowers around her shrivel. Dry pine needles fall off nearby trees. Somewhere in the darkness, a frog's chirp goes silent. "It's about more than money. You know that. Getting a bunch of idiot strangers to buy your shit doesn't make you lovable, or whatever sad thing it is she's looking for. It's pathetic, really. Needing attention like that. And then walking around like royalty when you have no actual skills that matter. I mean seriously, what has that girl accomplished? Reciting lines on a couple crappy sitcoms, singing some songs she didn't even write?"

Ash doesn't hear her. He is in that place where nothing touches him. Whatever potion Ivy gave him helped him get there even better than usual.

"And didn't she just get out of rehab?" Tami says. "She must have drunk two bottles of wine just by herself. And who knows what else she was on. What a mess."

That makes Ash laugh. "Why are you so concerned about Ivy Avila? You're one to talk."

"People like us know how to hold our liquor. People like us don't get out of control."

“People like us. People like us,” Ash sings in his smooth, low voice, with a melody like a children’s lullaby, and his laughter shakes the trees, pinecones knocking together like bells, creating an empty tinny ring, and it is the sound of Ash’s heart knocking around in his ribs, in its crisp, impenetrable shell.

That’s when Tami grabs the collar of Ash’s shirt, twists it tight around his neck, and pulls him toward her with a hard tug. His breath catches where she’s restricting his throat, and he closes his eyes and pushes into her as he gasps for air. She leans over and bites his lip as she slowly releases his collar, and he smiles between her teeth.

Their car arrives. The driver gets out and opens the door, and Tami climbs in. “Come on,” she says from inside, and I try to will Ash to stay. He stumbles, looks back in my direction, his eyes searching but not finding anything.

“Where’s Ivy?” he says, and Tami reaches her long arm out, grabs him by the belt, and pulls him into the car.

Where is Ivy? Not on this road, quiet and barren. Not on this driveway, surrounded by rustling branches. Not in the glass house, full of absence. Most of the party has started its sad procession home. Bodies slumped in the hallway. Asleep in the bushes. All these wind-up toys, unwinding.

Ivy is alone, sitting cross-legged outside on an oversized pillow, staring at the miniature palm trees she supposedly bought the house for, tropical plants that, years ago, would never have survived here.

“Look at those stupid trees,” she says as I slide silently beside her. “They don’t belong here.”

She is grinding her teeth. Her knee is bouncing. She is made out of chemicals.

“I wish I was like you, Fern,” she says.

“Me?” I say. “Why?”

“You have everything I’ve ever wanted. You’re exactly who I’d be if I could be anyone.”

“But I’m no one.”

“That’s the thing,” she says. “You don’t have to be. You don’t *want* anything.”

“Of course I want things.”

I don’t say, “I want Ash.” I don’t say, “I want you.”

“Do you want to hear a story?” She takes a swig from a bottle of something. I do not bother answering.

“I fell in love with Ash because he played me a song he wrote. That’s all it took. Three, maybe four minutes.” She is talking fast. Her mouth can barely keep up with her memories. “He doesn’t play them for anyone, his songs. He has a whole album’s worth now. He doesn’t let anyone see that part of him. Only me. Nobody knows it’s even there.”

I don’t tell her Ash has played me his songs too.

“It was beautiful, Fern. I mean it. Like real art. Not that bullshit I get paid to do. I know what it is. I’m not lying to myself. You know all those guys who were here? That band Ash was so excited about? I begged them to let me tour with them as an opener last year. I offered to take almost no money. But they pretty much laughed in my face. They'll come to my parties, the straight ones will fuck me, but they don't want me associated with their *brand*." Her fingers make sloppy air quotes around "brand." "Because my music is a joke. I'm a joke."

I remember the night at the old army fort, when Ash told her she wasn't crazy, how that made her melt into him. I want to do the same thing, want to tell her *you're not a joke,* but she starts talking again before I have a chance.

"Dr. Chen says I need hobbies, things I do just for fun, just for me. Something I'd enjoy even if no one was watching. But I don't even know what that means. Even when no one's watching, I pretend they are. When I'm brushing my teeth, when I'm fucking peeing, Fern, I imagine people watching me. I don't know who I am without an audience. So I perform for ghosts. I've grown up as a commodity. I don't know how to be anything else. I want to be expensive. Put a price tag on me, tell me how much I matter."

"You matter," I say. But I know she can't hear me.

"Who am I with no one watching? I'm nobody. I disappear. I turn into a fucking ghost screaming 'Look at me!' but no one can hear me, so maybe I get mad and start going around breaking stuff to get noticed and all those things ghosts do. I have to haunt people just so they'll pay attention to me. I have to scare them. That's the only way to get their attention. But there's nothing scary about me. That's the big joke. I'd make a terrible ghost. Or maybe I could be one of those ones who cry all the time, who you hear in the wind, who hide in the clouds—that one who's always wandering around looking for something she lost. But she's been a ghost so long she doesn't even remember what that thing is, just that it's missing, and she goes around wailing about how empty she is."

Finally, Ivy looks at me, like she just remembered I'm here. "Maybe I am a ghost," she says. "Maybe I'm haunting you."

She doesn't know that the real ghost is me.

"But that night on the beach, with Ash, with his music—I sang with him, and then he played the song again, and then again, and eventually it was me singing the song, and he was harmonizing like he was the backup singer, and it was the realest shit I'd ever done, and there was no one there to see it. Just me and Ash, and that was all I needed—for *him* to see me. Only him. No one else really sees me. And I'm the only one who sees him." She smiles, deep inside her dream. She is somewhere far away, on a different kind of island, a place where she is not surrounded by passed-out strangers, where the air is fresh and does not smell of things burning. "And then it started raining, one of those tropical downpours, not like it rains here. And he had to hide his guitar under an overhang, and we just started running on the beach through these sheets of rain, getting totally drenched, and lightning was flashing all over the place, lighting up the sky all kinds of weird colors, and we probably could have died, the lightning was so close, then it'd go black again, and we were just running blind in it, holding hands, completely free, and I could have kept running and running forever holding his hand like that, just running into the night and the lightning. All I want is to stay in that night forever."

But this is a different kind of night. It is a different kind of island where the water's freezing all year round and the beach is made of sharp rocks instead of soft sand and the rain is never warm.

She pulls on her nose. "Dr. Chen thinks talking about my pain will make it go away or something. But that's bullshit. Talking about my pain just makes me feel it again. The only thing that ever took away my pain was Ash. He was even better than drugs. Dr. Chen can take her PhD and shove it." Ivy tries to laugh but it sounds like static. "In rehab they're always talking about chasing the first high," she says. "That night was the best high of my life."

Ivy leans against my shoulder. "You're wonderful," she says. "It's like I made you up. I don't know what I'd do without you." She entwines her fingers through mine and lifts my hand to her mouth, kisses it, and the image of my skin flickers on and off, while the electricity of hers surges, and I fade while she becomes a light so bright, I'm almost blinded.

"Does anyone ever catch it?" I say.

"Catch what?"

"The first high."

I feel her harden next to me. She pulls her hand away from mine. "Go home, Fern."

I asked the wrong question. And just like that, I am no longer wonderful.

She stands up and wobbles for a moment, grabs the bottle and walks away, into the house, the bodies of unconscious strangers strewn at her feet.

I am left alone, surrounded by unmoving bodies. We are not much different, the bodies and me. Even the palm trees are still. But I know the stillness is an illusion. I know beneath it there are machines that never stop running.

I look up at the windows on the second floor, at the figures darting around behind the curtains, and I don't know if they are tonight's guests or the apparitions I saw before. They are restless, just like Ivy. They are shadows intersecting with other shadows. They are hungry ghosts on their endless quest for something to fill them up.

18

PANCAKES with Papa and Daddy. Gotami purring on the sofa. A ray of sun breaks through the window, hitting Daddy's crystal hanging above the kitchen sink and bathing us in a million tiny rainbows. This is where I learned how to be happy.

But something is off, like wallpaper peeling. Everything is frayed at the edges. Something hidden wants to be seen, something beneath the surface.

This little world at the end of the gravel driveway, this oasis in the forest—it is too perfect, too safe. I do not belong here. Not anymore.

Is this what it means to grow up? To realize you're broken and unsafe?

My fathers talk about something but I do not hear them. I am supposed to call Lily today but I will not.

When my phone buzzes with Ivy's text, I realize I was waiting for it all morning.

"I'm going for a walk," I say, and my fathers smile. Such a wholesome thing, walking.

When I arrive at Ivy's, a cleaning crew of half a dozen people is hard at work erasing the debauchery of last night. One woman sweeps up broken glass. One man aims a hose at a puddle of vomit. A private security guard carries an unconscious man down the front steps.

I climb the stairs to Ivy's bedroom on the second floor. It's the size of three of my rooms combined. Ivy sits in the middle of her king-sized bed, in a silky white slip, propped up by an elaborate construction of pillows. Light filters in through the thin slats of her wooden blinds, illuminating the dark room in brief, dusty segments. The place is trashed, covered with piles of clothes and boxes and bags, with the sour smell of spilled wine and old plates of food.

At first, Ivy doesn't know I'm here. I stand in the doorway for a long time, watching her face suspended in the darkness, lit by the cold glow of her phone. She is scrolling, in a trance, on autopilot, her world condensed to whatever appears on the tiny screen.

I close the door behind me, and the sound finally catches Ivy's attention. "You're here!" she says, her voice light with its practiced exuberance, but her face is blank, unmoving from her phone.

I stand in the doorway, waiting to be told what to do. Ivy finally sighs and puts her phone down on the dresser next to her, next to an empty bottle of wine and a couple red-ringed glasses and crumb-covered plates and crumpled-up napkins. "You know people go to rehab for phone addiction?" she says.

She looks up and smiles, and it's now that I notice the bags under her eyes and the sickly pale of her skin. She is not the sparkling girl of last night, not the one collecting shiny, useless things. This morning, she is bare, raw-skinned. She's what's left after that other girl is done.

Ivy pats the place next to her on the bed. I am beckoned. I am the last shiny thing left.

"Did you sleep at all last night?" I say.

"Climb in," she says, flipping open the blankets. I kick off my shoes and get in, feel something like sand on my bare legs, smell the unwashed sheets and the remnants of who knows what bodies, and I wonder if the housekeepers have been too scared to come in here.

"Spoon me," she says.

She lies down on her side and presents me with her back. She smells of alcohol sweat and cigarette smoke, but still I warm as I fit myself around her, as I turn into her shape.

"I can't find any sleeping pills," she says.

The thing she's wearing is not clothes. It's a thing women wear as a promise of what is underneath. She did not put it on for me, but it is me who is here now.

"Put your arm around me," she commands.

I press myself into her. She is only her back, these flimsy silk straps, the tiny hairs on her smooth skin. I brush my cheek against her shoulder blades. Maybe she will think it was an accident.

"Give me your hand," she says.

She smells like unwashed hair and miles and miles and miles between us.

She adjusts her hips, pulls up her slip, opens her legs just a little, and places my hand on the part of her that is burning in me. She guides my fingers to a place that makes me gasp, but I know she does not hear me.

She rocks against my hand, holding it in place with her own like I am her tool. And I am somewhere else, miles and miles and miles away, with all of my clothes still on, my yearning like a wound.

I imagine I become her, my skin is her skin, my body is her body, my other hand, my fingers, are hers, and I do to myself what I am doing to her, and she cannot see me as I press against her, as she pulls away toward herself.

It does not take either of us long. And then it is done. My work is finished. I am finished.

Ivy can finally sleep. And I am still, unbearably, awake.

19

THE parties are over. Cars show up to a locked gate.

It's getting hotter. Pine needles are turning brown and falling shriveled to the ground. The lake in the center of the island is shrinking. The earth is cracking.

I have not heard from Ivy in days. She has been too busy with Ash. They have been locked inside her house.

Socialites wander up and down Olympic Road, dressed for a party that does not exist, not quite sure what they're looking for—a secret entrance, a portal, a clue, any good reason why they took a boat and drove miles around an island to get to this nowhere place, why they're wobbling in heels on a rural road with no sidewalk or streetlights and no one to see how good they look.

. . .

People are saying she went off the deep end again. A breakdown. An overdose. A suicide attempt. People are saying she's not eating. She's strung out on a dozen different drugs.

But I know the truth. It is far less interesting than all that.

Ivy's mother swishes down the driveway with a picnic basket just like Daddy's, full of snacks and a thermos full of gin and tonics. She is one of those drive-in waitresses you see in black-and-white movies, the kind on roller skates that come to the window of your car to take your order. She goes car to car, charming the men here to make money off of spying on her daughter. She is on the hunt for the most handsome, the most bored.

I should be at work selling more fake antique watering cans to tourists. But I quit that job, and those watering cans are just for decoration. We're in a drought and not supposed to be watering anything.

Ivy has a story to try to salvage. I wrote the introduction, but I am no storyteller.

She is trying to make a fairy tale out of parched skies and scorched earth. She is trying to breathe life back into something dormant and almost dead.

. . .

There is a fine line between brave and foolish.

The paparazzi sit outside in their cars, seats reclined, windows open, breathing in the salt air, drowsy from their afternoon drink, waiting for the gates to open, waiting for a glimpse of the star, the waif, the junkie, the lunatic.

How do you make something real out of a secret?

I pick up my phone to text Ivy. I type a million things and erase them. There is no right thing to say.

I settle into my yearning and turn it into a prayer.

The paparazzi don't know about Ash's running trails through the forest, his feet as silent as a deer's. They do not know his stealthy, hidden path to Ivy's house, do not see him as he leaps across the road into the patch of trees that separates her property from the neighbors', as he scales the wall into her compound.

. . .

The forest fires in the north have spread, and now there are new ones popping up in the Cascades two hundred miles to the east. The sun hangs a sickly, bloody red in the hazy sky.

Lily keeps calling but I don't call her back.

If Ash is a deer, what does that make Ivy? What does that make her mom?

Tami keeps texting.

I tell her I am busy. I do not tell her that her boyfriend is a deer. That he has wandered through the forest away from home.

Hunting is forbidden on Commodore Island.

I sit at home at night, binge-watching *The Fabulous Fandangos*, binge-watching *The Cousins*. I listen to *This Is Me* on headphones while I wash the dishes. It is Ivy but it is not Ivy.

I try to see what everyone else sees, from the outside—first the precocious little girl, then the beautiful and mysterious teen, then the slightly edgy pop star still wholesome enough to fit the A-Corp brand.

The story of Ivy Avila, according to the world. But it is the wrong story.

Papa gives Daddy a look that says, "I'm not sure this is healthy."

What I want to say is, "If your friend wrote a book, you'd read it, right? What's the difference?" It is a sound argument.

If Ash recorded an album, I'd listen to it.

There is an episode of *The Cousins* where Ivy's character plays a game at a party where she's supposed to make out in the closet with a boy who turns out to be gay. The Coming Out Episode. That's the season the show won all those Emmys. Every award-winning show has to have a Coming Out Episode.

I wake up in the forest in the middle of the day. My eyes open to the canopy of leaves and pine needles, the mottled light seeping through. I do not know how I got here.

Tami texts, *Come with me to the city tonight to see Vaughn. It won't be as weird as last time. I promise.*

She wants me to be a witness to her secret. She wants me to make it real.

But I climb my tree instead. I am an eagle. I can see miles and miles and miles. Through the trees, on display behind glass walls, I watch the silhouettes of Ivy and Ash become a single shadowed thing, and I fly through the air to meet them.

20

I thought it might be cooler outside, but I was wrong. It's late afternoon, and the greens and squash leaves are wilting, curling in on themselves. The only plants people are allowed to water during the drought are food plants, nothing decorative, and only then after the sun's gone down. I helped Daddy pack the garden with thick mulch to help the moisture stay in throughout the day, but it can only do so much.

The house is stifling hot, even with all the windows open and the fans on. Daddy did not think to add air-conditioning to the old church when he rebuilt the insides. Even though it's been decades since it was true, old-school Seattleites still think they don't need air-conditioning. Living without it is their weird version of macho.

I don't hear any footsteps, but somehow I know Ivy is behind me, even before she says, "What are you doing?"

"Looking at dying plants."

"Sounds fun."

"How'd you get here without being seen?"

"I have my ways."

"Huh." I pretend to be looking at the plants some more, but mostly I'm waiting for Ivy to ask me if I'm mad at her. Papa would say I'm being passive-aggressive. Daddy would say something about honesty and practicing wise communication. Lily would say something about how Ivy's not even worth it.

Ash is out of town visiting his dad in rehab, so that means Ivy has time for me again. I'm the leftovers.

"Want to come over for a swim?" she says. "The air's clear today. Who knows how long that'll last?"

I don't say anything. I am looking at dying plants.

"I need your help with something," she says. "Are you still my assistant?"

I turn around and look at her, and for a second she seems so normal—beautiful, but normal—with her long dark hair around her bare shoulders, her black tank top, her cutoff shorts, her sandals, her face raw and free of makeup or pretense, maybe with even a hint of loneliness. When no one else is looking, maybe she is more like me than anyone thinks.

"Okay," I say. So she is not perfect. She is someone who can neglect a friend for a few days while she's distracted by a boy. How much more normal can you get?

"Oh good!" she says, and seems genuinely excited. "I've missed you, Fern." And her voice turns my name into music.

She is more comfortable in the forest than I expected she'd be. But she walks fast, with a purpose, a destination, while I usually meander, trying to notice every little thing, identify every mushroom and slug and sprout with the names Daddy has been teaching me since birth.

These are different trails than the ones I walk on the interior of the island, the ones Ash runs. We're on the other side of the forest, between my house and the waterfront. Our feet follow the narrow paths made by generations of deer and raccoons, smaller and wilder than the ones I'm used to. The paparazzi cannot find us here.

We reach Olympic Road far from her house, past where the street curves to the right, hiding us from where the handful of cars are parked outside her house. Funny how the paparazzi are allowed to camp out there all day and night, but if island security even suspects someone of living in their car, or if they just think the car is an eyesore, the vehicle is impounded and the people are arrested, no questions asked.

Ivy peeks out of the forest and looks both ways, then grabs my hand as we dash across the street into the bushes on the other side. The branches grab at me, spiderwebs twist around my wrists and ankles, and I am stumbling blind through brambles, Ivy leading me through some hidden back way to her house that she and Ash created. Now I am in on the secret too.

An old stump sits at the foot of a wall, just high enough for us to use as a boost to throw ourselves to the other side. Ivy is unscathed, but I am covered with scratches and mosquito bites, the crosshatching of thin lines of blood all over my arms and legs, leaves and dirt stuck to the sweat on my skin, like I am some kind of magnet for the earth, and she is impenetrable, only made for sparkling things. "Come on," she says, and I follow her across the manicured grounds to a sliding glass door, where I can see all the way through to the other side of the house, everything inside the glass walls flawless and still.

Upstairs, there are thick plastic sheets on the floor, everything covered with a layer of white dust. "My mom's redoing some rooms neither of us ever use."

"Why?"

"What else is she going to do?"

"She does the work herself?"

Ivy doubles over herself with laughter.

"Oh my god," she says after she calms down. "Fern, you're hilarious. No, she does not do the work herself. She hires people to do it and then tells them how to do their job."

Ivy loans me one of her many swimsuits and we get changed in her bedroom. I can tell a housekeeper has been here recently because I can actually see the floor. Everything is put back in its place. All the broken things have been thrown away. I try not to look at the unmade bed, try not to think about what has been happening in there since I was here last, try not to picture Ash under those sheets, in the place where I once, briefly, was. Where Ivy probably faced him, looked into his eyes, and touched him back.

I wonder if she even remembers the morning she called me to her bed. Maybe she was in a blackout. Maybe what happened has been erased, or maybe it was never even recorded.

I look at myself in the full-length mirror, in the tiny bikini I would never choose for myself. I do not recognize the girl I see, this girl with so much skin, with long legs and curves all over the place. I am not who I used to be. I am not my fathers' daughter.

"Hey there, beautiful," Ivy says with a grin, locking eyes with me in the mirror. I can't tell if she's serious or if this is some joke imitation of a catcall, but either way, I blush and look away.

"Don't be so modest," she says. "You're one hot mama." I laugh at the sheer ridiculousness of her words.

"'Hot mama'?" I say. "You're such a nerd." And she smiles like that's the nicest thing I could ever say to her. Ivy Avila has been called many things, but "nerd" is probably not one of them.

It's almost too hot to be outside, but the pool makes it bearable. Ivy pours us mimosas, heavy on the champagne, in cups that fit nicely in the cup holders of our inflatable rafts. We lie on our backs, drifting until we get too hot, then we roll into the water. We do this again and again, falling into a kind of rhythm of swimming, then floating and drinking until our skin dries, then swimming again until we cool off. And I realize this is some people's whole life—plenty of people on this island—just moving from one lovely thing to the next, trying to get a little more comfortable. And still they find things to complain about.

"It's working, Fern," Ivy says dreamily. "Ash is turning back to the boy I knew. His real self."

I wonder if his "real self" according to Ivy is the same Ash

I remember from when we were kids, the one who, even back then, already knew the rules of being perfect, but would crack that shell for a select few so we could see inside, just a little.

"Tami really fucked him up," Ivy says. "She's abusive. I'm serious. She belittled everything good about him until he just packed it away, put all his feelings and creativity into little boxes inside himself that he keeps locked up so he won't get hurt. His whole 'I'm too cool to care' thing is just how he protects himself. It's how he tries to stay in control."

So what does that mean? Is being out of control the solution? But I don't ask.

"I've got him all figured out," Ivy says.

"Okay," I say.

"I'm getting better," she says. She reaches out and grabs my hand over the water. "I feel strong. I think I'm ready to start working again. You've helped me more than any shrink."

"How?" I say.

"Just being here. Just listening, without judging me. You don't tell me to be anyone different."

"Okay," I say. I am useful for doing nothing. This is what she pays me for.

"People like Tami, they always win," Ivy says. "But not this time."

I don't know how much I drink because Ivy keeps refilling my cup, but after a while I realize I am drunk. I am under the water, eyes open, watching how Ivy's shadow moves across the bottom of the pool, erasing the glittering web of the water, how everything pops and bubbles in my ears, how it's so peaceful down here, I almost don't mind not breathing. But my survival techniques get the best of me and force me to the surface.

I suck in air and the world comes back into focus. Champagne sloshes in my stomach as I bob in the water. I open my mouth to call to Ivy but stop when I realize she is talking to her mother standing at the side of the pool. The brightness of the day has suddenly turned oppressive. Chlorine burns my eyes, and the acid of champagne and orange juice burns my esophagus. I find the side of the pool and walk myself to the shallow end with my hands. I am hiding.

"Ivy, get out of the pool," her mom says. "I want to talk to you."

"You can talk to me right here."

Ms. Avila sighs, puts her hands on her hips. "Dr. Chen says you haven't been returning her calls."

Ivy's sigh is identical to her mother's. "Dr. Chen is not a good therapist. She shames me."

"What the hell are you talking about?"

"She doesn't trust me to make my own decisions."

"Why would she? You're a fucking mess. I pay her good money to help you make decisions."

"Are you serious? *You* pay her good money?"

"Don't start that again. I've worked my ass off for you since you were nine. I've earned that money."

"Jesus Christ."

"Where do you go all day when you disappear?"

"None of your business."

"Are you using again?"

"Mom, shut up." Ivy pushes off the wall with her foot and glides across the pool.

"Why hasn't Ash been over today or yesterday?"

"I told you already. He's visiting his dad."

"I don't think you're making enough of an effort with him. You need to work harder."

"He's my boyfriend, not yours."

"No, he's still Tami Butler's boyfriend. That's my fucking point. You already lost him once. But you've still made it further with him than any of the other ones we tried."

"You're obsessed." Ivy glides across the pool again.

"Listen to me," Ivy's mom says. Her heeled rhinestone sandals click on tile as she stomps around the pool. She catches Ivy's floatie under her foot and wedges it against the side so Ivy can't move.

"Hey!" Ivy says, grabbing on to the side of the pool. "You're going to flip me over."

"I know you don't believe me, but you're not going to be young and beautiful forever. Your career has a shelf life, and it's shorter than you think. For all we know, it may already be over. You have to start thinking about your future. Our future."

"Let me go, Mom," Ivy says, pushing against the pool wall, but she's not going anywhere.

"You're damaged goods, Ivy. Girls like you are fun for flings, but no one wants a crazy girl long term. Maybe we set our sights too high with this one. Maybe it's time to forget about Ash Kye and find someone dumb and rich who'll be grateful to have you."

Ivy stops pushing. I feel her heart stop beating in my own chest.

"Work harder with Ash," Ms. Avila says, and then kicks Ivy and her raft into the middle of the pool. "You need him."

"You mean *you* need him."

"I'm going to get a massage," Ivy's mom says as she walks away, her heeled sandals clicking on the patio tiles.

"Of course you are. Go relax after all that hard work you do." No one hears Ivy but me. No one else hears the crack in her voice.

Ivy slides off her raft into the water. I wait a long time for her to surface. Is she down there thinking the same things I was, watching the shadows and the light, questioning if she even wants to come back up again?

When she finally comes back up, I gulp in air with her, and I realize I was holding my breath the whole time she was under.

"Are you okay?" I say when we've both caught our breath.

She doesn't answer me right away. I watch her climb out of the pool, the water glistening as it rolls off her skin. She walks a few steps to the outdoor bar, leaving puddles in her wake.

"She's leaving the day after tomorrow," Ivy says, her back to me as she pours vodka into a glass. "For two whole glorious weeks. I just focused on that the whole time she was talking. I've made an art form of tuning her out."

"Where's she going?" I ask, even though that's not anywhere near an important question.

"Some overpriced health spa where rich women pay a bunch of money for bullshit treatments to cure their meaningless lives. Like getting sound healing and putting crystals in her vagina and eating nothing but juice for two weeks is going to make her any less repulsive. Maybe one of her colonics will backfire and she'll end up in the hospital. A girl can dream."

Ivy pours a splash of club soda and squeezes a lime into her glass. "Are you making one of those for me?" I say, even though I have a headache, even though the sticky remnants of orange juice and champagne have turned my mouth sour, even though my stomach is still sloshing.

"Of course," she says with a smile.

I am sitting on the side of the pool with my feet dangling in, my ass burning on the hot tile. I can't decide if I want to be in or out.

"Ash is getting back tomorrow," Ivy says as she hands me my drink and sits beside me. "You should hang out with us. With me and Ash."

“I don’t want to be the third wheel,” I say.

“But what if we’re a tricycle?” she says, weaving her fingers through mine. “Did you ever think of that?”

21

THERE are three rafts in the pool now. We make an island, hands clasped. Three is the strongest number in nature.

Ivy dresses like she's at the beach, eating nothing but tropical fruit. She's stocked the outdoor bar with a blender and fresh juices and coconut cream and tiny paper umbrellas. She flits around, bringing things to Ash, earning his kisses.

"I have this fantasy," she says, sipping something fruity. "Where everything turned out different. My mom actually listened to me when I told her I didn't want to move to LA and quit school. Or sometimes she isn't even my mom at all. She dies in a car crash and I get adopted by some really nice family, and we go to Disneyland and they help me with my homework and I'm on the school soccer team or something."

Ash laughs. "I'm picturing you in a soccer uniform running around with a swishing ponytail. It's pretty hot."

"Shut up, I'm being serious."

"I know." He rolls off his raft and pulls himself up to sit on the side of the pool, where he dries his hands on a towel and starts rolling a joint.

"But even my fantasies turn to shit eventually," Ivy says. "I'm some character whose grandma dies and she goes into a deep depression and starts acting out. She starts shoplifting for some reason. She sleeps with a teacher and gets pregnant and it's this big scandal. Something stupid happens and she loses everything. That's where my thoughts always go. It's like I can't even imagine what a happy, normal life looks like."

"That's tragic," Ash laughs, sucking on the joint.

"It is!" Ivy says, pulling the joint out of his fingers.

"Stop, you're going to get it wet," he says, half-playful, half-irritated.

"I don't care," she says, trying to inhale, but the whole thing is drenched. The ember has gone out.

I smell something too sweet, almost rotting. It must be those drinks Ivy keeps making. The sugar and alcohol are seeping out of her skin.

I think about Vaughn. I think about Raine. What are they doing now, as we laze around a waterfront pool getting drunk in the middle of the day?

Ivy is sparkling, as usual. Small, shiny objects stick to her skin. They jingle as she stands, like tiny bells. She doesn't even seem to notice. Neither does Ash. He is solid, impermeable, all tendon and bone and muscles that always seem flexed.

The problem is we are too sober. It is too bright out. I can see it in Ash's face; he can't quite relax. Does Ivy see it? Is she just pretending everything's okay? Does she think if she acts hard enough, we'll believe her?

"Have another drink, Ash," she says.

"I'm tired. Let's go inside. It's nap weather." And then his smile is something different than his usual smirk. Then there is the briefest of openings, and Ivy takes it, and they are gone, and I am left floating in the pool, on the verge of sunburn.

Maybe I stay here. Or maybe I turn into a ghost and go inside to watch them, unseen. Either way, it is not my body being touched.

Days and nights pass. There are times when even Ash must go home. He must tend to Tami. He must not be too conspicuous. But Tami has her business too. Her secret lets him have his.

There are times when I must go home. Must turn back into my fathers' daughter.

The news says something about the gray whales that keep washing up on the beaches. The whole Pacific coast smells like rotting flesh.

The white supremacist separatists in Alabama have expanded their territory to five counties. Several towns are now under their rule.

More protests about A-Corp private prison labor. Another chemical spill in the Midwest. Another oil spill in the Arctic Circle. Another shootout between militias in Montana.

More refugees piling against our border walls even though they know no one's going to let them in.

The protests in Seattle are getting more violent.

Papa and Daddy watch me while I eat. They look at each other and say things with their eyes.

I don't tell them where I've been spending my days. I don't tell them I quit my job.

I sit in my tree and wait for my turn to come again.

It is getting harder to stay in my body. I feel more comfortable without skin, floating, watching from above. I have to make the conscious decision to return to the ground, and sometimes I don't want to; sometimes I wonder if I could just stay here forever, without form, just observing, not participating. I think I go whole hours without speaking. Just listening. Just watching. IvyandAsh. AshandIvy.

Lily leaves me voice messages. "I'm worried about you, Fern. I'm afraid something bad's going to happen."

I don't care what Lily thinks anymore.

"See," Ash says. "I brought it, just like you wanted." Ivy has been nagging him to bring his guitar, said she wanted to hear his new songs, said she wanted to sing them.

Did she not notice the way he kept avoiding the issue, kept weaseling out of it, changing the subject, kissing her to shut her up?

It is not just alcohol and weed tonight. More magic needed to be conjured.

Ivy's knee is bouncing and Ash is even harder than usual. He is leather drawn tight and she is a top, spinning.

He plays. His dark hair hides his eyes as he bends over the guitar, as his fingers pick the strings in impossibly beautiful arrangements. He lays his notebooks of lyrics out like flower petals. These are not the songs of the gangly thirteen-year-old boy I used to know. The lyrics are poetry, dark, full of metaphors I don't quite catch but am certain mean something important. His voice is gravel and Ivy's is moss. Gritty and soft. Made of the earth.

Ivy is radiant. I have listened to her album a million times, but she never sounded like this, not like someone with weight, with gravity. She has only ever been a puppet.

But is this any different? She is still twisting herself into someone else's melodies, someone else's words. She is still the shape of the script she's been given. The only difference now is that she's been given a better script.

"It's beautiful," I say when they take a break, but she and Ash only smile at each other.

I want to believe that this is some kind of intimacy, that I have witnessed some great reveal, but I feel further from them than ever.

Maybe this is the curse of all artists. Maybe they all desperately want to be understood, but they only know how to communicate in riddles.

Or maybe they can only ever understand each other.

A sweet smell fills the air, like something overripe, on the verge of turning.

We have two weeks while Ivy's mom is gone. We are somewhere near the middle now, but I'm not sure where.

Daddy says he's starting to worry I'm staying out too late. Have I been eating? Have I been taking my supplements? Have I been drinking enough water?

I have no idea what day it is, what time. My phone ran out of battery days ago and I haven't bothered to plug it in.

Ivy is always talking, eating, drinking, smoking, laughing. I watch her lips, the things that go in and the things that come out. There is a science to her mouth.

She won't stop talking about Ash's music. She won't stop talking, period. This new drug has sped everything up.

"It's only real if it punctures your heart," she says. "That's how you know you're alive." She's hunched over a mirror. She goes *tap tap tap tap*, organizing the white powder into tidy rows.

Daddy would remind us we're not our thoughts and feelings.

There is no permanent self when our perceptions are constantly changing. There is no isolated self when we are connected to everything.

"It's only real if it threatens to kill you," Ivy says.

The only sure things are loss and death.

She inhales. She passes the mirror to Ash.

"I'm reckless when I'm with you," he says, bending over with a straw in his nose.

"Not reckless," Ivy says. "Free."

"You make me weak. You make me do things without thinking."

"Why is that a weakness?"

And then there is no space between them, and I feel myself squeezed between their bodies, and I slide out and begin my retreat into the shadows. They are arms and lips and torsos, and I am mostly mist now, suspended droplets of liquid, tiny particles of myself.

But then Ivy removes her mouth from his, whispers something, and I am made solid again as she reaches out her hand. She does not need to speak for me to know when I am beckoned.

Somehow, I know how to do this. I have not had much experience, but it is like my body holds all of Ivy's knowledge. I know because Ivy knows.

She touches Ash and I feel him in my fingertips. Her lips kiss and I feel his tongue in my mouth. His hands, her breath, on me, on them, everywhere. There is not a part of me that is not touched.

There are four legs entwined, then six, then four, then six again. There are arms at all angles, hands finding the darkest places, a hand finding me, and I gasp and arch my back, and I hear her laugh from far away, and Ash is on top of me, his perfect chest with all its ribs and muscles and smooth brown skin, the musk that I inhale. Someone bites my shoulder and I call out. We are consuming each other. We are ravenous. Every cell in my body is on fire. I want to feel everything.

The earth shakes but none of us notice.

This is exactly what I wanted.

And then silence. Then all of a sudden, I can't feel my skin being touched, or touching. I am in the sky looking down at the pulsing, entwined bodies, and I am gone, all the pieces of me turned into tiny porcelain replicas—an elbow, a collarbone, a toe—the hard parts of me transformed into beads that Ivy has strung with strands of her own hair and now wears in a bracelet dangling around her wrist. Her naked body glitters with all its adornments. I am mesmerized, watching, as she makes love to a shadow, a mirror, and then a shadow again.

I wonder: Does this mean they're mine?

At home, a few brief hours in my own bed.

I get a text from Ash: *Are you awake?*

I double-check. It is not a group text with Ivy. He sent it just to me.

I can't stop thinking about you, he writes.

I miss you, he writes.

It must be a mistake.

I miss you too, I write back.

It is night. I don't know which one. My body is sore in brand-new places. We are on our backs, spent, lying naked on a blanket on the dry, brown grass in Ivy's backyard, between the water and her house with all its decks and patios. We are concentrating on the sky, waiting for shooting stars. But the lights of the city are too bright and the haze from new fires is pulling everything out of focus.

"My mom is having a meltdown about not being able to water," Ivy says, sitting up. She never stays down, or quiet, for long. "She's like, 'Why'd I pay all this money for a garden I have to let die?'"

"She could put in a rock garden," Ash says. "That's what people are doing."

"A rock garden is not a garden. It's a bunch of fucking rocks."

Ash looks at Ivy and laughs lazily. "Your mom is something else," he says.

"She wants us to get married," she says, then looks at Ash, sees him closing. "Isn't that crazy? Marriage, at our age?" she says quickly, her voice tight with an attempt at a laugh, but it is too late.

And just like that, Ash turns into something already burned, like coal. "Don't say things like that," he says.

How did we get here? How can everything shift so quickly?

"You're alive when you're with me," Ivy says. "You're free. Isn't that what you want? Isn't that what everyone wants?"

Is it? I'm not so sure. Freedom is full of choices. Maybe things are easier when no one has to decide anything.

"You're not free when you're with Tami."

"I am not going to talk to you about Tami," Ash says. "That was the rule. You promised."

"But she doesn't even want to know who you really are."

But maybe that's safer than freedom. Maybe that's the exact reason he stays with her. Maybe that's the reason no one's heard his music but me and Ivy.

"Ash," Ivy says. "She's seeing someone else."

He turns on his side and faces her. She thinks she's used her secret weapon, that she can hurt him into choosing her, but he just sighs. "I know. I've always known." He doesn't seem upset by this. Just tired. Just numb. "We don't talk about it, but we have something like an understanding."

What I want to say is, "How can you have an understanding about something you don't talk about?"

What I want to say is, "Ivy wants to be more than your side piece."

But I say nothing. A ship's horn blows somewhere in the distance, and it's the loneliest sound in the world.

"I don't think we're going to see any shooting stars," Ivy says.

"Nope," Ash says.

"Let's swim," Ivy says, jumping to her feet. "Let's swim in the ocean." Sitting still is death to her. She's like a shark that must keep moving to breathe.

"It's the Puget Sound, Ivy," Ash says. "Not the ocean."

"Come on." She takes his hand and pulls him to his feet, pulls him to her naked body, presses her mouth onto his. Her kiss will erase her questions. She will not be too difficult, too demanding, too high-maintenance. She will make him stay.

"I want to show you something," he says. And just like that, he is back.

As we run down a small hill to the dock, the dry grass and plants seem to shrivel a bit more. What little color I can see in the darkness seems to drain out as soon as Ivy passes by, as she absorbs it and adds it to her collection. She leaves a graveyard of decimated things that used to be beautiful.

Ash collects rocks along the way and Ivy is full now, completely covered. Her shiny things have run out of room. They start cracking, falling off, leaving a trail of shattered glass and porcelain. I step on a shard and feel a sting deep in my foot, feel a warm wetness seeping out. I look behind me as we walk and see a trail of bloody footsteps, and I feel a strange, twisted pride that there is now proof that I have been here.

We sit on the dock and Ash deposits his pile of rocks. "Look at this," he says. "We can make our own shooting stars." He throws a rock into the water and an explosion of light follows it down as it sinks.

"Holy shit!" Ivy says. "How'd you do that?"

"It's bioluminescent plankton. There's a bloom right now. It lights up when it feels movement."

"Can we swim in it?" Ivy says.

He grins. "Yeah."

My splash is silent. I feel the shock of cold water all the way to my bones. Everything is sharp, in focus. We yelp and laugh as the glow of millions of microscopic organisms define the outlines of our bodies as we move, as they mark our existence, as they make us shooting stars.

We emerge, sticky with salt water. Ash's skin sparkles in the moonlight. I don't know if it's Ivy or me who licks him, but I can taste the salt on his skin along with something metallic, like blood, and I imagine the tiny glowing creatures inside me, lighting me up. Is this what Ivy tastes when she consumes people the way she does? Is this what it feels like to be made out of hunger?

22

OUR two weeks are abruptly cut short when Ivy's agent calls about a series of meetings with some new casting directors in LA she's never worked with before. "This could be big," she says, throwing clothes into a suitcase. "This is what I've been waiting for. A new opportunity. A chance to reinvent myself."

She says nothing about Ash, how Tami insisted on "quality time" with him today, how he is somewhere else, in his other life, while we have to go back to being a secret. She says nothing about how she's going to be gone for four days, how I have no idea what to do without her.

I walk outside with Ivy when her car arrives. The grass is brown and dry. No one has cleaned up my bloody footprints.

"Are you sure you don't want me to come with you?" I say. "As your assistant?"

"Stay here and relax," she says. "You should still use the house when I'm gone. Everything that's mine is yours."

"Okay," I say.

"I mean it."

The air is bad today. The driver is wearing a mask. He says nothing as he hoists Ivy's suitcase into the trunk of the car.

"Are you going to be okay?" I say.

She laughs. "Of course I am. I'm a professional. I've done this a million times."

Of course she has. I don't know why I'm so afraid of her being alone.

Or maybe I'm just afraid of myself being alone.

She kisses me on the cheek and says, "Be good," then gets into the car.

"I always am," I say, but the driver has already closed the door.

Ivy is gone, on her way to the ferry, to the airport, to a hotel in another city, to a series of offices where she will meet men who hold the keys to her future.

And where am I? Subterranean.

Ivy disappears across the water, then into the sky, and I disappear into the forest. I am on hold. Waiting until she comes back and we can be whole again.

Maybe I am home. Maybe I am watching nature documentaries with my fathers. Maybe it is a seamless transition. Maybe nothing's changed all that much.

Maybe I drive to the coffee shop in town by the ferry terminal. People stare at me as I wait in line, hiding behind my sunglasses. They whisper. I am now the girl who hangs out with Ivy Avila. I was no one before.

Maybe Ash texts me and I text him back. Maybe he calls me on the phone and we talk like old friends. We do not mention the night we became other things. He tells me how he's considering majoring in music at Yale next year instead of economics, how his mom will throw a fit but will eventually become too distracted by her own work to care, how his dad will probably secretly be proud. Maybe I ask him what Tami will think. Maybe he says we don't talk about Tami.

Or maybe it is not that easy. Maybe I am sick and sleep deprived, poisoned, emptied, turned completely invisible, all the pigment and weight sucked out of me. But somehow Daddy can still see me. When I was a kid he always knew I was getting sick before I did. He feeds me smoothies with mysterious green powders. He juices anemic veggies from the garden.

Maybe I am still my fathers' daughter. Maybe all the fresh green foods clean me out from the inside and fill in all the places I am missing, maybe I am nourished, and a surprise rainstorm bursts out of the afternoon and calms the heat and clears the air, maybe all the plants are given another chance to live, and I go into the forest and roll on the soggy ground so the coating of mud will tell me where my skin is.

After I am clean and fed, I find a pair of tweezers. I shine a light on my foot. I poke at the swollen place where the shard of Ivy's glass is lodged, digging in, trying to find something solid inside my flesh. Jolts of pain shoot through me, but they are not unpleasant. With each one, I think, *This is how I know I'm alive.*

I put the tweezers down. The glass is unfindable. Skin will grow over it, this tiny fragment of Ivy that is now a permanent part of me. I will turn it into a pearl.

23

DON'T have too much fun without me while I'm gone, Ivy's text to us says in the morning.

Impossible, Ash texts back.

We exchange various heart emojis.

Today is the day of her first big meeting. I feel like I should be doing something. Praying. Doing some kind of magic. But before I can figure that out, my phone rings. Ash. It must be a mistake. I pick it up but say nothing, expecting to hear the swishing of pants moving, jostling in a bag, some evidence of this call being an accident.

"Hey," Ash says. Bubbles pop inside my chest.

"Hey," I say back.

"Are you busy right now?"

"Not really."

I pretend I am a girl in a show. I pretend I am Ivy in *The Fabulous Fandangos* when she was still wholesome. A nice girl talking to a nice boy on the phone.

"I just wanted to hear your voice," he says.

"What do you want me to say?"

Her room on the show looked just like mine.

"Sing me something," he says.

"I can't sing."

"You're ridiculous."

What is happening right now? Why is he talking like this is totally normal?

"I wish we could just go out for coffee or something like normal people," he says.

"You're not allowed to have coffee with girls?" I say. "What is this, the 1950s?"

"People talk," he says. "This island is so small."

I have done so much in the last few days, but I have never done this.

"Maybe we could go hiking," I say. "No one could find us in the forest."

"I get so frustrated with hiking," Ash says. "It's so slow. I always want to run."

"What's your big hurry?" I say.

He laughs. "That sounds like a joke my dad would make."

Something constricts in my belly and I don't know why. Like for a split second, I miss my dads more than anything in the world, even though they're just in the other room.

Dad jokes. What a wonderful thing.

"How is your dad?" I say.

There's silence for a long time. "Thanks for asking. No one ever asks."

Not even Ivy? What do they talk about when I'm not around?

"I think he wants out of this life, like he wants to do something crazy. My mom's been moving all the money to different accounts so he can't do anything with it without her permission. She thinks he wants to join one of those communes where they take all your money and you go live in a yurt in the middle of nowhere and no one ever hears from you again."

"What do you think about that?"

"Honestly, I don't think it's a bad idea. It'll kill him to go back to his old life."

Can anyone ever really do that? Go back to their old life after they crack? Some holes are too big to patch back up.

"I was thinking about asking my dad if he could pull some strings and hook me up with some A-Corp music people," Ash says. "I bet he'd do it, even if it's just to piss off Mom." He laughs. "She *wanted* me to be part of the A-Corp family dynasty, didn't she? People should be careful what they wish for."

I feel the crush and squeeze of something inside me. Why is everything so easy for him? Just a few phone calls by his dad and he has a music career? Why doesn't he have to work his way up the way Ivy did? All he has to do is decide what he wants and it's his.

"I like talking to you like this," Ash says. "When things are calm. I can talk to you about stuff I can't talk about with anyone else."

I am a secret being kept from a secret.

. . .

In the afternoon, Ivy sends a group text that she's coming home early.

When are you getting back? Ash texts.

I don't know. When I can get a flight. I'm taking a nap now. Turning off my phone.

How'd the meeting go? Ash texts, but she does not answer.

Are you okay? he texts. But she is gone.

I am waiting for Ivy at her pool, floating in the water in her bikini, drinking her drink, willing the sun to turn me the same shade of golden.

The last she told us was she was still trying to get a flight out of LAX. Something about another government shutdown. Something about protesting airport employees. Something about a bomb scare at O'Hare.

There is an air quality advisory because of the smoke. The elderly and infirm and small children are supposed to stay inside. I don't know what I am doing out here. I am pretending things are different than they are.

I hear a rustling in the bushes. I see a pair of eyes. Long limbs emerging. A deer found its way here through the forest.

Ash is shirtless, covered with sweat. "There you are," he says. He takes off his running shoes and socks and dives into the pool. For a moment, there is silence as he glides underwater toward me, and my body bobs up and down from the waves he made. He pops his head out of the water just inches from mine.

Deer know how to swim. They can go from island to island. That's something not everyone knows.

"Hey," he says.

"Hey," I say. "I was just going to get out."

"Okay."

We stand in the shade, toweling off.

"You shouldn't be running in this weather," I say, watching a drop of water run from his shoulder down his chest across the ridges of his ribs and stomach.

"You shouldn't be swimming," he says, hooking his finger under the strap of my swimsuit and pulling it down over my shoulder. He steps closer, puts his other hand on my hip and pulls me to him. My head goes cloudy. All I can feel is my body pulsing, pulling toward his, the heat where we make contact, the need for everything to touch.

But then I think of Ivy, alone, in a big city even more polluted than this one. I see her wearing a face mask on her way to her meeting, trying not to mess up her makeup and hair. I feel the timid hope inside her chest as she steps out of the car, as she walks, a little wobbly, to the sliding glass doors at the bottom of a skyscraper. Maybe she says something like "I have an appointment" to the security guard behind the podium in the middle of the giant, windowed space that was designed by some architect for awe and intimidation. She takes an elevator up, to a different part of the sky where powerful men reside. The receptionist at the front desk eyes her with a smirk and Ivy gets a sinking feeling this is nothing new at all.

I pull away from Ash. His fingers are still tangled in the strap of Ivy's bikini. "Aren't you supposed to be hanging out with Tami today?"

He looks stung. He drops his hand. "I played sick. I wanted to be with you."

"Why?" I want to ask him. "You have Tami, you have Ivy, why do you need another girl?"

"Are you in a bad mood? Did something happen?"

Did something happen? I don't know. So many things have happened. So many things keep happening, and I can't keep track.

Where is Ivy? Why isn't she home yet? What happened that made her have to leave early?

"I think I have to go," I say.

Ash looks confused, like I am some upside-down version of a girl, not a species he recognizes. He is not used to being rejected.

Something in me burns, but it is not passion. This is a different kind of fire, one that wants to destroy, one that wants to see him burn, wants to see everyone burn. Who does he think he is that he can have whatever and whoever he wants?

"But where are you going to go?" he says.

I look at him, at his beautiful, perfect face, and I try to

remember the boy I used to know, the one who didn't yet know the power he had. The skinny boy. The awkward boy. The sweet boy. The boy I loved.

That boy is gone, just a story now. We are all just stories.

Where am I going to go? Where else is there but here? And what exactly am I stopping myself from doing?

Ivy said everything mine is yours.

I close my eyes and imagine we are on a different island, one far away from here.

I feel the whisper of his lips, the press of his body against mine. I am solid. I am not a ghost, floating around, watching these bodies move together. This is my body and only my body. I can do with it whatever I want.

I am not letting him have me. This is not about him at all.

It's not just the boys who get to take. It's not just the boys who get to want.

Ash is just a body with nothing inside it.

It's my turn now.

I'm sorry, Ivy.

But I'm also not.

"I never know who I'm going to get," he whispers into my mouth, and I don't know what or whom he's talking about—me? Ivy? Tami? Which one of the three girls he has on rotation now? Or is he talking about which version of me—this person who exists without Ivy, or the one who's nothing but an extension of her.

But there are different versions of Ash too. There is one who loves Ivy, and there is one who needs Tami. And there is one who thinks he's entitled to yet another. One who thinks he can have us all, that he doesn't have to choose. There's a version of me who hates him as he touches me, as he leads me into the house and up to Ivy's bed, the sheets still tangled from before her leaving.

Hate and want are not exclusive. They can partner. They can feed each other.

Now here I am, claiming Ivy's bed for myself, and now my body will add to all the stories that have already been told here. My want will add to all the other wants.

But still, I will imagine she is here, with us. She is telling our stories with her body. She is conjuring us into being.

I wake up in the forest, alone, and I know that Ivy is home. It is time to find her. It is time to start again.

Little mushrooms sprout out of my skin, and I pluck them off. Their names are on the tip of my tongue, but I can't remember what anything is called.

24

It is near sunset when Ivy comes back. The sky is orange and the sun is the color of blood.

I wonder if she can tell, if she has a sense of what we've been up to. If she can smell us on each other's bodies.

She will not tell us about the meeting. She makes us promise to not ask questions. All her shiny things have fallen off and her skin is raw.

She returns with more bottles, more vials, more pills, more potions to conjure magic.

"I did everything he wanted" is all she says. "I did everything I know how to do."

My rage is big enough for both of us. Its source is infinite, as old as skin.

The fires have gotten worse. They are coming down the mountains, eating up the small towns a hundred miles away. We have to stay inside. Outside the glass walls is a thick soup of smoke. The world is on fire.

. . .

We don't bother with fancy drinks anymore. We don't bother with clothes. Time is running out. We burn the tiny paper umbrellas in the sink. Garbage piles up around us.

My foot throbs. I think it's infected.

"Are you happy?" I ask Ivy.

A glass shatters on the floor. I cut my finger as I try to clean it up.

"Who said anything about happy?" she says. "I'm just trying to survive."

She takes my hand and puts my finger in her mouth. I feel her warm wetness close around me and pull. My blood is inside her now. There is a piece of her inside my foot, turning into a pearl. We are fused. Whole. We can never be separated.

It is better this way. I am not enough on my own.

Our teeth grind themselves into stardust. Sparks shoot out of our eyes.

"We are bottomless pits," we say. "We are black holes."

. . .

Ash says: "But you're a star."

We say: "Stars and black holes are related."

We look it up. We read, brow knitted: "'A black hole is a massive star that runs out of nuclear fuel and is crushed by its own gravitational force.'"

Ash says: "Look who's an astrophysicist all of a sudden."

Some stars have twins. From far away they look like a single star, but when you get closer, you can see there are two orbiting around the same empty center.

There is not enough to go down our throats or in our noses. There is not enough to fill us up. There is not enough to put the fire out.

"Black holes are invisible," we say.

. . .

Ash says: "Huh."

There is never enough of anything.

"A black hole is a star dying."

Ivy has told the housekeepers to leave us alone. Outside, everything is brittle tinder. Inside, the smell is earthy, moist.

Ash pulls us toward him. We pulse with the chemicals inside us. We move in and out of each other's bodies and lose all our edges. We keep going and going, always just on the verge, but never finished.

We are made out of want. We are made out of always needing more.

Is this what I wanted?

. . .

We have turned. We have gone rotten.

We are a mess of body parts. We are blood inside and out. We are gaping mouths. We are animals. We are holes.

We remember: Men. Expensive suits. Expensive couches.

The couches are always leather. They tear at bare skin.

I know because Ivy knows.

I look at my foot. It is reddish purple. It is swollen and bubbled with something wet just barely inside.

Elevators into the sky. Receptionists who say nothing.

We are eighteen. We are fifteen.

We are twelve.

More things in our noses, in our throats. In our other warm and empty places. We are desperate to be filled.

. . .

We are made out of fear of losing it all.

Ash paints us with his breath. He does not know we are only our body parts.

This body part remembers. So does this one.

All the vials, all the pills, all the bottles in the world will never make us forget.

The hands, the mouths. The men.

Now Ash is done. His glassy eyes close and he turns to stone, unreachable. He is leaving us. He is going inward. He is going the wrong direction.

This body part remembers too.

We are afraid of falling asleep. We are afraid of that space between sleep and awake when everything opens.

. . .

We remember: That time with our dislocated shoulder, our bruised ribs.

We remember: That time we tried to tell Mom, that time we tried to ask for help.

We remember: That time with Mom's slap across our face.

We can never un-rot. We can never un-break.

Everyone in the world is asleep except us. Our heart beats inside our chest at a troubling rhythm. We want to scream, but there's no point. Ash cannot hear us inside himself. The glass walls are thick and shatterproof. We are protected by gates and walls and smoke and mirrors and the best security money can buy.

What does a heart attack feel like?

We remember:

. . .

Mom already knew. Of course she knew. She's the one who made it happen.

A black hole is a star dying.

25

I don't remember how I got home. I don't remember leaving Ivy's house. The last thing I remember was not knowing where my body stopped and hers started. I remember anger turning into passion into anger again. I remember claws and teeth and broken skin. I remember sleep seeming like an impossible lie. I remember thinking I was having a heart attack.

But somehow I sleep for fifteen hours. That's what Daddy says. I wake to fresh fruit and a pile of scrambled eggs. I have never been so hungry and thirsty in my entire life. I drink three glasses of water. I eat half a dozen eggs and almost an entire cantaloupe.

My nose is raw and starts bleeding while I'm brushing my teeth. I wonder if I've done permanent damage. I wonder if I'm one of those people who have no cartilage left in the middle of their nose, if I burned it all away and now have only one nostril. I reach into my nose to check. I pinch the space in the middle, and it is solid, but it stings so bad, my eyes water, and now my fingers are covered with blood.

It hurts to breathe. I feel like I've spent the last ten days inhaling tiny shards of glass. My body aches in all kinds of weird places, and my foot has gotten worse. The swelling and weird purple discoloration have spread and my pinkie toe looks like a fat, inflated grape. Parts of my brain are missing and have been replaced with clouds of smoke. The world is flat and gray where there are supposed to be curves and color. I think I died a little over the last two weeks.

"I think you need to stay home today," Daddy says. There is something almost stern in his voice. This is the closest he has ever gotten to "You're grounded." But instead of being mad, I'm filled with an overwhelming sense of relief. He is saying no so I don't have to.

Before I settle into bed with my laptop cued to binge-watch mindless shows, I text Ivy just to make sure she's okay.

You alive? I text.

I think so, she texts back. *Just barely.*

Then a few minutes later: *I think I'm going to call my therapist today.*

That's a good idea.

I think maybe I will call Lily too.

We have family dinner, but it feels like a lie. My fathers want to talk about college, but I cannot think beyond the fork scraping at my plate and the throbbing in my sinuses. The future seems so far away, impossible. A dark cloud fills our awkward silences. I've never had to keep secrets before, and now that I have them, I can't meet my fathers' eyes, and the cloud grows thicker and they are miles away and no amount of small talk will ever help us cross that chasm.

After another night of sleep, I feel almost normal. I blow my nose and scabs come out. That means my body is healing. That means I am growing new skin.

I look at my phone and there is a text waiting for me.

Come over, Ivy says.

I get dressed quickly, grab a mask from the hook by the door, and walk to her house, barefoot. I close my eyes to keep the smoke out, feeling my way down the hill. I am pure instinct. I am a wild animal. My body tells me where I need to go.

Ivy's mom is home, but she doesn't even notice me as I enter the house. I crawl into bed with Ivy and wrap my arms around her. I bend my leg between hers and pull her close. She closes her eyes as I kiss her neck, her collarbone, and I can feel something new inside her, a different kind of pulse, something that wasn't there before she left. Her body is hotter. It is getting ready to explode. Implode. It is ready to collapse under its own weight.

"Do you ever think about how fucked up it all is?" she says.

"How fucked up what is?" I ask. Ivy lifts her arms as I pull her thin tank top over her head. She is pliable. Compliant.

"What people get away with. The people who look the other way."

"Uh-huh," I say as I brush my lips across her breasts.

"What if we could hurt them back?" she says.

I don't know who this is that's driving my body. I don't know when I became this girl who wants, and gets, and takes.

"Are you even listening to me?" Ivy says. But I am lost inside her legs.

And then pain shoots through my scalp as Ivy pulls me up by the hair. It pulses through my whole body and turns into something else as she pushes me onto my back, and I moan as she pins me down, her legs straddling me, her hands tight around my wrists.

There is a fine line between pain and pleasure. Sometimes they smash into each other. Sometimes the line breaks.

Does she know what I did with Ash? Is she punishing me?

We are animals. We are ruthless. We are tired of being prey.

Her nails tear into me.

Punish me, Ivy. Do whatever you want.

Imagine justice. Imagine revenge.

There is a fine line.

Her teeth break skin.

She is drawing blood. She wants to hurt a body and mine is the only one that's here.

I deserve to be punished.

These sheets will have to be bleached. They will have to be burned.

26

ANOTHER morning, another text waiting for me, sent in the middle of the night. From Ash, inviting us over to his place this afternoon.

It was a group text. Tami was on it too.

I think it must be a mistake. But it is a mistake that can't be undone.

Tami replied, *Can't wait to see you Ivy! It's been too long.*

Or maybe it's not a mistake. Maybe this makes sense according to some logic only Ash knows. Inviting over his girlfriend and the girl he's cheating on her with. And me, whatever I am.

All I want is to be back in bed with Ivy. What if we don't need Ash anymore?

I got what I wanted, and now I'm not so sure I want it anymore.

Maybe he's only ever been a mirror with nothing behind it.

Maybe Ivy and I are the only ones who are real.

Daddy still doesn't know I quit my job. I get dressed and tell him I'm going to work, even though I have nothing to do until the afternoon. I drive aimlessly around the island. Everything seems dull, the color less saturated, everything with a matte finish. I've lived here my whole life, but suddenly I feel like a stranger, like a tourist in my own hometown.

I get some fast food from the island's one drive-through and eat it in my car at a park by the ferry terminal, windows rolled up and the AC on full blast, with a hazy view of the boats going back and forth. I guess I fall asleep, because I wake up to a couple of tweens wearing particle masks standing outside my window taking pictures of me with their phones. I scream, and they scream, and then they run away.

A text from Ivy is waiting from me when I wake: *I'll give you a ride.* So even though I'm parked only a few minutes from Ash's house, I drive all the way around the island again.

I wait for her in my car and watch the workers inside the house, through the glass walls, cleaning up the mess we made over the last two weeks. It's been three days and they're still cleaning. There are a couple outside with bandanas wrapped around their faces, braving the noxious air. Someone is hunched over, covered with sweat, finally scrubbing my bloody footprints off the walkway.

Ivy's mom is standing at the kitchen counter, drinking a cup of coffee. She does not look any different than when she left. Even at rest, even when she doesn't know anyone's looking, there's something mean in her face, something desperate, calculating.

Ivy comes out the front door, avoiding the kitchen. She is

stunning in a yellow sundress, a picture of health, as if the last few days never happened, as if she was never wild-haired and red-eyed. She waves me over as she runs to her car, and I am hit with a wall of heat and smoke as I open my door, like a force trying to keep me in, but I make it across the driveway to Ivy just as her mom turns and notices us, as she runs to the door screaming something, as Ivy turns the car on and speeds away.

"I need to tell you something," I say as we pull onto Olympic Road. I need to tell her about what Ash and I did. I can keep secrets from everyone else, but not her.

"I'm getting so sick of this smoke," she says. "I wonder when the fires are going to stop." As if it's that easy, as if there's no possibility we're in danger, even though people in the suburbs have already started evacuating. "Maybe I'll move to Iceland. There's hardly any trees there. There's hardly any ice either."

"Something happened while you were gone," I say.

"If I have to stay trapped in that house with my mom for one more day, I'm going to kill her."

"Ivy, are you listening to me?"

She drives a little faster. "I don't want to talk about it. I don't want to talk about anything that happened while I was gone."

"But there's something you need to know."

"Don't tell me what I need to know." Her voice is sharp. This conversation is over.

But then she looks at me and smiles and takes my hand. "Let's go see Ash," she says, and something in me lightens, and something in me drops. What if we were enough? Just Ivy and me?

IvyandFern. FernandIvy.

"We're a team," she says. "You and me."

And what about Tami? Where does she fit into all of this?

"Oh, I have plans for Tami," Ivy says, like she read my mind.

Ash has a different kind of house than Tami and Ivy. It is old, originally a summer home for some big lumber family back in the day when there was still old-growth forest on the peninsula. It's all dark wood and stone, plush furniture you sink into, rich colors and soft rugs. A huge fireplace as tall as me is the centerpiece of the living room, and that's where we find Tami and Ash sitting together on a couch, her legs draped over him, her favorite position.

"Long time no see," Tami says. She is drinking iced coffee. There is a tray of fruit and pastries on the coffee table. Somehow Ash can make even sweatpants and a T-shirt look sexy. Tami is in her casual chic getup, looking like a sportswear model. "We just came from yoga class," she says, picking at some fruit.

"You do yoga?" Ivy asks Ash with a playful smirk on her face. She is enjoying this game of pretending they are acquaintances.

"Only when Tami makes me."

Everyone laughs for exactly one second. It is all perfectly normal. It is afternoon, and we are drinking iced coffee and eating fruit, and everyone's sober as far as I can tell.

"Grab a chair and get something to eat," Tami says, as if she is the hostess, as if this is her house.

"Ash, your house is beautiful," Ivy says.

"Wait till you see the wine cellar," Tami says. "It's as big as a poor person's house. Isn't that why your dad bought this place?"

"Yeah," Ash says. "Everyone at rehab says he needs to get rid of his collection, but it's his prized possession. There's like half a million dollars' worth of wine down there."

"I don't blame him," Tami says. "He shouldn't have to get rid of anything."

"You're not helping," he says.

"What? Your dad has run a multibillion-dollar department of A-Corp for years. He can stay sober if he wants to. All it takes is willpower."

"I don't think it's that easy."

She rolls her eyes. "You want to make everything complicated."

"I wish we could go swimming," Ivy cuts in. "I brought my suit."

"No one's going swimming today," Tami says. "Unless you want to die of asphyxiation."

"My mom's having a meltdown because the lawn's brown," Ivy says, her voice too high, too perky, like she's genuinely trying to befriend Tami. "She keeps trying to bribe the gardeners to water it."

"It's ridiculous," Tami says. "How can the government tell us what to do with our own water?" She smiles at this thing they have in common, whatever it is. That their mothers have a similar disdain for environmental protections?

"It's shared," Ash says lazily. "Everyone shares the same water. It all comes from the same place. Nobody owns it."

"Well, that's stupid," Tami says.

"Tell that to Mother Nature," he says.

"My boyfriend, the armchair activist," Tami says, then leans over and kisses him, and I can feel Ivy tense next to me. But what did she expect? Tami is his real girlfriend. Ivy is not.

Tami's phone buzzes. She looks at it and smiles, angles her body so Ash can't see the screen as she texts back.

Despite all her training and experience and awards, Ivy right now is a terrible actress. She keeps looking at Ash with a face that says everything. Ash is the real actor here. He barely even looks at us. He runs his fingers up and down Tami's perfect, smooth leg, as if hers is the only body he's been touching lately.

How can he make this look so easy? How can he act like he doesn't even care?

"I have to make a call," Tami announces suddenly. She catches my eye with a covert smile as she hops up and glides out of the room. The second she's out of sight, Ash walks over to our couch and kneels between Ivy's legs, and she pulls his face to hers, and I am just sitting here next to them as they inhale each other, but I am miles and miles and miles away. I am who they touch when the other isn't around. But I am invisible now.

I hear footsteps. "She's coming back," I whisper, but they do not separate right away. Ivy has to push Ash's chest to get him to go back to his seat. It's almost like he wants to get caught.

He is not fast enough. When Tami enters the room, he is falling into his seat, still staring at Ivy, and she is staring at him, and I am looking back and forth, at their wet lips, their panting mouths, the want in their eyes, and I am filled with a sudden, shocking anger. How could they be so stupid? So reckless? This is mine to lose too.

Tami stops in her tracks. She looks at Ash, then at Ivy, and a wave of recognition passes over her face. Her hand squeezes around her phone. She takes a tight, shallow breath. Then she smiles. A sickly anything-but-sweet smile.

"I'm bored," she announces. Her voice is too loud. She is a bad actor too. "Let's get out of here. Let's go to the city."

No one moves.

"Right now!" she commands, her voice cracking with anger. I have never heard Tami raise her voice before. She's never had to.

"Um, okay?" Ash says. Tami squeezes his shoulder, hard. "Ouch!" he says, rubbing it as she walks toward the front door and picks up her purse from the table there.

"We're going *now*?" Ash says. "Like this? Can I at least change out of these fucking sweatpants?"

"Fine," Tami says. "We have five minutes to change our clothes."

"I think I'm going to stay back," I say. "I'm not feeling well."

But Ivy looks at me and shakes her head, her eyes pleading. She cannot do this without me. And even though I have a feeling something terrible is going to happen, I know I can't leave her.

"This is going to be bad," I say after Tami and Ash have gone to change their clothes.

"You don't know that," Ivy says.

"How could it be anything else?" I say.

"The truth is going to come out," she says. "Isn't that a good thing? Tami's going to lose." She takes my hand, and we just sit there in silence for the next few minutes, looking out the window at the poisoned sky.

I don't know what Tami and Ash talk about while they're gone, but I can feel the tension as they emerge from the hallway. Ash immediately goes to the liquor cabinet, pulls out a bottle, and stuffs it in the oversized purse on Tami's shoulder. She just nods and says, "Let's go."

Ivy and I stand up in unison. Ash doesn't even look at us.

"Ivy, let's take your car," Tami says. "I've always wanted to see the inside of one of those monstrosities. It's so entertaining to see the ridiculous things new money will buy."

27

WE drink in the car. We drink on the ferry. By the time we are in the middle of the Puget Sound, halfway between Commodore Island and Seattle, everyone except Tami is on the verge of drunk, and it's not even dark yet. We are in a private VIP room on the boat, which I never even knew existed before today. "For privacy," Tami says. "We don't want anyone to bother our little star, do we?"

Tami talks constantly, as if hearing her own voice will crowd out the reality of what's right in front of her, as if she can make it go away by sheer force of will.

"I cannot wait to get off this fucking island," she says. I don't mention we are on a boat floating in the middle of the Sound. "Right, Ash? We're going to have the perfect life." She takes his hand and holds it to her chest, and I have never seen anything more fake in my life.

We are all actors. We are all terrible fucking actors.

"Huh?" He is looking out the window. He has gone away from us. But his shadow is heavy on the floor, somehow darker, thicker, more substantial than ours.

Ivy and I are sitting across from them. She is pinching the flesh on the underside of her arm so hard it's bruising.

"Life is really going to start when we get to Yale. Even though it's in Connecticut." She laughs, but no one else does.

"What's wrong with Connecticut?" Ivy says.

Tami sighs. "Have you ever been to New Haven?"

"No."

"Well, it's certainly not New York. And it's half underwater now anyway."

"I don't really like New York," Ivy says.

Tami looks her up and down like she's some kind of alien. "How could anyone not like New York?" she says.

"It's too crowded. And it's scary how it's just those storm walls that are keeping the ocean from covering the whole island."

Tami rolls her eyes. "If the walls broke, the water would just go up to the second floor. And anyway, the important parts of the city are elevated. I wish Seattle would get their shit together and elevate downtown the way they did in Manhattan. It's so much more civilized."

"Walls and gates aren't enough for you?" Ash says, still looking out the window. "Some might say that's elitist." His shadow seems to tremble, almost like it's laughing.

"If other people want in the elevated city, they can pay the toll like everyone else. What do you have to worry about? You can afford it."

A voice comes over the loudspeaker and announces we are approaching Seattle.

"Let's go," Tami says, standing up.

"Where are we even going?" Ash says.

"Back to the car, dummy."

"Then what?"

"I have a stop to make."

I feel myself shrivel like all the dying plants outside.

The news keeps saying the protests in Seattle are getting worse. Daddy says they just flare up when it gets hot and the air gets bad, but Papa says we're going to end up like Portland soon, like so many other cities that have either given up to the separatists or been put under complete police lockdown. He said I shouldn't go into the city for a while. But he doesn't know I'm here.

People have broken through one of the gates that separates the restricted toll area of downtown from the rest of the city. There are protesters everywhere. The police have managed to set up barriers along the street so cars can get through. A line of cops in full riot gear protect us from the yelling crowd.

It could be anything, what they're protesting. It could be so many things. There's so much to protest that protests have become meaningless. One sign says something about refugees from El Salvador. Another says something about refugees from

Mississippi. Another says something about debtors' prison and A-Corp slave labor. Something about reproductive rights in the south. Child brides in Kentucky. A little girl is carrying a blown-up photo of Penelope the Polar Bear, the last known wild polar bear on earth, who died nearly a decade ago.

"God, people really need to get over that fucking bear already," Tami says.

Then limbs start flying and the crowd surges. The police drones circling overhead start shooting sedative darts into the crowd, and people start falling. The line of riot cops move in, and there's something almost graceful in their precision. They know what they're doing. They've done it so many times before.

One by one, the protestors' hands are zip-tied behind their backs, and they are lined up on the sidewalk side by side, waiting for their turn to be hauled into the police van.

And just like that, the fight is over. It is so fast, this taming. All of this while we're driving along in Ivy's beautiful tank, untouchable. The glass of the windows is so thick, we couldn't even hear anyone scream.

The child with the polar bear sign has disappeared. Maybe her mother whisked her away. Maybe she got trampled by the crowd. Either way, she is gone.

"They're better off now," Tami says. "Non-violent protesters get sent to one of those nice prisons along with the debtors. They're practically resorts. Most of those people were probably trying to get arrested on purpose. They do that, you know. Have you seen photos of the rooms they get? Everyone has their own TV with all the channels. They have internet. They get time to socialize and take classes. They're even allowed to get passes to visit each other's rooms to fuck. When you think about it, their lives aren't that different from the guards'. They're both owned by A-Corp. The only difference is the prisoner doesn't have to commute to get home."

"You're horrible," Ash says.

Ivy takes a gulp of liquor, and then so do I.

When is this going to be over? What are we even doing here?

"If you make the prison comfortable enough," Tami says, "no one tries to get out."

The protestors are gone, like they were never here. The police have gotten so efficient at making them go away. Unconscious bodies have been loaded into a police van. Beauty Bots begin sweeping up all the trampled protest signs. The blood. The lost shoes. The poster-sized photo of a polar bear.

I remember this route. I know where we are going even though Tami won't tell us.

"I want to go to a show," Ash says. "I'll see who's playing tonight." He begins poking at his phone.

"We're not going to a show," Tami says.

I'm in the back seat with Ivy. She let Tami drive for some reason, probably so she can drink in peace. She's cradling the half-empty bottle of liquor in her arms.

"What is this place?" Ash says as we pull up in front of

Vaughn's house. Daylight illuminates the ratty old couch on the sagging porch, the rusty chain-link fence, the sheets over the windows, the trash cans askew on the sidewalk. Tami opens the car door without explaining, and we all follow. Ivy's already having a hard time walking in a straight line. Ash says, "Are you limping? Is something wrong with your foot?"

"Vaughn said you were coming," Raine says when she opens the door. "I sent him to the store, so he's out right now, but I can help you."

"He's not here?" Tami says.

But before Raine has a chance to say anything, we're met with a squeal and a "Holy shit, that's Ivy Avila!" from two people sitting on a couch in the living room, a guy and a girl, probably nineteen or twenty, eating out of the same takeout container on the coffee table.

"I'm so sorry," Raine says apologetically, coughing a little. "I should have told my roommates to not be weird." She turns to the people on the couch. "Don't be weird, okay?"

The girl puts her chopsticks down, but the boy is still holding his midair. A piece of what looks like teriyaki tofu falls from them onto the floor. "We should have cleaned up the house or something," the girl says. The guy nods, still staring at Ivy.

Ivy smiles and stands up a little straighter, somehow brought back to life, maybe even sobered a little by the attention.

I expected the familiar relief of air-conditioning when we entered the house, but it's even hotter than outside. Even with fans all over the living room, the air is thick and stifling. Raine and the roommates are practically in their underwear, and the girl has her feet in a bucket of ice water. I feel sweat form a sticky film all over my body.

It's then that I notice Raine doesn't look so good. She has huge bags under her eyes and her face has a grayish tint. She wheezes every time she takes a breath in.

"Are you okay?" Ivy says.

Raine pulls an inhaler out of her pocket and puts it to her mouth. She sucks in the whoosh of medicine.

"Just asthma," she says. "The smoke is making it bad."

"Just asthma?" says the boy. "We practically had to do CPR on you last night."

"Why don't you go to the hospital?" Tami says. Even she is sweating.

"No insurance."

"But aren't there those hospitals that have to take everyone?"

"Yeah, but they still send you a bill."

Ash pretends to be interested in a book he randomly took from the bookshelf. Ivy sits on the couch across from Raine and looks like she's about to either cry or have a panic attack. Tami is still standing, like she's afraid to touch the furniture, like she's afraid of catching something.

Raine coughs and pulls a box out from under the coffee table. "So how many do you want?"

"How about twenty," Tami says. "You guys want some Freedom?"

I shake my head. Ash is still pretending to read the book.

"Do you have anything else?" Ivy says. "Anything stronger?"

Raine looks at her sadly. "We don't sell stuff like that. I'm sorry." But not sorry that she doesn't have the drugs Ivy wants; more like she's sorry Ivy had to even ask, like she feels sorry for Ivy. "But maybe Freedom will help you realize you don't need those other things?"

Ivy's not listening. She's staring at Ash over by the bookshelf. She's watching every move he makes.

Raine counts out the pills and the roommates whisper to each other. The girl looks at Ivy and says, "Okay, so this is probably totally annoying and you can totally say no, but would you mind if we took our picture with you?"

"Are you serious?" Tami says.

"Sure," Ivy says, all smiles. "No problem." She gives Tami a look that would make anyone else wither, but Tami just gives her the same look right back.

The roommates squeeze themselves onto the couch where Ivy and I are sitting, one on either side of her, with me on the outside. I try to scoot myself to the edge so I won't be in the picture, but Ivy reaches out her arm and pulls me into the shot as the girl holds out her phone for the selfie. She says, "Cheese!" and I try to smile.

Tami mutters, "Yeah, cool. Just taking selfies in a drug dealer's house. Real classy."

"We are not drug dealers," Raine says, and starts coughing again.

We all lean in to look at the picture. "It's great," says the boy, but the light is terrible, everyone is disheveled and sweaty, and the roommates are half-naked.

But the worst part, which no one else seems to notice, is that in the place where I'm supposed to be, there's nothing but a shadow. It's like I've been erased.

I think maybe I'm hallucinating, maybe I need to take another look, maybe it's just a combination of bad lighting and too much alcohol, maybe a part of my brain is permanently broken from those two weeks at Ivy's house, but the roommates have already returned to their couch with the phone and the picture of me and possible proof that I really have finally turned completely invisible.

Raine hands the plastic baggie of Freedom to Tami. "You know we're moving, right?" she says.

"What?" Tami says, her fingers clenching around the baggie in her hand. The side of her lip twitches. "What are you talking about?"

"Vaughn and me. We've been talking about it for a long time, but it's finally going to happen. I can get my degree online. I think we're going to one of the Midwest states where they have all those mega-prisons. Vaughn can get a job there easy. We need to go somewhere it's not so expensive to live. We wouldn't need roommates, you know?" She pauses for a second. "It'll be miles of A-Corp–owned sprawl. But we're all owned by something, right? And anything's got to be better than this. It's toxic here. Vaughn has been . . . It just isn't good for him. It isn't good for us."

"You can't do that," Tami says. "You can't just make someone move like that."

Everyone looks at her, strands of her white-blond hair sticking to her face, black mascara smudged under her eyes, as drenched with sweat as the rest of us.

First Ash, and now Vaughn. Tami is not used to things being taken from her.

"I'm not making anyone do anything," Raine says slowly. "But you should start looking for somewhere else to get your Freedom."

"Let's get out of this fucking shithole," Tami says, standing up and grabbing Ash's arm, hard.

"Ow!" Ash says, his first word in a long time. He's been as quiet as me. "That fucking hurt, Tami."

"Don't touch him like that," Ivy says.

Tami leans forward so her face is only a couple inches from Ivy's. "I can touch him however I want."

Ivy is the first to look away. I don't know what her plan is, how she expects to win this game with Tami, but so far it's not looking too good for her. Even with all her money and fame and beauty, even with Ash's love, Ivy is still the underdog.

Somehow we all make it back to the car without killing each other. Tami gets into the driver's seat again. Ivy immediately opens the bottle she left in the back and we all take big gulps.

"Why'd you get so mad back there?" Ash says. "You can find somewhere else to get the pills, can't you?"

"It's the heat," Tami says. "It's getting to me. And why the hell can't those idiot firefighters put out those fires?"

"Really?" Ivy says. "You're going to talk shit about firefighters now?"

Ash laughs, but Tami gives him a look that shuts him up.

Tami starts driving before any of us has a chance to put on our seat belts. I am the only one who looks behind us and sees Vaughn pull up in his busted old car and get out carrying mismatched canvas bags full of groceries. He watches us as we pull away, probably wondering at the sight of this kind of car in this kind of neighborhood, and then I see his face change with the realization of who's probably in it, and he drops the groceries and starts running, waving his arms like a madman. We turn the corner, out of sight, and I say nothing.

28

THE smoke is turning a darker shade of orange. The sky is closing in. The mountains and skyscrapers and Sound are all disappearing, getting erased by the falling night.

It is amazing how much a person can drink on the way from one side of a city to another. Ash, Ivy, and I pass the bottle around while Tami drives. By the time we get to Tami's condo, the three of us are wasted.

The night is still young. There are still so many more things that could happen.

"Why are we going here?" Ash complains. "I want to go *out*."

Those are almost the exact same words Vaughn said a few weeks ago.

Has it really been just a handful of weeks since that night? Is that all the time it takes to turn a person upside down?

We ride the elevator up in a heavy, whiskey-soaked silence, and I feel the familiar feeling—or lack of feeling—of myself floating, of my feet not touching the ground, of losing my connection to gravity. I wonder what I'm even doing here. Ivy doesn't need me. This is between her and Ash and Tami.

I will not get out of this elevator when we get to Tami's floor. I will ride it all the way back down and be done with these people forever. I don't love Ash. I can't stand Tami. There is no good reason to have them in my life.

But then Ivy reaches for my hand, like she could read my mind, like she could sense a distance forming, and she squeezes, and I feel it all the way up my arm and into my heart, and Ivy pumps through my veins and fills up every space in my body, and I feel the truth in every atom of my being: We are impossible to separate, whether I like it or not.

I will stick around a little longer. In case she needs me. In case things get out of control. Nobody knows what Tami's capable of.

"Why did we come all this way to sit inside?" Ash says as he collapses into a chair. Tami goes to the bar and I sit by Ivy on the couch.

"We have to stay inside," Tami says. "You know that. The air is toxic."

"But so are you," I want to say. "So are all of you."

"But we could be inside somewhere else," Ash says. "Like we could go to the Science Center or something. We could go to the aquarium."

"What are you, nine years old?" Tami laughs.

"We could at least go shopping," he says.

"Now that's an idea," Ivy says.

"You're already drunk," Tami says. "I need to get drunk."

“That’s a good idea too,” Ivy and Ash say in unison, and then they look at each other with a glowing surprise, and for the briefest of moments, they are inside a bubble where time stops, and we are out here, in real time, watching it.

I cannot read Tami’s face as she stares at them. She is calculating something in her mind. She is always calculating.

“What is this?” Tami says. She sucks down her drink and immediately pours another one.

This is finally happening. Saying something out loud makes it real. I feel Ivy buzzing next to me. The lights in the condo flicker. Something inside me flickers.

“What is what?” Ash says.

“This. Between you two. What is going on?” There is an air of condescension in her voice that only people like her can pull off.

“We’re drunk,” Ash says. “You need to catch up with us. Finish your drink.”

“Don’t tell me what to do.”

I can’t feel most of my body, cannot find where I touch the couch, but I can feel my foot in sharp focus, unconnected, disembodied, and throbbing with infection. The piece of Ivy is still in there, poisoning me from the inside.

The wound is the part of me that is dying, and it is the part of me that feels most alive.

Something is rotting, way past sweet.

“Give me one of those pills,” Ash says.

"They're in my purse," says Tami.

"I'll take one too," Ivy says.

"You owe me two hundred dollars," Tami says.

"So sue me," says Ivy, swallowing the pill as soon as Ash hands it to her.

I look at Ivy and her shiny things are long gone. She has lost her powers. She's just a girl now. Someone like me. Someone breakable.

"You need to talk," Tami says. "Right now. What's going on between you two?"

Ivy looks at Ash, calmer than I've seen her all day, but a feeling of dread washes over me. She is so sure of the righteousness of her heart, so sure she's going to win, but it is a naïve and foolish kind of confidence. This world is not made for people who think with their hearts. And people like Tami don't like to lose.

"You didn't tell her we knew each other from before?" Ivy asks Ash.

Ash just sits there with his mouth slightly open. His beautiful, empty mouth.

"We met a year and a half ago," Ivy says. "On an island in Brazil. We fell in love."

This is supposed to be Ivy's triumphant big reveal, but Tami just laughs. It is a hollow, grating laugh. Tami is not someone who admits to being caught off guard. She acts like none of this is news to her. "Love?" she says. "Is that what you call a vacation fling?"

"It was more than that," Ivy says. "It *is* more than that."

"I know the vacation you're talking about. Ash and I were already dating by then. He was depressed when he came back. I helped him recover from whatever you did to him. *That's* what you call love. Not some two-week romance when you were a junior. Jesus, you really are nuts."

"She's not crazy," Ash manages to say, but just barely, and then he retreats into his shadow, like he used up whatever tiny amount of courage he had for that useless statement and now there's nothing of him left. He is hollowed out and gone. Now it is just Tami versus Ivy.

"Who needs a drink?" Tami says with false cheer, like this is all so small, it doesn't even bother her. "I'll make everybody drinks."

"No one needs a drink," Ash says. "Let's all just go home."

"Giving up so soon?" Tami says. "We're just getting started. I want to hear everything Ivy Avila has to say."

"Ash doesn't love you," Ivy says. "He's never loved you. He loves me."

"My god," Tami laughs. "You're batshit."

I wait for Ash to interject, to at least say Ivy's not crazy again, the one thing he seems capable of doing, but he stays silent, wide-eyed, watching this scene unfold before him like something he has no intention of participating in.

Ivy jumps up, wobbles slightly on her feet. "You don't even know him. He only chose you because he gave up on real love, because he gave up on the life he actually wants. Because you and your fake little world sucked the life out of him. But he's not going to do that anymore. Right, Ash? Tell her. Tell her she's a mistake."

But Ash is gone. He has a "Do Not Disturb" sign etched on his face. Everything Ivy says bounces off of him and falls flat at her feet. His shadow collects itself and sneaks away.

I try to get up to leave, but I am stuck in this place, tied to these people. They will not let me go.

"What's going on, Ash?" Tami says, in an absurd imitation of kind. It would be comic if any of this was funny. "Tell us the truth."

"I told you the truth," Ivy says.

"I wasn't talking to you," Tami snaps.

"Almost two years," Ivy says. "He's loved me the whole time."

"Really?" Tami says, eyebrows raised, with contempt so thick, it's practically dripping off of her. "You were in contact that whole time? You were seeing each other behind my back for two years, while we were away, *together*, at school?"

"Well, no. We lost contact for a while, but—"

"That's not love. That's not a relationship. That's a fling. You're a fling. No one loves girls like you. You're just candy."

"That's not true," Ivy says. "Ash, tell her that's not true. Show her who you really are. Tell her you don't want to get an MBA and be another A-Corp executive. You have dreams."

But he's just sitting there, a statue without its shadow.

"Oh, are you talking about his little music hobby?" Tami says.

"It's his passion, which you would know if you gave a shit about him at all. You would support him being who he really is."

"Yeah, and what? End up like you? Some washed-up child star whose career is already over at eighteen? You know you're never going to work for A-Corp again, right? No one's going to want to pay the kind of insurance you require. You're not worth it anyway. There are so many girls like you, pretty little nobodies with desperate mothers who think they've got something special, some ticket to success. But you're nothing special. There are thousands of girls just waiting to take your place."

"That's uncalled for," Ash manages to say.

"Oh come on. What do you even see in her? Do you actually buy it, her whole tortured artist thing? You think being next to her, maybe some of it will rub off on you. You can pretend for a little while it's you who's the star. But I hate to break it to you, honey, she's not a star anymore. That light's gone out."

"He doesn't love you," Ivy says again. She will keep saying it until she makes it matter to anyone but herself. "And if you supposedly love him so much, why are you cheating on him? He knows about it, you know. He knows all about it."

"Of course he does," Tami says coolly. "But he understands sometimes people need to decompress. Sometimes we're under a lot of stress and need something uncomplicated. But it's never about love. You know that, right? Ash? I've never cheated with my heart."

"You're a monster," he says, barely a whisper.

"But you make everything so complicated!" Tami yells. "Give me a fucking break."

Ivy walks over to the chair where Ash is sitting, kneels down beside it, and puts her arm around him. But he does not bend to her, does not lean in. He stays stiff, unmoving.

"Ash," Ivy says, facing him. He cannot look her in the eyes. "It can all be over now. Just tell Tami it's over. Tell her you never loved her, that your whole relationship was built on you following the rules. But you don't want to do that anymore."

"I never loved her?" he says, but his eyes are turned down, and there is a question at the end of his statement, like he's saying it because he was instructed to, like he's reading it off of a script and is not sure it's a good line.

"You love me," Ivy says.

"Yes."

"You're done with Tami. You're coming with me. We're going to start a life together."

"Oh, don't be ridiculous," Tami says. "He's not going anywhere with you. You know why? Because *you're* not going anywhere. You think he's going to run away from home with you? To do what? To wait tables and live in some studio apartment and take buses everywhere so you can play at being authentic artists or some bullshit? That'd be fun for about a week, tops. You think he's going to run away from his future for *that?* For *you*? People don't do that. Honestly, I feel sorry for you. Some of us have a future, some of us don't."

"I want to go home," is all Ash can say.

"Do you realize what a luxury you have?" Tami says to Ivy. "That you get to fall apart? It's almost part of your job. And people care enough to keep watching. It's part of the show. It makes them even more interested in you. Other people don't have that privilege."

"Tell her you don't love her," Ivy says to Ash. She can't hear a word Tami says.

"Don't say something you'll regret," says Tami. "Don't say something you can't take back."

"Tell her!"

"I can't," Ash says, burying his head in his hands.

"I think we should go," I say, but no one hears me. A toxic sludge of liquor and stomach acid burns in my guts. I try to stand up again, but I am not connected to any of my limbs.

"What do you mean, you can't?" Ivy says.

"I need time to figure things out," he says, staring at his lap.

"This isn't something to figure out," Ivy says. "It's not about thinking. That's your problem, Ash. You need to let yourself *feel*."

"Jesus Christ," Tami says. "Do you realize how ridiculous you sound?"

"Show us how you're really feeling," Ivy insists. "Stop trying to control it."

"What?" Ash snaps. "And be out of control like you?" He is finally looking at her. His cracks are showing for all to see, but it's not light behind them now. It's just more shadow.

Tami laughs and laughs and laughs.

Finally, I manage to stand up. A giant mirror on the wall behind us reflects the vague glow of the city's lights through the thick smoke outside, with Ivy, Ash, and Tami frozen in the foreground. I am nowhere to be seen. I wave my arms around, but the only thing that moves is Tami's eyelashes as she blinks.

"I don't understand," Ivy says pathetically, and I think no truer words have ever been said.

"God, what a waste of a day," Tami says, pulling out her phone. "I'm not going to let you two ruin my night. Take that ridiculous car and get out of my face."

Ivy and Ash just stare, confused, unsure of what to do.

"I'm serious," Tami says, looking up from her phone. "I want you both to leave. Now."

But what about me?

29

AN elevator. A dropping through space. All I am is one pulsing foot. The rest of me is ether.

We are three people, not looking at one another.

"Why didn't you tell her?" Ivy whispers. "Why didn't you tell her you're through?"

"It's not that easy."

"But love should make things easy."

Ash looks at Ivy with disbelief. "You don't really believe that, do you?"

And I think this is it. This is the moment he confesses he never had any intention of leaving Tami, that he never planned to give up being a prince. Being different was only ever a hobby, a place he went when he felt moody and misunderstood. But being understood is not his goal. What matters is being worshipped, being surrounded by special people. Ivy was once one of those special people, but she has lost all her shiny things.

"Ash," she pleads. "I—" But then her voice cuts off and her face softens. Her eyes turn slightly dull. "Oh," she says.

Ash is smiling, his eyes as dull as hers. "Yes," he says.

"I think the Freedom just kicked in," Ivy says. "What were we talking about?"

"It doesn't matter."

With the right pill, nothing matters. With the right pill, all you are is a body falling through space and you don't care if there's anyone to catch you.

In the parking garage, Ivy's car comes to greet her, drives right up, headlights blinking in some automated, false friendliness, loyal like a pet dog.

"Get in," she says. "I'll put it in self-driving mode."

"I want to drive," says Ash. "I've always wanted to drive one of these."

How can he think about cars at a time like this?

I get in the back. We sit in the car, unmoving, as Ash runs his hands over everything, eyes sparkling. It is so easy to forget the world is on fire.

Ivy is in her own little world, miles and miles and miles away. "It's going to be okay," she says. Then she says it again, and again, and again, and every time she says it, I believe it less.

"Why have I never tried this pill?" Ash says.

Ivy smiles and meets his eye. "We're free."

But I don't believe either of them.

"Car, on," Ivy says.

"Would you like to engage automated driver assistance?" says the car.

"No," Ash says. "I want to be in control."

We peel out of the parking garage, and for a split second everything is weightless, and the world shifts and there is no gravity and the constant pressure in my chest turns to bubbles, and I think I can feel the Freedom too, and now, yes, I believe in them, I believe in us, I think this could really happen, Ivy and Ash could really happen, Ivy's dream could actually come true, this could be a world with possibility where people can transform themselves and start over and go anywhere. We are flying onto the street, wheels not touching the ground, and I think we may just keep going, up and up until the car transforms into a jet, with a course set straight for that island in Brazil that the ocean has not claimed yet, with the perfect beach where true love was born and where fruity drinks with umbrellas will be waiting for us.

But the car is just a car, and whatever air we temporarily gained was only centimeters, and now we are on the ground again, heavy with all we have done, heavy with laws of nature and truth we cannot outrun, and there is a thump of something else, something soft and rounded, in front, then beneath us, not road, not something tires are supposed to touch.

"What was that?" I say.

Ivy says, "Keep driving."

We cannot hear the people on the street, so many anonymous, masked faces, some bare, braving the smoke, their mouths open wide like fish, fingers pointing, other hands pulling out phones.

"Did I hit someone?" Ash says.

"Keep driving," Ivy says. Calm, so calm.

I say, "Stop!" but no one hears me.

Ivy and Ash are somewhere manufactured, in a present moment unburdened by shame. Is this what Daddy is always talking about? Is this equanimity? Is this what it means to be at peace no matter what happens? Are they islands made out of rock, unmoving in the storm? Is Freedom the shortcut to awakening?

No. They are running. They are made out of fear and want. They are always leaning forward.

There is a fine line between feeling shame and having a conscience.

I am the only one who looks back.

I am the only one who sees the body on the ground, the pool of blood, the muscled arm bent at an unnatural angle. I see the familiar tattoos, those corporate brands he paid to be advertised on his skin, images and words and patterns made meaningless from being repeated on so many bodies. Now this body, this life, has been made meaningless.

Of course he was on his way to Tami's condo. He missed us at his house by only seconds. If only he had arrived seconds earlier, or later. If only he had stayed with Raine. If only he had never started wanting what he couldn't have.

There is a theory that souls travel in packs, across lifetimes, repeating the same stories together over and over again, everyone playing the same roles, everyone on their own karmic journeys, waiting for someone to wake up and break the cycle.

Of all the thousands of people who could have been walking in front of the parking garage at that exact moment, of all the anonymous people who could have gotten caught under Ivy's tires, of course it was Vaughn.

None of us will ever wake up.

I scream, but of course no one hears me. I scream so hard, my throat, already raw from the smoke, tears itself to shreds. That is where it starts, the splitting, at my throat, the place where my voice lives, the pressure valve that opens and closes to let me out or keep me in, the place where my voice dies.

The tear slices through me. I am unzipped, cracked, split down the middle. I am two halves, no longer connected.

30

CAN I be two places at once? Is it that easy to split me? Half of me here, in the car with Ash and Ivy, half of me back in Tami's condo.

I have gotten used to not feeling my body. I've gotten used to being unseen. Maybe I am a ghost again, haunting Tami now, following her as she paces around in her tower, clutching her phone, texting everyone she can think of, every single person who could get here fast. There is no app for ordering friends. There is no app that cures loneliness.

I keep glancing in the mirror every time I pass it, but I'm still not there.

This feels like my memories, something I have pulled out of the recesses of my mind, something saved in black and white but that I have colored in, am coloring in now, blindfolded, making it new.

This is not real. My memories are not real. I have imagined all of this.

All I know how to do is make stories. There is a fine line between fact and fiction.

I don't know where my body is.

Tami texts Vaughn a million times. Maybe his phone is crushed, broken bits in his pocket below. Maybe Tami's messages will be stuck in limbo in some channel forever, her desperation reduced to ones and zeroes that never land.

What happens when your destination is erased?

She downs her drink and puts the phone to her ear. "Vaughn, I'm here waiting. You know it must really be serious if I'm *calling*. You know I hate talking on the phone." She laughs, but I can hear the sandpaper in her throat. Her face goes blank and the laugh stops abruptly as soon as she hangs up. She is still for a moment as she looks at the windows that used to show a panoramic view of the whole world beneath her but now just push up against a flat wall of smoke. Now everyone gets the same view, no matter how much they're paying.

Tami's shoulders slump. Her face contorts and turns red like she is straining, and it is the first time I have ever seen her look ugly, even if this whole scene is just my imagination. I think maybe she is trying to cry, but she doesn't know how. Maybe her face cracks, just a little, but it's too late. Girls like her get everything they want, they don't deserve my sympathy too. She throws her glass at the window in frustration but it doesn't even break, and now there's a mess of ice cubes on the floor that will soon melt and make a puddle.

She takes a deep breath. She forces herself to smile.

She leaves the spilled glass for someone else to clean up.

I follow her out the door, down the hall, into the elevator, down through the sky to the ground level she despises. What if Seattle had two levels like New York? What if people like Tami could stay in the sky all the time? Would she have ever even met Vaughn? Would their lives never have intersected at all?

Is that the destination? Is that what would make all of this complete? For some people to never have to land?

Tami pauses in the lobby, taking in the scene outside the glass doors. The crowd on the street has grown. Police lights pulse in the smoky night, like the whole world is throbbing. People crowd around a barrier made of yellow tape. Tami checks her phone but no one has texted her back.

We step into the night without masks. Red and blue flash across the scene like some morbid dance club, the tense chatter of onlookers our music. One cop is putting Vaughn's wallet in a plastic bag. Another cop is talking about informing next of kin. I think of Vaughn's wife, Raine, wheezing in their oven of a home, making plans for their new beginning in a place that is also dying. I think of Ivy and Ash, who stole Raine and Vaughn's new beginning on the way to theirs.

Medics lift the stretcher into the ambulance. They are in no hurry.

The white sheet snags on something and reveals the gnarled and bloodied meat of the body. The whole street groans, like some spectator sport, and I think of Vaughn's failed career as a fighter, and I can't help but think that he finally got the audience he was waiting for.

And there's his arm, there are his generic tattoos, and here is Tami, standing eerily quiet beside me. She starts walking, calmly, her chin in the air, parting the crowd with all her entitlement. "You can't go in there," someone says, but of course she can. Girls like her can do anything they want.

"It was like a spaceship, man," someone says to a cop. "The car that hit him."

"Did you get a look at who was driving?" says the cop.

"Nah, man. Those windows were all mirrors."

The ambulance door closes. "Miss?" a cop says to Tami. "Miss?" But she doesn't hear him. She is kneeling next to the pool of blood, staring at the reflection of the police lights in the glassy surface like a red liquid mirror. I lean down and put my face next to hers.

Can she see her face there? Does the reflection tell her she's real?

31

"IT'S going to be okay," Ivy says, again and again, like a mantra. "It's going to be okay." The thing about mantras is, after a while they lose all meaning. After a while they're only sounds.

"It was an accident," Ash says. "It wasn't intentional. We didn't mean to hurt anyone."

"But you did," I say. "You did hurt someone. Your intention doesn't change that."

"It's not our fault," Ivy says.

"But it's still your responsibility," I say.

She acts like she doesn't hear me, but I know she does. Ivy can always hear me. She's the only one who can.

"Where are we going?" Ivy says.

"We have to get rid of the car," Ash says.

"Tell him he can turn himself in," I say.

"You can turn yourself in," Ivy says. "It was an accident. You'll get the best lawyers. You'll be fine."

"People like him are always fine," I say.

"We'll hide the car," he says. "We'll say it was stolen."

"But they'll question us," Ivy says. "When they find the car. They'll question me."

“Ivy, turn the autopilot on,” Ash says calmly. Too calmly. She does what he says.

He turns and grabs Ivy’s arm. “I can’t get in trouble.” He puts his hand on her cheek, trying to be gentle, but I feel it burn on my own skin. “Help me,” he says. “If you love me, you’ll help me.” He kisses her and I want to spit in his mouth.

“No, Ivy,” I say. “Tell him no.”

“Yes,” she says with her eyes closed. “I’ll drop you off at the ferry terminal. Go home and pack your stuff. Get ready to go. I’ll get rid of the car. I’ll buy our plane tickets.”

Ash doesn’t say anything, just looks ahead into the night, his hands back on the steering wheel even though he doesn’t need to drive. He has gone somewhere else and I don’t know if he’s coming back.

Ivy tells the car to take us to the ferry terminal. She gently uncurls Ash’s fingers from the steering wheel and holds his hand in her lap. Their faces are serene. Neither of them is scared. The Freedom they swallowed is doing its work. But I wonder if it’d be any different without the pills.

The billboards shine their advertisements. The bots do their cleaning. The drones do their watching, but no one is looking for us yet.

The car pulls up to the ferry terminal and Ivy kisses Ash goodbye. Their lips are just paper against paper. Everything is dried up.

He does not look either of us in the eye, just turns around and goes.

"Make sure people see you," Ivy calls after him. "It'll give you an alibi."

Something's over now. Ivy doesn't know it yet, but I do. Something else is beginning. That's how things work.

As we drive away, I see Ash pull out his phone. Somehow I know he's calling Tami. He has the look of someone who has no intention of doing the right thing.

Ivy tells the car to take us to the warehouse area south of downtown.

"You need to turn him in," I tell her. "You need to save yourself."

"Why should I save myself?" she says dispassionately. "What's the point?"

"So you don't have to go to prison. It's not like debt prison, Ivy. When you kill someone, it's different."

"There are worse things."

"Like what? Death?"

"Maybe I'm already dead."

"Don't be so dramatic."

Ivy laughs a hollow laugh. "That's all I know how to do."

"He's not worth it," I say.

"Yeah? Well, neither am I. Don't you get it? I've lost everything. He's the only thing I can't lose."

"What about me?"

"I'll never lose you."

Maybe she is right. But maybe she is wrong. Or maybe all of

these things are true. Maybe there are other truths we haven't even considered.

Maybe it is not about losing at all. Not about the clinging and chasing and holding on for dear life, not about something getting taken away.

Ivy, what would happen if you just let go?

And that's when I get out. Or part of me gets out. Maybe I split once more.

I am unbound, released.

How many pieces am I now?

It is a dark street south of downtown, outside the toll gates. It is a world where people like us don't go. But what does that even mean, *people like us*? We are all made out of the same things.

I walk among the shadows. I am a shadow. I fit right in.

The only open businesses are dive bars, liquor stores, and a few twenty-four-hour recruitment centers for cults. Police drones fly overhead. Streetlights flicker. Rats scurry. Blanketed figures huddle in doorways behind shopping carts that contain entire lives. Somewhere, glass breaks. Somewhere, there is yelling. The world smells like smoke and piss and garbage. Somewhere above, stars are shining, bright and constant, but they are blocked from view, and none of the light filters down here.

I don't know where my shoes went. My foot is raw, bare flesh. The wound has opened. I have no protection from the sidewalk. There is no layer between me and the grime of this part of the city that no one wants to see.

I walk through blocks and blocks of identical shadows and mask-covered faces. They go on forever. The streets and the faces are infinite. The pain in my foot travels up my leg and into my entire body.

Eventually I reach the boardwalk, the ferry terminal. The Ferris wheel and vendors are all shut down because of the smoke. The postcard view of Commodore Island has been wiped out, the view Ivy's mother supposedly looked at as a child, the view that made her dream of a different kind of life, that made her use her daughter as a tool to get that dream. And she got her mansion on the island, she got her money and fine things, she got to live inside the view, and now she's trapped inside that glass house while the world burns down around her.

I am the only person on the boat's outside deck. There are no tourists taking pictures of the Seattle skyline. There *is* no Seattle skyline. The ferry horn blows its sad announcement into the night: *I am here. I am coming.*

The fires are getting close. The dusty ash falls from the sky and makes a shape around my body, and I am a brittle shell with nothing inside.

32

I do not need roads. I will walk through the forest. I will walk miles and miles and miles. I will cross through the middle of the island where the giant estates have not yet taken over, where there is still wildness, where, despite the smoke and shrinking lake and cracked earth, the animals and plants have no idea what any of us have done.

I try to call Lily but no one answers. I don't know what time it is in Taiwan.

You can see so much through glass.

The window into Ash's living room glows like a computer screen in the dark. Tami has cleaned herself up. She is sitting on the couch, in the same place I first saw her this afternoon. How is it possible this is the same day?

She is drinking one of the good bottles of wine from the prized collection in the cellar. The giant screen in the corner is turned to one of those reality shows where a bunch of nearly identical women fight over a man none of them know.

She is so sure she's the winner.

I am walking blind, barefoot. Nothing but shadows and texture and sounds I cannot name. Branches grab at me, scratching my legs, my arms, my face, tugging at my hair. This is not a trail. I may not be going in the right direction. But I am moving. That's the point. I am not standing still.

Tami's almost done with the bottle of wine. Her lips are stained purple. Her eyes are slits.

On the television, it is time for the elimination ceremony.

Tami says to no one, "I am not a loser."

How long have I been here? Did I go into the forest only to come out in the exact same place? Have I been walking in circles this entire time?

Why can't I get away from these people?

"He's in there breaking up with her," Ivy says. We are in the bushes together. We are on the outside looking in. Where did

Ivy come from? I thought I'd left her too. Why is she so hard to get rid of? Why does she always know where to find me?

"It doesn't look like they're breaking up," I tell her.

"I want to make sure he's okay," she says. Her skin is scratched and bleeding. "I want to make sure Tami doesn't hurt him. He's going to need me as soon as she leaves."

"I don't think she's leaving," I say.

"He'll need me to help him pack."

She is looking right through me. From this angle, she cannot see Ash walking into the living room with a towel wrapped around his waist, his hair wet from the shower. She cannot see Ash and Tami kissing in the living room. She cannot see him not thinking about her at all.

"You have to turn him in," I tell her. "You have to tell someone what happened. People saw your car. It's only a matter of time. The cops will think it was you."

"We'll say the car was stolen. Someone took it for a joy ride. They abandoned it in SODO. It happens all the time."

"But whose fingerprints are on the steering wheel?"

She says nothing.

"He's dead, Ivy. Vaughn is dead."

"I already bought the plane tickets."

My feet are bleeding. My skin is coated with pine needles. Spiderwebs are stuck to sweat and blood. My lungs are clouds of smoke. We are not supposed to be outside like this.

. . .

This is what it looks like when Tami breaks someone down. She dials a three-digit number into a phone and then hands it to Ash. I know what Tami's smile means. He takes a deep breath and looks her in the eye as he begins talking. I can't read all the words, but only one is important. I know the shape of Ivy's name on his mouth.

I turn to Ivy and her face is changing, morphing, twisting. I feel the weight of her, the light sucking in and disappearing. She will collapse under her own gravity.

A black hole is a star dying.

"Ivy," I say.

The sun is starting to rise. Metallic blue peeks over the treetops.

"Ivy," I say again.

Then she starts running.

Deep in the forest, there is no dawn. It is still too dark to see any edges. Ivy is far away and I cannot see where she stops and I begin.

I have lost her.

I am lost.

I wake up in the forest. It was all a nightmare.

Maybe Ash and Ivy are already on that plane, high above the smoke, watching the rest of us suffocate.

Here's my favorite big rock. Here's my climbing tree. Here's the pear tree and the apple tree and the Italian prune. Here is my familiar clearing in the forest where the sky opens, where the sun reaches down into the garden and helps Daddy's garden grow. I feel relief, but it is short-lived.

The garden is overgrown, unrecognizable. The deer fence is down, the metal wires pulled into the earth by layers of plant life, generations upon generations of growth and decay.

And there, where my house should be, is nothing but vine-covered ruins.

33

I wake up to the smell of smoke. I should be used to it by now—the smell of the world on fire, even with all the doors and windows closed, even with all the ways we try to shut it out.

Please come over is the text I find from Ivy. I am in my bed, Gotami curled up in my armpit, my head pounding. Hazy images flash through my mind, and I don't know if they are memories, or my imagination, or random neural firings. Daddy thinks our dreams are our subconscious trying to tell us things. Papa says they're just waste products from the trash compactors inside our brains that clean things out when we're sleeping. He thinks dreams are literally garbage.

What if Papa's right and the subconscious is not made out of symbols and messages and meaning that needs to be deciphered; what if it's just chaos and nonsense? What if there's nothing inside us but dust and specks, and we keep trying to connect the dots because we're desperate for a path? But what if there is no path? Maybe we're all just specks floating in space, infinite and vast and alone.

I sit up in bed, wondering if anything I think I remember

about last night is real, or fake, or something in between. Maybe I was here all night, watching TV with my parents. Maybe the sickness I feel in my body is not a hangover but a freak summer flu. Maybe no one is dead and no one is in trouble.

Maybe I am going crazy. Maybe I have always been crazy.

I look at my phone again: *Please come over*. I try to read meaning between the letters. Was this a message sent in haste as police cars showed up at Ivy's gate? Is she getting hauled away in handcuffs right now? Am I already too late?

Or is she sitting up in bed like I am, wondering what happened last night, wondering if her dreams are real?

Does she need me to hold her? Will she turn around this time and face me? Will she be gentle? Will she just let me love her?

I'm coming, I text back. I get dressed fast and brush my teeth. But when I get outside, my car is gone. Maybe Papa drove to work today instead of getting a ride to the ferry from Daddy.

I walk down the hill in the smoky air, and by the time I get to Ivy's house, I think I will never be able to get the burning smell out of my nose. It is permanently absorbed in the membranes still chapped and raw from the week of excess with Ivy and Ash. I should have worn a mask. Pain shoots from my nostrils through my sinuses and into my eyes, like thick needles sewing through my cartilage and flesh.

There are no cop cars at Ivy's. Her mom's car is gone.

Everything is still. It could be any other day, not a morning after someone may have died. Maybe I had a bad dream and I can't tell the difference between that and my real life anymore. Maybe everything I think is just meaningless neural garbage that I believe is true.

When I get to Ivy's room, the first thing I notice is a suitcase standing upright next to the bed, the handle raised, the strap of her purse wrapped around it, ready to go at a moment's notice.

I can tell she hasn't slept. She's still in the yellow dress she wore yesterday. Her eyes are red and swollen, like she's been crying, and her skin is covered with a crosshatch of dried blood from scratches all over her body. She looks at me, and for a moment I see a terrified young girl. And I know, definitively, that last night was not a dream. Someone innocent died, and we are all responsible.

Ivy glances at her phone as I crawl into bed with her. She sighs as she sets it on the nightstand and lies down with her back to me as I put my arms around her. She smells sour, poisoned.

"Ash still hasn't called me," she says. "He must be sleeping. He was so tired."

"What are you going to do?"

"What can I do? I have to keep waiting. I can't leave without him, can I?"

I remember seeing him through the window last night, Tami's arms around him. I remember seeing how well they fit together. Why had I never noticed that before? Why had I always assumed he was too good for her?

"But what if he's not coming?" I say.

"He probably has to handle some things before we go."

"What if he's staying here?"

"He's not staying here."

"Have you called the police yet?"

Why aren't they here yet? How hard is it to track down the owner of a car that looks like a spaceship? Is Vaughn's life that low of a priority for them?

Ivy just sighs again and rolls over to face me. "I'm going to miss you, Fern. After we leave. Maybe you can visit us after we get settled. You should. When you're on a break from college. Wouldn't that be wonderful? The three of us, on a beach, all of this, gone?" She waves her hand in the air limply.

"Okay," I say. Her hair is wild and tangled. I pick out a twig, a gum wrapper, a small piece of moss. I try to pat it down, but it won't be tamed.

"Keep doing that," Ivy says, closing her eyes. "That feels good." So I keep petting her hair, like she's a young child needing to be soothed by someone trustable and sturdy, needing someone to keep telling her that magic is real even though she's old enough to know better.

Everything is quiet for a while. I assume Ivy's asleep, so I close my eyes to join her, but then she speaks: "You know I had another job besides acting. You figured it out."

"Yes," I say.

She rolls over to face me. "This one producer, the one who gave me my breakout role in *The Cousins,* he liked to introduce me to his friends. I think he got off on that more than anything—*distributing* me." Her voice is monotone, emotionless. "That was years ago, but every time I'm with someone, it feels like the same thing over and over again. It's like my soul leaves my body. It makes it easier. They use me like a tool. I am a tool."

"You are not a tool," I say. Her eyes are just inches in front of mine, but I know she doesn't see me. She is looking straight through.

"But Ash was different. He wasn't using me. We had this perfect container of time, this perfect little island where nothing could touch us, where who we were in the real world didn't matter. It was just us on the beach talking and singing and sometimes just lying there in silence, and for once in my life I didn't have to perform, and for once in my life I wasn't powerless. And when it got dark, when he couldn't see me, I still felt like I existed. Do you know what I mean? I didn't plan to love him. I saw him on the beach that first day and thought he'd be a nice fling. I wanted to use *him*. But he was perfect. Everything was perfect. My soul didn't have to leave. It was the only time in my life I wasn't terrified."

I don't tell her what I'm really thinking, that she has every reason to be terrified. There is no island remote enough to keep us safe.

"Ash isn't afraid of anything," she says. "Have you noticed that? He lives in a world where nothing can hurt him."

I don't say, "Except Tami. He's scared of Tami."

"You should see some of the stuff he wrote me. He's a poet, you know? For a while, we were writing multiple times a day. I would check my messages constantly. I would wake up in the middle of the night and do it. Then after a few weeks his notes started coming less often, and they got shorter and colder until one day he said he was in a serious relationship with someone who made more sense. He said I was just a fantasy, that we'd never survive in the real world. He picked the real world over me. Do you have any idea what that feels like? To be un-chosen? To just dissolve?"

I do. I know exactly what it feels like to dissolve.

"Dr. Chen has this thing she says all the time: You are not your trauma. It's something that happened to you, it's something you have to work with, but it's not who you are."

"Dr. Chen sounds wise."

"Dr. Chen is a bitch. She doesn't know anything. Everything I have, everything I am, is because of what happened. I was nobody before that. Those casting couches are where I was born."

"No," I say. "That's just where your career was born."

"But what else is there?"

I have nothing to say to that. I look at Ivy and notice she has started a new collection. But now instead of shiny things, she is covered in garbage. Here is the oily sheen of someone else's forehead, the crust of dried skin from somebody's lip, the acne from some girl's hairline caked over with concealer.

"People think that when you're famous you're surrounded by people who worship you. But it's not you they worship. It's the package they want, and the package is all bullshit. But the people who are really running the show, all those guys in power, they're even worse. They're surrounded by so much celebrity and beauty, it doesn't even impress them anymore, so they get hungry for something else. Tami's right—girls like me are everywhere. We're disposable. What the guys in charge want is more than to just consume us. That's easy. They want the power of creating us, the power of making or breaking a life. And they know they can do it, because our hunger turns us into puppets. It's our hunger that makes us vulnerable. It will make us do anything."

"Fuck your hunger," I say. "Don't blame your hunger. You didn't *do* anything. You were a child. Those people raped you. Your mom let them rape you. Your hunger or whatever you want to call it had nothing to do with that."

Ivy has tears in her eyes. She says, "That pill wore off."

"And the dealer is dead," I say.

She rolls over and screams into her pillow. She sounds like someone being murdered. She sounds like someone's insides being torn out, a throat being ripped open. I watch her back heaving, the notches of her spine and the bones of her shoulder blades trying to break through her flesh. She is a cornered animal trapped inside a beautiful girl's skin, thrashing and pounding on the bed, gnashing her teeth, tearing herself apart, ripping open the barely healing cuts from last night, turning herself into a giant wound. She is want and pain and hunger and skin and bones and blood. She is other people's garbage. Even if her fantasy comes true, even if she flies away with Ash to some paradise, that will still be all she ever is, and I am the only one who can hear her screams.

Ivy finds a half-empty bottle of something under her nightstand and gulps it down, eyes closed, liquid streaming out of her mouth and down her chin. Her body is here but she is gone. Her soul has flown to that safe place it found so many years ago, away from all the people who would hurt it. I will never know where that is. The map is locked deep inside her where no one is allowed to go.

I want to tell her she's not garbage. I want to tell her Ash is wrong, everyone is wrong. But I know she cannot hear me.

I should remind her of the inevitable. I should remind her the police will come soon with their questions. But she is trapped inside her little world, where all that exists is the storm inside her own mind. Everything else is just a prop, disposable.

So I drift away, through the smoke, up my hill. The sliver of Ivy is finally out of my foot, but now I can't feel my feet at all. Who needs feet when they're floating, a ghost, invisible, forgotten?

Ivy, I can't remember if I told you I love you. Perhaps the breeze will bring you the message. But by then, you may already be all the way gone.

You have already given up.

But I have not.

34

THERE are infinite stories and infinite endings, but they all lead to the same place.

Daddy thinks we all get reincarnated to repeat suffering over and over again until we figure out the magic trick to not worry about our pain anymore.

Papa thinks we turn into dirt, into dust, and eventually back into atoms, into energy. We turn from biology into physics. We are stardust that will eventually get turned back into stars. The universe is expanding now, but it will probably reverse course at some point, like a rubber band that gets stretched too tight and snaps back in on itself. A reverse big bang. Nothing into something into nothing again. Energy gets recycled, but not souls.

Daddy calls it samsara. Papa calls it science. Daddy says the Buddha was the original psychologist. Papa just sighs.

Some endings have a surprise twist. Everyone loves surprise twists, even the tragic ones.

Of course the police figure out who owns the car. Ash called and told them it was Ivy. But still, they take their time, and Ash is already on a plane going somewhere without us, on his way to some frozen island like Iceland, somewhere Tami won't have to break a sweat. In first class, they will have their own room, their own bed with satin sheets, walls to separate them from their neighbors, and the noise of the plane's engine will drown out any sounds they might make to distract themselves from what they've left behind.

There's a fine line between feeling shame and having a conscience, and maybe Ash and Tami have always been able to buy their way out of both.

They end up together because that's how destiny works. You're born on a path and it does not diverge, no matter how much you want it to. It is a law of science that the simplest solution is the best one. A river always finds the easiest path to the ocean.

In the end, there is always equilibrium. There is always balance in the universe. Vaughn is dead and Ash's punishment is he will give up Ivy. In the logic of their world, that will make him and Tami even.

And what about Ivy?

There's the version we all know, the classic: Pick the most innocent among us and destroy her. Find the victim and throw tragedy at her. Or worse, make her the destroyer too. Beat her up so bad, she breaks. Turn her into one of us.

That's the choice when you are broken. Either you turn into dust, or you start breaking things.

But what is left for us to break?

I wake up to the smell of smoke.

This ending is different, but it leads to the same place. In every ending, someone always has to pay.

I hear the gunshots. Somehow I run down the hill even though I still can't feel my feet.

Some people have lost so much, they don't have anything more to lose.

I beat the police to Ivy's house, but someone else got there first.

You would almost think someone colored the pool water pink on purpose. A few drops from some giant squeeze bottle of food coloring, mixed around with one of those long nets people use to pull out leaves and dead bugs. If only there weren't that bullet-ridden body floating in the middle of it, facedown, long dark hair fanned out like a shroud.

And there, a few feet away, is Raine, Vaughn's newly widowed wife, a handgun next to her, lying on the burning tile in a pool of blood with half her face gone.

What were Ivy's final thoughts before she died? Was she still waiting for Ash? Did she still think they were going to run away together? Was she planning their escape to that other island half a world away, the place where all this began, where she believed she could go back in time and become unbroken? Did she die with her dream intact?

Or maybe that is just the story we think we know.

Maybe she finally realized Ash wasn't coming. That she had packed her suitcase for nothing. Did she ever figure out that he was never worthy of any of this?

Maybe someone else had to figure it out for her. Maybe she was too far gone to realize it for herself.

Sometimes we need help to make us see the truth. Sometimes it has to hurt.

Maybe Ivy did figure it out in time.

Maybe someone helped her.

Did we ever really believe Ash loved Ivy? Or did he merely see someone beautiful and charming, another name to add to the long list of people who worship him? Someone warm and open, someone who would sometimes listen? Someone who made him, for the briefest of days, more complicated?

But Ash has chosen to not be complicated. He likes comfort too much. And he's not that brave after all. At this very moment, he is somewhere above us all, unburdened by the weather or the people he left behind, in first class with the girl who doesn't trouble him with wanting to know who he is.

And now, if Ivy didn't figure it out, if no one could help, then

Ash has this story he can tell, the story of a star who loved him so much, it killed her. He can take that trophy with him wherever he goes. That will be the extent of his depth and damage.

He's gone, back into Tami's arms where he came from, the privilege of his destiny untarnished, and Ivy has met the tragic ending waiting for her at the bottom of her dream.

Ivy and Ash were my dream.

Alive or dead, they're both gone.

So what does that mean for me?

35

WE are made out of our stories. We are a collection of creation myths. But this one was never really mine.

I wake up to the smell of smoke. I will never wake up to anything else. The world is on fire and I am on fire, and we are all burning.

Your house is surrounded by fire trucks, police cars, the brittle hedges belted by flapping yellow tape. Olympic Road is a parade of onlookers and paparazzi. The deer and raccoons are in hiding.

I watch the smoke rise from your house to join the smoke that has made its way down the mountains. I wonder about the glass walls. Are they still standing? Are they melting? Are they charring black? How does glass burn?

That house was never your home. It was a glass box meant to keep the shame in and the smoke out, but it failed at its job.

I float above it all. I inspect the pool. The water is still clear. You are not floating, alive or dead.

No one knows where you and Ash or Tami are. But I know. I know everything. I am omniscient.

I am the author of all these stories.

The story is over. The fire has done its damage. It has burned itself out.

In some parallel universe, there is such a thing as happily ever after. In a place where we have evolved beyond human, there is such a thing as getting what you want and having it be enough.

Maybe all of Daddy's Buddhist philosophy is wrong. Maybe the goal is not to end the clinging and yearning. Maybe it's exactly those things that tell us we're alive. Maybe we're nothing without our hunger.

All we have now are burned ruins, with glass walls still, miraculously, standing. People have found Ash's secret deer path; they have made it onto the property; they are hiding in the bushes, getting scratched by the same branches that drew bloody cross-stitch into your skin. People are out on the water, in kayaks, on Jet Skis. They are watching. They are recording.

They are waiting for the big reveal, when a firefighter will pull your lifeless, charred body from the wreckage. Your grand finale.

Your mother is in her bathrobe. She has no gin and tonics to share with paparazzi this time. This time, they're all for herself.

"What am I going to do?" she says. To nobody. To me. "She was everything. God, she could have been something. She could have done so much."

Everyone assumes that you're dead. How could you not be? That is how these stories always end.

The smoke says: "You have her money now, don't you? You're her next of kin. You'll be fine."

This is the woman's defining moment. This is her origin story. With your death, the royalties from your work would come pouring in. This is when your mother would graduate to become one of the people, like Tami and Ash, who will always be fine.

She blinks. She doesn't know where my voice is coming from.

The smoke says: "Isn't this what you wanted? Look around. This is everything you always wanted. This is everything you sold your daughter for."

36

I find Ivy in the pool, just after dawn. She is floating on her back in her bra and underwear. The water is clear. The glass walls are still standing, uncharred. The fire is somewhere close, but it is not here. Not yet.

Someone has died, but it was not Ivy. We are back at the beginning.

"You shouldn't be outside," I tell her.

Her arms lift lazily above her head and then back down again. Her body glides through the water. She makes such small, pointless waves.

"You know about the giant redwoods?" she says.

"What about them?"

"You know how they propagate?"

"What are you talking about?"

"They need forest fires to grow. The pinecones—that's where all the seeds are—they only open after they've been burned. And the seedlings can't grow unless a fire comes and wipes everything else out, because they need lots of space, and lots of sun. Without fires, they get too crowded and they suffocate."

"Why are you telling me this?"

"Maybe some things just need to burn down."

"I'm going to call the cops," I say. "I'm going to tell them it was Ash who killed Vaughn."

Ivy laughs. "They won't believe you. No one's going to believe your word over his."

She glides over to the stairs in the shallow end and gets out of the pool. She coughs as water drips off her body.

I pull out my phone as she walks toward me.

"His life is worth more than mine," she says.

"How can you say that? How can you not want justice? He used you. They all used you. They used both of us."

"Oh darling," she says. "You're so naïve." Ivy's wet hand closes over mine and squeezes, hard. I feel my bones getting crushed. "Don't you know you don't even exist?"

I push her away and she nearly falls backward. Something changes in her face, and I see myself reflected in the mirrors of her eyes, distorted.

I have become the enemy. I am a substitute for Ash, for Tami, for her mother, for all the men in those offices in the sky, for everyone who looked the other way. She needs someone to hate, and they are all too big, and I am the only one here.

My only job was to love her, and I have done my job well. But now she has given me another job.

She lunges for me and I fall back on the concrete patio. I feel the skin on my shoulders scrape as she tackles me, as she reaches for the phone and grabs it out of my hand. I manage to push her off. I grab her hair as she tries to crawl away, still clutching my phone. She is on her hands and knees, painting a trail of blood to the edge of the pool.

“Why are you protecting him?” I say. “People like him get away with everything. You can’t just let them destroy you.”

Ivy has reached the water. She turns around and faces me. Her hair is a tangled wet mess. Her knees and forearms have been scraped raw. She is wet with a pink cocktail of pool water and blood.

“But that’s what they do,” she says. “They can’t help it. They don’t know how to do anything else.”

“But you still get to decide what *you* do. You have choices.”

“I’m done making choices.”

“But if you let them win, they get me too.”

Ivy looks down at the phone in her hand. “I’m so much stronger than you,” she says. “I always will be. You don’t even have a name.”

And that’s when I lunge for her, and she falls back into the pool, the phone going with her and sinking to the bottom. But I don’t care about the phone. There are more phones. Ivy’s in the water and I’m on solid ground, and my hands are on her head, and they are pushing her down.

“I have a name,” I say. “Tell me my name.” But she cannot speak.

You are not stronger than me, Ivy. You will not let them win. You will not let them destroy us. Again and again and again, they destroy us. Because we let them. Because we let them into our minds, because we let them fracture us from the inside, in the only place we have any real power to keep them out.

They broke the world, but they will not break us.

It is my job to protect her. To protect us.

I hold Ivy under the water. Her arms thrash and grab but there is nothing to hold. Her heart is not in it. She's done fighting. She's done making choices. She said it herself.

Sometimes peace requires a fight. Sometimes you have to push and pull before you can agree.

"I love you, Ivy," I say, and even though she's underwater, I know she can hear me.

For a moment, there is silence. Ivy is weightless under my hand. There is no smoke. There is no history. There is no story. There is just Ivy's face, under the water, looking up at mine.

We can speak to each other without words. We are in each other's heads. We always have been.

She tells me, "It's your turn now."

She tells me, "Thank you."

She is smiling, finally at peace. I look into her eyes and watch as her sparkle fades, as her lights go out.

She is gone, but she is not dead.

We are free.

There is a world outside and a world inside. One is on fire. The other is submerged, underwater. Sometimes it is dark. Sometimes I can't breathe.

We are parts and pieces. We are whole. We are a tapestry. A mosaic. A stained-glass window.

I emerge from the water, gasping for air.

We are reborn.

I crawl out of the pool, like those creatures at the beginning of time. The first webbed things that decided to have feet. How many lives did I live to get to this one? How many first breaths have I taken?

The thin fabric of my bra and underwear clings to my skin. My lungs are full of smoke and water. I cough up everything I can. I empty myself. I make myself new.

Who are you when half of you drowns?

Who are you if you are the one who pushed her under?

Who are you when you merge and become whole?

I look down at the water and nothing is there but a thin reflection of Ivy's face staring back at me. My own face.

This is what really happens.

This is my story now.

37

"YOU'RE too late," I say.

Raine is pointing a gun at my face. Her hands are shaking.

I don't know how long I've been sitting here on the edge of the pool. I am looking in the water. There is nothing there but my phone lying dead on the bottom.

"It's not me you're looking for," I tell Raine.

She is so close. How did I not notice her coming? She is so close, I can hear the rattle in her lungs as she breathes.

"You really shouldn't be out here," I say. "What about your asthma?"

Raine is real and I am real. I was Ivy but I was never Raine.

"You killed him," she manages to say through her wheezing. "Everyone saw the car. Your car. You ran over him like he was nothing. We're not nothing."

We are all nothing.

We are everything.

"How many of those pills did you take?" I say.

Freedom. What a stupid name for this nonsense.

"Swim with me," I say.

Daddy says our true selves live in the silence between our breaths.

But what if you can't breathe?

"Ash was the one driving," I say. "He kept driving even though I told him to stop."

That's what they do. They keep going when you tell them to stop.

I can tell Raine wants to believe me. She knows exactly what I'm talking about.

"I knew he was cheating on me," she says. "But he went there to see *you*? Why him? Don't you have enough?"

"Me? Oh, no. You have the wrong girl. That was Tami."

TamiandAsh. AshandTami.

"Don't you know that if you shoot me, they win?" I say. Again and again and again, they win. "Don't you know you'll just be another fucked person in prison?"

Don't you know it's the women who always pay? The sick women. The poor women. The dark women. The women, scorned. The women, forgotten. The women, beaten and used.

But look at us now. We are the ones who can make or break a life. We are the ones who start and end everything.

Maybe Raine drops the gun on purpose. Maybe it is a choice. Or maybe she just gets tired and her body makes the decision for her. Either way, the gun lands in the water with a splash and joins my phone at the bottom of the pool.

"Sit with me," I say. What else is there to do?

So Raine sits. We stare into the water. Who knows what will happen to us now.

"I thought the pills were supposed to make it stop hurting," she says.

"No pill can do that," I say.

I take her hand. We lean into each other. We hold each other up, just a little. Sometimes that's all we can do.

Maybe we are just dust and specks floating in space. But no matter how infinite and vast it is out here, somehow we find each other. Gravity pulls us in. We crash into each other, over and over and over again, we connect and fuse and change matter, we touch and make explosions. We touch and it changes everything.

We dissolve and we come back together, re-formed into something new. Something better.

"I don't understand," Raine says. "The pills. Something is wrong with the pills."

But they only affect shame. Not loss, not grief, not this.

Sometimes we need to dissolve. Sometimes we need to go back to fragments, to dust and specks. Sometimes that's what it takes to build a new path.

Tami and Ash in their private first-class cabin, clear sky ahead. They think they can coast. They think they can trust their path forward will be easy because it has always been easy.

But paths intersect with other paths. New paths are born where we've dissolved and collected and built something new.

"He was mine and they took him," Raine says.

"Yes," I say.

"They're not going to get away with this," Raine says.

"No," I say.

And then her hand becomes a vise, and mine breaks inside its grip, all the bones of my fingers crushed into fragments, needle-sharp, tearing from the inside.

Sometimes new stars smash into old stars. Sometimes whole galaxies collide. Sometimes everything changes and it lights up the universe.

And I tell her, "Keep squeezing. Squeeze as hard as you can."

38

IT'S possible to build a whole life out of other people's stories. You can fill in the details with imagination and hope. You can make a new childhood to replace the one you lost.

I wake up to the smell of smoke. It is night again, and I am in the forest, naked, covered with dirt. My skin inhales it through the cuts all over my body. I am absorbing the earth. I am putting down roots.

Something is different this time.

I can't stay here. I am not wild, not made for the forest. It is time to go home.

The forest whispers its gossip. I don't care what it says about me. I don't care what anyone thinks. I have built a life on caring too much. That life is over. That life has burned away.

The trees grow impatient. They grab and scratch and pull at my hair. I run, but they trip me with their roots. My knees scrape and burn, soil pushing grit into my blood. I break out of the forest into the clearing, and I brace myself for what I know I'm going to see: my favorite rock, my climbing tree, but nothing else. Where Daddy's garden should be is only a bent, rusted fence protecting a plot of overgrown, dry weeds. I call out to my fathers even though I know no one's here. All I hear is the trees mocking me. A feral cat steps out of the shadows. I say "Gotami!" but it just hisses and runs away.

And there, in the place where I painted a memory of my home, is an old abandoned church at the end of a gravel road in the middle of the forest, years' worth of ivy creeping between the crumbling stones. The windows are long gone. There is no tasteful Episcopal stained glass left. Everything of value was stripped long ago.

The heavy wooden door is rotting off its hinges. I step into a dusty, cobwebbed cavern barely lit by pale moonlight streaking through the glassless windows. Overturned pews, an old wasps' nest hanging in a corner of the ceiling, decaying floorboards sprouting ferns, the tendrils of ivy reaching up the walls like bad veins.

I follow the smoke down the hill. I tell the trees I will join them soon. The blood on my feet will nourish the soil, I will drop my roots and fuse with theirs, and I will learn their secret language.

I know the deer trails. I know my way around the crowds and the cameras and police lights. I know my way around in the dark.

The house is on fire and so is the world, and no one's trying to put it out.

I rise with the smoke. I climb up the stairs to our bedroom.

I find our packed suitcase at the foot of the bed with nowhere to go. I look in our purse. I find a whole bottle full of glittering, golden pills. What did these thousands of dollars' worth of Freedom buy us?

Our phone is on the nightstand. I pick it up and dial Lily's number, but no one answers. What time is it in Taiwan? What time is it here? I look at the phone as I throw it on the bed and the name *Dr. Lily Chen* shows on the screen.

Everything is pain. My lungs are full of knives. My skin is so hot.

I set the fire. It was time to burn this prison down.

Are we free yet?

There is our mother, fortified by gin, standing close to the most handsome police officer. We must be on fire, because everyone starts screaming when they see us come out of the burning house. Flames must be shooting out of our eyes. Our skin must be melting off. We are only a charred skeleton moving across this scorched piece of earth.

This is my origin story. This is my creation myth. This is me being born from the ashes of everything I destroyed. The police are yelling, but I can't hear them. The sound of the fire is too loud in my ears. I can see them draw their guns. I can see the way they look at me, like I am dangerous.

How does it feel? I would ask them if I could speak. *How does it feel to be afraid?*

They draw their guns, but I do not care. I am done caring. All

I know is everything is on fire, but I am not afraid. Sometimes things need to be burned down. Some seeds only open and grow when they've been through fire.

I see myself in a garden, working alongside a man who looks exactly like Daddy but is not Daddy. He is telling me about soil, about what makes it rich, what nutrients it needs to make things grow. He looks up and meets the eye of one of the therapists on his way to the outdoor group circle, a man who looks just like Papa but who is not Papa. Their smiles make the sun burn brighter; the tomato vines stretch, their fruits darken. I wish I was theirs.

I wonder what it would feel like to be born in the middle of that glance. What would it feel like to be caught inside that love, to be created by it?

There is no garden. There is only fire. There is only my mother's gin-drenched voice: "Ivy, what have you done?"

At the end of this story, there is just me, surrounded by flames. Everything I built is gone. There is no home, no Papa, no Daddy, no Lily.

There is no Fern. There has never been Fern.

There are strangers looking, talking, taking pictures, posting my new story into the world. My eternal audience, making me, destroying me, then making me again, over and over, our own little ecosystem, our own little universe. Nothing to something to nothing again.

There has always been Fern, but that was never her name.

Ivy. Evergreen. The most aggressive weed. Adaptable. Impossible to kill.

It has not rained. It will not rain. There is water all around this island, but none to put the fire out.

There are sirens painting the night into a hallucination. With every rotation they say: *This is not real. This is not real.*

But this *is* real. This is the only real thing.

There's a police officer saying, "Ivy Avila, you are under arrest," and then he says all the other things cops say on TV shows as they lead the girl to the police car, as they put their hands close to where they shouldn't just to let her know that they can.

But this is real and my show has been canceled, and now there's nothing left of me but a charred shell in the shape of a girl who used to be somebody, full of dust and specks already forming something new. Something solid. Something better. Something mine.

39

A pool can be drained. It can be scrubbed with bleach. But not us.

You will never really be gone. But we've made an agreement.

Maybe you will come back. Maybe you will get scared and want to take control again.

But I am here. I will always be here.

My job is to love you.

We are broken and we are whole. We are discarded and we are loved. We are worthless and we are special. We are everything in between.

All of these things are true.

All lies say something about the liar.

I am Ivy and I am Fern, and I did not kill a man.

But I took the pill. I let Ash drive. I did not kill Vaughn, but I am complicit. My silence makes me complicit. Every moment I do not tell the truth, I am letting a boy get away with murder. I am letting those men on leather couches break girls' lives before they even start. They do everything they can to convince us that we have no choice.

But they are liars. And we know the truth.

No one can stay in the sky forever. Not Ash. Not Tami. Not the men who make or break lives.

There is no such thing as destiny. There are only choices made and choices not made.

Everyone has to come down sometime.

Truth is contagious. It catches and spreads like wildfire. The whole world is tinder.

Everyone can see through glass walls. We just pretend that we can't.

When glass walls get too hot, they shatter.

Fire. Ash. Glass shards. This is the world we were given. But I want something better.

Go home, Raine. Go home and claim your grief. Go home and scream about the people who stole your life. Tell everybody. Tell them who hurt you. Keep speaking no matter what they do to try to shut you up.

There are so many endings. There are the ones we think we know. We know what makes a tragedy—the hero dies. But what if someone dies and he's not the hero of anyone's story? What do you call that?

How much money was Vaughn's life worth? What a vulgar question, and yet we ask it, we attempt to put a number on it, and that number is delivered to the young widow wheezing in her crumbling, crowded home, and that number will be deposited in the bank, where it will collect interest for the rest of her life.

That's what money does. It makes more money.

This is not justice. This is not salvation. But maybe Raine will be able to breathe now. She will be provided for, but it will never be enough.

Money can buy bodies, but it can never bring back the dead.

Money can buy lawyers. But what is the price of justice? What is the price of salvation?

The rain will fall as it always eventually falls. The ashes will be washed away and what is left of the world will emerge sparkling once more.

But the fires came closer than ever to the island this time. What will happen next year, and the year after that, when things get hot? What will we do with the flying sparks that travel miles on the wind? How do we keep them from landing?

Miles of forest, gone. Whole lives, erased. Whole towns, flattened. Suburbs of suburbs of suburbs. The world expands and then it contracts. We are the big bang. We are the massive black hole at the center of everything.

And still, there are years ahead for those who remain. Life will sprout out of the ashes. Whole mountains are empty, waiting to be filled with brand-new life.

Maybe the world is not built for us, but we are still in it. The moon still pulls the tides even as the sea rises, and we keep beating toward the shore, desperate for contact.

Our fathers, the real ones, they never leave us, even if we have to build them out of earth and ruins, even if they are salvaged from broken things. They live somewhere inside, caring for the girl who was taken, but whose outline is still discernable, faint whispers of her memory echoing in our empty spaces, her need like smoke, untouchable but yearning to be held.

"Help me," the ghost of myself says. "Help me," she will always say. And maybe sometimes the best we can do is create other ghosts to listen.

There's an ending we've been sold, the one we've been taught to think we want, the happily ever after—the girl ends up with the boy, or some other similar configuration. Two halves, joined, made whole. The origin of love.

But girls have been taught all sorts of wrong things.

That ending is a lie.

Maybe the only real happy ending is this:

The girl ends up with herself.

We are here. We are everywhere. We will be here, even as the sea threatens to swallow up our islands, as the fires close up around us. But we will not be burned. We will not be drowned.

We are not done yet.

There is evidence. There is truth. There is Dr. Chen, testifying in court, telling the world what happens when you've been hurt like we have. There are the men we sculpted into our fathers—the gardener, the counselor—telling the world we are worthy of being salvaged.

I am there, speaking. I am telling the world I am worthy of being salvaged.

This is our best show. These are our highest ratings.

Raine, this will not be your headline. You will get away. You will be the one to survive this. Even if the world is on fire, you will live a life and it will mean something.

I am the star now. Something to nothing to something again. I am the sun orbiting the black hole.

I will not be quiet.

Acknowledgments

FOR a long time, I was convinced this book would never get published. It was too weird, too risky, too unlike anything I'd ever written. My deepest gratitude goes to my brilliant agent, Michael Bourret, for believing in me and my book and our weirdness, and for finding us the best home.

Big love to my editor Jessica Dandino Garrison. From the moment of our first phone call, I knew you were the one. Thank you for challenging me to be better and for putting so much time and heart into this book. I lost count of the rounds of edits, but I think we finally got it.

Thank you to everyone at Dial/Penguin: cover designer Kristin Boyle, especially for your at-home glitter photo shoot when the world changed our plans; interior designer Cerise Steel; copyeditor Regina Castillo; Doni Kay; Shannon Spann; Lauri Hornik; Nancy Mercado; Michelle Lee; and Rosie Ahmed.

My humble gratitude goes to Anna Long, Amanda Starr, and Crystals, for your expertise and insight into the mind of Fern and Ivy, and for your wise guidance in helping them be more true.

To my Nebo girls, who have patiently been listening to me talk about this book for years: Jaye Robin Brown, Amber Smith, Frankie Bolt, Jocelyn Rish, Rebecca Petruck, Rebecca Enzor, Robin Constantine, and Joy Neaves. Thank you for being my yearly dose of peace in the chaos of this publishing world. May we dance to Lizzo in the kitchen for years to come.

And finally to my daughter, Elouise. For being my hope, my reason for everything. I'm dedicating every day to you.

Author's Note
(spoilers ahead)

WHEN I started writing this book, Fern and Ivy were two distinct people. My original intention was to follow *The Great Gatsby*'s story line pretty closely, while expanding its themes based on our evolution as a country and culture in the hundred years since its publication:

How have the shadows of the American Dream darkened even further since then? What happens when we look at it through the eyes of young women rather than men—when we add climate change, the further consolidation of wealth and power, white supremacy, the corporatization of politics and media, the commodification of young women's bodies? And how do we burst through the coded homoeroticism in Nick Carraway and Jay Gatsby's relationship and make it hella queer?

But something happened in the middle of my first draft that threw me for a loop. One morning, out of nowhere, Fern and Ivy told me they were the same person. Or more correctly, Ivy told me that Fern was a manifestation of a self she did not yet consciously know how to access, but desperately needed. (It may sound strange, but these are the very best, and most elusive, moments of writing—when our characters surprise us and take the lead and start telling their own story.)

I have lived with trauma, dissociation, addiction, and mental health issues my whole life. And while I do not have the experience of living with Dissociative Identity Disorder (formerly known as Multiple Personality Disorder), I have done a lot of therapy known as Internal Family Systems work—or "parts" work—in my own healing journey. This is the idea that we all have several parts, or personalities, inside us, all with different roles. There are parts of us that are still little children: maybe they are terrified, or ashamed; maybe they act out in various ways. There are parts of us that are more grown (or more awakened, if we want to take the Buddhist psychology approach), that we can rely on for compassion and love and wise guidance.

I became interested in exploring Fern as a part of Ivy, as a personality inherent within her, one that maybe the scared, reactive, and traumatized parts of Ivy would both yearn for and fight against.

This book is not meant to be a literal depiction of Dissociative Identity Disorder, which can manifest differently for different people, but a fictionalized interpretation of what might resemble aspects of that experience. I did a lot of reading, I consulted with psychologists who specialize in personality disorders, and I asked a person with DID to read a draft and give feedback. If

I have failed at representing the experiences and struggles of those with DID in any way, the failures are my own.

Though I do not have the experience of multiplicity, I know what it is to need to listen to my parts, to find compassion for them, to challenge them, to ask them for help, to tell the ones that are scared and wanting to act out that the grown-up me can take care of things. That I can take care of her.

May we all find this power, and this courage. May we remember that we are not alone. May the wise and resilient parts of us assure all our scared and wounded parts that we will be okay, and that together we will find a path to healing.

Love,

Amy

If you or someone you love is experiencing Dissociative Identity Disorder (DID) or want to learn more about it, here are some recommended resources:

Beauty After Bruises:

An organization dedicated to providing survivors of childhood trauma with access to, and funding for, therapeutic and in-patient care; while creating professional and public awareness for Complex PTSD.

beautyafterbruises.org

International Society for the Study of Trauma and Dissociation:

A professional association whose main goal is education and furthered research. They provide an extensive database of therapists and resources for survivors while hosting seminars and trainings for therapists.

isst-d.org

Sidran Institute:

An education and advocacy group that provides information and support to survivors, loved ones, professionals, and the general public.

sidran.org

For survivors of rape and sexual trauma:

RAINN (Rape, Abuse & Incest National Network):
The nation's largest anti-sexual violence organization.
rainn.org

National Sexual Assault Hotline:
1-800-656-HOPE

For those struggling with addiction and/or mental health issues:

TWLOHA (To Write Love on Her Arms):
Non-profit dedicated to presenting hope and finding help for people struggling with depression, addiction, self-injury, and suicide.
twloha.com

National Suicide Prevention Lifeline:
1-800-273-8255

Recovery Dharma:
A Buddhist-based program of recovery from addiction.
recoverydharma.org